P9-CSW-826

WITHDRAWN

THE
LIGHTNESS

THE
LIGHTNESS

A NOVEL

Emily Temple

WILLIAM MORROW
An Imprint of HarperCollinsPublishers

This is a work of fiction. Names, characters, places, and incidents are products of the author's imagination or are used fictitiously and are not to be construed as real. Any resemblance to actual events, locales, organizations, or persons, living or dead, is entirely coincidental.

THE LIGHTNESS. Copyright © 2020 by Emily Temple. All rights reserved. Printed in the United States of America. No part of this book may be used or reproduced in any manner whatsoever without written permission except in the case of brief quotations embodied in critical articles and reviews. For information, address HarperCollins Publishers, 195 Broadway, New York, NY 10007.

HarperCollins books may be purchased for educational, business, or sales promotional use. For information, please email the Special Markets Department at SPsales@harpercollins.com.

FIRST EDITION

Designed by Elina Cohen

Library of Congress Cataloging-in-Publication Data has been applied for.

ISBN 978-0-06-290532-1

20 21 22 23 24 LSC 10 9 8 7 6 5 4 3 2 1

FOR MY PARENTS

THE
LIGHTNESS

i

Once, not so long ago, a woman on the street told me my fortune. She said it was good news: I'd live a long life. I'd be happy. Bouncing babies, etc. I was past thirty by then, and I'd had these things on my mind. But there was a catch (well, isn't there always?): *You'll never get your good, long life if you keep asking the wrong questions*, the woman said. I wanted to know: *Which question is the right question?* She passed my fingers between her palms, my palms between her fingers. She said, *Not that one.* But I was only teasing her. I knew which question to ask.

ii

A suicide, they said. Nothing to suggest otherwise. If not a suicide, perhaps an accident. The steep cliff, the shifting rocks. *When you see hoofprints in the forest*, the authorities said. *What would horses be doing in our forest*, we wanted to know. *Accidents happen all the time*, the authorities said. *We know you had nothing to do with this.*

iii

I've found the authorities to be, in some matters, unreliable.

1

The man who drove me up the mountain in the first month of my sixteenth summer looked nothing like my father. He had thick black hair, a thick red neck, and a rosary wrapped around his rearview mirror, but instead of a cross, a miniature naked woman, whose breasts seemed not quite to scale, dangled from the coil of synthetic beads. She bobbed in the flow of the air vents, twisted and slapped two-dimensionally against the cheap black cab plastic, and I was reminded, again, of the shapes of women, the impossible geometry into which I was meant to fold myself. I couldn't look at her for long. Not because of my own monstrous reflection, which I kept catching in the rearview—also not quite to scale, I thought—but because my stomach was weak in those days. Whenever the car hit a quick dip or banked a long curve, it felt as though parts of my body (throat, liver, one thick thigh) were left hovering, separated, while the rest plummeted, or swerved, or bumped, or whatever.

It was a long drive, our trajectory relentless. *Even approaching the Levitation Center is an exercise in antigravity*, people used to say, and it's true: the Center was high enough in the mountains that

I felt the air thin out long before I even saw the main build-ing, with its paper-white stucco walls, its red-tipped roof, its enormous golden seal. The atmosphere loosened steadily as we drove; I could feel all that nice, thick sea-level air pooling at my ankles and then abandoning me, even through the churn of the air-conditioning.

In the end, I spent most of the ride staring at an amoebic mole on the back of the cabdriver's neck. That was my mother's wisdom: to combat motion sickness, look unwaveringly at some-thing inside the car, something small and still. If it's decidedly cancerous, dark purple, spreading out at the edges, no matter. Say nothing. Try not to move your eyes.

I know a lot of people who can't remember themselves as teen-agers. They look back and see only smoother, pinker versions of themselves, the actual feeling of those frantic years replaced by anecdote and snapshot. Oh, look, weren't we babies, weren't we thin, remember the time we, etc. We were so *bad*! We weren't so bad. Who can say? Me, I can't forget. I remember the girl from that summer as though she were sitting beside me: a fear-ful girl, but insatiable too, possessed of a fundamental savagery. Well. Can we blame her? It had only been a year since her father had disappeared.

As soon as I started to become nihilistic about my nausea, the cab crested through a final bend and pulled into a white sand driveway the size of a swimming pool. A woman was waiting there, wearing a white dress. She introduced herself as Magda and took my hand, as though she knew me. For a moment, I tried to pull away, but she held on tight, and I was unsteady enough in the thin air that I let her. By now, we were almost eight thousand feet up.

I was late, Magda told me. I was the last, the very last to arrive.

She led me across the driveway toward the Center's main building. Paths lined with globular pink peonies scribbled out in the grass to either side, but we didn't follow any of them. Instead we strode, hands linked, across the white expanse. The duffel bag on my shoulder felt heavy, much heavier than I remembered, and I wondered, briefly, if someone could have hidden something inside of it at the airport, when I wasn't paying attention—a hard-packed pallet of powder, say, or a recording device, or the body of a small child. No, no. Don't be silly. That's not what this story is about. (Isn't it?)

Magda began talking, pointing out all the different buildings, the different trails, listing the daily activities, the times I'd be expected for meditation and meals. I couldn't follow any of it. *Commissary, dormitory, promontory, bedtime story.* I stumbled on a bright white rock; it sparked across the sand like a popping kernel. Magda only tightened her grip. She gave an overall impression of linen and salt. They say everyone faints at least once during their first week at the Center, before they acclimate to the altitude. (*Altitude* is a perfect word for itself, don't you think, all peaks and valleys and places to slip.) But I'd been drinking steadily from my battered canteen, the one my father had given me years before at a place very much like this one, and so I didn't fall. Besides, I was busy looking back over my shoulder.

Back over my shoulder, the wind had caught in the loose white sand of the driveway, and was coaxing it upward into a steamy funnel. A group of strange-looking girls, who had clearly been installed at the Center long enough for their heads to become utterly untethered from the old brown world down below, appeared as if from nowhere. They yipped and laughed and took turns running through the snow-white mini-twister, holding hands, shrieking like children at a water park, coming out the other side with thick white eyebrows and heavy white eyelashes and red, sand-scratched cheeks, an instant aging. Magda turned and called out to them and, after a few more furtive whoops and peals, they ran past us toward the main building, sand streaming off their bodies like water.

During most months of the year, the Levitation Center was a panspiritual contemplative community that held meditation retreats, organized talks by spiritual leaders of various lineages, and offered programs with names like "Intermediate Mind-fulness Training" and "Open Sky Intensive" and "Walking the Path of Indestructible Wakefulness." Its visitors practiced Buddhism, Hinduism, and Taoism, among other things. Dowsing, psychology, iridology, judo, aikido, tae kwon do, oil painting, law, yoga, croquet, bodywork, vegetarianism, Reiki, piano, lucid dreaming, crystal healing, palm reading, gratitude, abstinence, tantric sex. The usual assortment of practices for people like these: people who are looking for something.

The Levitation Center wasn't its real name, of course. That's just what everyone called it. According to legend, it was the only bit of land left in America where levitation was still possible, at least for those with the correct set of aptitudes. They said there was something about the place—a balancing aura or geological phenomenon or holy spirit, depending on the *they* in question—that made it easier for anyone with the potential for levitation to achieve it. It was like one of those thin places you stumble across once in a while on sea-beaten cliffs or in toothy grave-yards, where the ancient pagan Celts would have said heaven and earth nudged even closer than their usual three feet. Most people walking by would feel nothing. But a bare few might find room there, space for upward motion, for unfurling like paper.

My father was a Buddhist. He too was looking for something. All my life, he'd flown across countries and continents, visiting meditation centers and monasteries, temples and contemplative schools, their names strange and musical: Paro Taktsang, Vajrapani Institute, Dechen Chöling, Samyé Ling, Naropa. I sounded them out to myself in bed while he was gone, spelled them in wet fingertip on my thigh. No one but us knew words like these. He'd go for a week, sometimes a month, while I did homework and ate breakfast and sat alone in my room, and then he'd come home, sliding his suitcase under the bed in the manner of turning a latch. He always seemed different to me in the days following his return: there was a new delicate rawness there, a lingering sense of sublimation, as if his external layers had been steamed loose and peeled away. After a while, they would grow back. A while after that, he'd leave again. It was not dissimilar to ecdysis.

My mother called these trips his *retreats from reality*, to which my father would say, when he returned, *reality is a construct, consciousness an illusion*, and my mother would either laugh or turn away, depending on how long he'd been gone that time. After a while, she stopped calling his trips anything, and a while after that, he moved to a small house one town to the east of ours. The direction seemed significant at the time; I see now that it was not. It was from this small house that he would eventually vanish entirely, without a word, without saying goodbye.

Of course: a vanishing preceded by a goodbye is no vanishing at all, though it can be just as incomprehensible.

The beginning I know for sure. Once upon a time, my father went to the Levitation Center. I also know the next part: and he never came back. He missed his weekend with me, and then the next. I remember my mother's silence filling the car as we waited outside the darkened windows of that new eastern house,

engine running, pretending the pile of plastic-wrapped news-
papers breeding steadily on his porch meant nothing, nothing
at all.

disappear (v.) from *dis-* "do the opposite of" + *appear* "come into
view," from the Old French *aparoir, aperer* "come to light, come
forth"; see also: vanish, die out, abandon; see also: no letter, no
call; see also: a year and more without a single message to your
daughter, who is wondering what could have happened, who is
alone with her furious mother, and who misses you.

"You've missed the welcome talk," said Magda. Her bare feet
were thin and coated in white dust from the driveway. They
looked dead. "Are you hungry?"

My stomach recoiled. The cab, the mole. The slap slap slap
of the body on the dash. I shook my head.

"All right." She shrugged with one shoulder and I wondered
how old she was. "Let's drop off your bag." She led me inside the
building and down a short hallway. Most of the program participants slept in four small dormitories, she explained, though
a handful would spend the summer in tents a half mile or so up
the mountain. The tents were private, and more comfortable in
the heat, but they also cost more, and, as I would soon find, few
parents sending their daughters here wanted to grant them any
extra comforts. Most of us were here to be punished.

The dormitory was unlit when we entered, but I could see
that the wood supports of the bunk beds had been painted a
dark green; the effect was of an encroaching forest, a bedroom
Birnam Wood. The only single bed was positioned next to the
door we had come through; Magda stepped protectively in front
of it. The space was littered with sharp-colored detritus: suit-
cases half-gutted and abandoned, bottles of shampoo laid out on

beds, sneakers all over the floor. But it smelled like cedar, and it was dark and cool, and there was a wide mirror on the back wall that reflected the door. Even then, before it all happened, I'd been the kind of girl who needed to be able to see the door in every room, to clock the exits, register all potential avenues of approach. It wasn't cowardice, not exactly. I just wanted to see my murderer first. I wanted to see the blade, or the gun, or whatever it was going to be. Noose, wrench, kitchen knife. At home, I would bare my throat to the tight-latched door of my bedroom, eyes on the shadows until I fell asleep. But you know what they say: curiosity killed, etc.

The Center's annual summer program was called "Special Teen Retreat: Becoming a Warrior in Body, Mind, and Heart." The website had boasted that we'd spend eight weeks *exploring the possibilities that unfold when we are fully present in the moment*, and also that we'd *deepen our awareness of our actions and their effect on the world*, and also that there'd be lots of *heart-cleansing activities*. There was no air-conditioning. There was no internet connection. There was no cell service. We would be carefully supervised at all times. That "Special" was code, you see. Privately, I called it Buddhist Boot Camp for Bad Girls. I was looking forward to the *heart-cleansing activities*.

So the girls at the Center were trouble. I knew that going in. They were slick-finish girls, cat-eye girls, hot-blood girls. They were girls who reveled. They were girls who liked boys and back seats, who slid things that weren't theirs into their tight pockets, who lit fires and did doughnuts in the high school parking lot. They were girls who left marks. They were girls who snuck. Girls who drank whiskey and worse by the water-front, looking out at the smeared reflections of the streetlights, making plans instead of wishes. They were girls who ran away, who inked their own arms with needles and ballpoint pens, who got things pierced below the neck. Below the neck, ladies, can you believe it? Only whores, etc. etc., as my mother never tired of telling me. They pierced too, these girls, and hit, and were sent out of gym class for raising bruises on the girls whose daddies brought them to school in Porsches, though some of their daddies had Porsches too. That wasn't the point. That wasn't the point! They had their problems. They had their demands. They were shoplifters and potheads, arsonists and bullies, boy crazy and girl crazy, split and scarred. They were, some of them, cruel. They were, more of them, angry—angry at their parents, at their schools, at their congressmen, at their bodies, at the painted white lines they saw everywhere, telling them no no no when they wanted yes—they were girls who were bored, so bored, or they were girls who were the opposite, who were so full up of feeling that they couldn't simply do their times tables or learn their French conjugations or go to the movies on a Saturday night and discuss the relative cuteness of so-and-so's haircut and let the age-appropriate boy next to them drag his sweaty palm around and around and around their pretty knees. They were too full up for that. They were too full up for caution. So they were girls who got caught. And they were girls who got sent away. They were girls whose mothers couldn't deal with them for one more minute, not alone, not without help, not this summer while you sit in the office all day and come home late after "golf," Carl, really, I can't; girls whose fathers thought maybe some Good Clean Mountain Air and some Good Far Eastern Religion would cure them, since nothing else had. You know the girls I mean, because every school has them, every neighborhood, including yours, especially mine. I was not one of them, of course. Not yet.

• • •

There were some sixty of these girls in the Center's main shrine room when Magda led me inside, all jostling and laughing and shouting at one another. I stood blinking for a moment in the doorway. This was an enormous version of a space I recognized: my father's own personal shrine room, which had once been tucked in the attic of what was now my mother's house. Here, as there, the white walls were hung with gold silks, the wood floor was patterned with red cushions, and there was a squat shrine at the front, which held candles, sticks of incense, framed images of old men and green goddesses, and several unidentified objects—one was definitely a cookie—stuck into little bowls of rice. Here, as there, I had to remove my shoes to enter. Here, as there, I was required to bow as I crossed the threshold.

But no one else was paying any attention to the room, or to the shrine, or to the threshold. No one else was holding their breath. Nearly every body I saw was in motion, girls scrambling to touch one another, shoulders and hair, all of them seeking the best positions, the best friends, the long-desired faces of their age-old enemies. The sounds—shrieks of recognition, cracked-jaw chattering, spiraled laughter—bounced busily back and forth between the walls, building to a cacophony that sparked around me like an electrical storm. To say hyenas is too pat, but: hyenas. They have the same stalk, the same hysteria. They are equally dangerous; this much should be obvious to anyone. At least here no one knew me, or knew I was any different from them. No one even looked in my direction. I found a safe, silent cushion and sat.

It was then, in the midst of the racket and rough, that I first saw her. She sat unmoving in the far corner by a wide picture window, her thick black hair like a calligrapher's mark, swiped straight down her back, nearly to the floor. Next to her was a tall blonde, perched and pretty as a bow, and on the other side, a smaller girl with messy purple hair and something that looked like a crown painted on her cheek. But my eyes kept sliding to the girl in the middle. She wore a faded floral sundress in a room full of girls out to prove their grit; her brown shoulders shone. She was calm, expressionless: the small black eye of the storm. I felt a pulse of something as I looked at her, the same feeling you get when you turn a corner and are confronted with something unexpected: a magnificent mountain range, maybe, or the slick, fresh corpse of a deer. *Direct experience*, my father would have called it. When what you see bypasses language entirely. A slap to the face, for instance. A sudden fall. Don't be fooled by the language I'm using now, that simply can't be helped. She was beyond it, yes—but only for a moment.

A warm ringing filled the room. There was a woman sitting cross-legged next to the shrine. She wore a loose blue dress and a jade necklace so large and heavy-looking I couldn't help but imagine the indents it must have been making on her breasts, which were large and heavy-looking themselves. This was Shastri Dominique, the Center's program director, who would lead us in our meditation practice for the summer. She was probably in her early thirties, I think now, though the girlish braids she wore, thrown casually over her shoulders, made her appear far younger. "The basics of meditation are simple," she said. "You sit, you follow the breath. Keep your eyes open, but soft, resting gently on the floorboards in front of you. You are trying to gain control of your mind." She spread her hands for a moment before letting them fall back to her knees. "Do not force your thoughts away: simply watch them as they arise, note them, then let them fall away. If you notice yourself drifting off, say to yourself *thinking* and come back to the breath. That's all you need to do, for now." She struck the singing bowl again.

I relaxed a little. This was something I knew how to do. I assumed the posture my father had taught me. The girls around me groaned. The girls around me sighed. The girls around me fidgeted and tittered and poked one another behind raised palms. But the three in the far corner sat as straight as Dominique, as silent as my father, their palms resting gently on their knees, their eyes on the floorboards in front of them. Even then I could tell they knew not only what they were doing, but why. Even then I could tell that they believed in all of this. For this reason, I couldn't pry my eyes from their upright spines, their parted lips. For this reason, I knew I had come to the right place.

It was despite my mother's protests that my father had taught me to meditate at all. I remember her standing in the doorway of his shrine room as he arranged me on the cushion, her arms crossed. I watched her, not without prejudice, but confident she wouldn't enter unless invited. She wasn't, she didn't. But she didn't leave, either. My father taught me to focus on my breath by imagining a little girl, my own age but in miniature, with silver, sparkling hair, who rode the air out of my body like it was a wild horse, her hands loose above her head, my out-breath squeezed between her thighs. I still imagine her sometimes, though meditation is harder now.

My mother rolled her eyes at this instruction. She did not approve of religion, of this kind or any other. But meditation was not religion, my father explained. "Nor is it relaxation, despite what people think," he said. "It is *preparation*." He and I sat beside each other on our cushions, the thin stick of incense turning to ash on the shrine. My mother had finally gone from the doorway. It looked smaller without her. I noticed for the first time that the clean white paint on one side was chipped, revealing a grimy taupe underneath, and I felt a small plume of anger, as if she'd broken something that was mine.

"Preparation for what?" I asked.

"For waking up to the true nature of things."

But when I asked what the true nature of things was, he only smiled and held a finger to his lips.

It wasn't that I expected to find my father at the Center that summer, of course, or not literally: waiting for me on my bottom bunk, say, soft hands folded in his lap. Too much time had passed for that. There were too many places to go. He had never been loyal to a single meditation community, or temple, or school. Retreats, plural. (Realities, plural too, if we're being honest here.) My father drifted. My father sampled. But he had come here, to the Levitation Center, and it was here that something had changed. His pattern, once so familiar, had been broken. You know what they say: once you find what you're looking for, you stop looking. If you're smart, that is.

So once the world he'd left twice over became unbearable, I followed him. I thought the Center itself might have the answer—an old diary, a forwarding address, that sort of thing. I'd seen the movies. But more than that: I thought that if I learned this place, I would also learn *him*—that if I did what he did, loved what he loved, believed what he believed, I too might be transformed. Into what exactly, I didn't know. Something new and pink-skinned, fresh and holy: a girl worth coming back for.

Maybe the Center had that power, maybe not. But I knew I couldn't go home, not to her, not anymore, not unless I found a way to change everything.

• • •

So I sat. I followed the breath. I tried to gain control of my mind. But a few minutes later I found myself staring through the picture window, watching a tall man with a black beard and a black topknot digging a hole in the lawn beside a wide path, a plant on the grass in front of him, exposed and unpotted, its roots a bouquet of bare legs, and thinking about the man's strong digging arms, wet with sweat and reflecting the warm evening light, hairier and harder than my father's, hairier and harder than any man's I'd ever seen, then—*thinking*—thinking about thinking about the man's strong digging arms, and then thinking about thinking about thinking about the strong digging arms, and then thinking about thinking about thinking—

I closed my eyes. When I opened them, I saw that two of the girls in the corner were watching the man through the window too: the smaller girl impassive, her head barely turned, the blonde leaning forward, biting down hard on one blood-red lip. The dark-haired girl was not looking at him. She hadn't moved at all since the bowl had been struck.

I turned back to the man, wondering who he was, and who he was to them, but he was gone. There was only a sunburst of loose soil on the close-cropped grass where he had knelt. I couldn't even tell which plant was new.

After what felt like hours, Dominique coaxed a long, final note from the bowl. I felt it settle in my stomach, as if swallowed. "Get some sleep," she said as girls stomped past her. "Doing all this nothing is going to be hard work."

I was the last one to leave the shrine room, except for Dominique, who continued to sit, her eyes soft and unfocused. I bowed again in the doorway and followed the frantic sounds back to the dormitory. The dark-haired girl was nowhere to be seen, but her friends had claimed a bunk bed only two away from mine. The others seemed to give them a wide berth. Needless to say, this only made me curiouser.

The blonde was tacking photographs of her friends to the green supports around her pillow, positioning one over another and then changing her mind, matching a red tack to a boy's red sweater, then putting a yellow tack where the red one had been. The other girl had climbed to the bunk above and lay motionless on the thin mattress, her sneakers dangling. I was sitting still on my own bottom bunk, thinking about what I could say to them, how I might start, when a head swung down and introduced itself as Harriet.

"I hope you don't snore," Harriet said. "Because I've been known to smother people in my sleep." She grinned at what must have been my look of horror and reached out to pinch my cheek. How easy these things are for some; I still have not learned how to be so bold with strangers. This was Harriet's third year at the Center, she told me. "It's this or summer school. Math being much worse than meditation, in my opinion." She rattled off the names of everyone else in the room, and I listened politely, though of course I only cared about two of them. The girl with the purple hair was named Janet and the one with the photos was Laurel. The other one, Harriet told me unprompted, maybe seeing the look on my face, was called Serena. None of them were to be approached.

When I asked, as casually as I could, why not, Harriet yawned and flipped back up onto her bed. "You'll wind up regretting it," she said. "That's all I can say."

For organizational purposes, we had been separated into four groups named after the four Tibetan dignities: Lions (traditional associations: joyfulness, freedom from doubt), Tigers (satisfaction, unconditional confidence), Garudas (freedom, boundlessness), and Dragons (power, ultimate wisdom). Our dormitory of twelve had been assigned the Garuda as our emblem, and once I saw its picture, I thought I understood. Lions, Tigers, and Dragons (oh my) were one thing, but the Garuda was the only one of the four that was truly a monster, an enormous birdlike, humanlike thing with wings and arms and a beak, a fat belly and breasts and an unruly look on its face. (The word *monster* comes from the Latin root *monere*: "to warn." Gruesome creatures are always, by etymological necessity, portents.) It seemed right that I had been put into this group, that I would spend the summer marching under the flag of this patched-together thing. My body felt to me the way the body of the Garuda looked: bulged and bulbous in all the wrong places, bones and fat in unholy organizations that seemed ready to tear or terrify.

Of course, there was no point in thinking this way. Our group assignments were random, or perhaps alphabetical. Of course Laurel, who brushed her hair a hundred times each night, who had brought her silk sheets from home, who would wear that bright red lipstick every day that summer, right up to the horrible end, was no monster. (Though certainly, in retrospect, an unheeded warning.) It was only that I had a soft spot for metaphor, for the laying on of language, especially when it could be used against myself. I may not have entirely outgrown this habit.

That first night, I couldn't sleep. The wooziness brought on by the altitude was supposed to make sleep easier, or at least that's what Dominique had told us. Our bodies craved rest to reorganize their expectations, to build new blood cells to combat the sudden oxygenlessness. But unfamiliar physical sensations have always driven me to distraction. It's the reason I have never succeeded at doing drugs—other than the little pills that, these days, I need to get any kind of sleep at all. Now I can tell you that the equation for the physiology of altitude sickness is

$V_{gas}=A/TD_k(P_1-P_2)$ and that really, we had it easy; we weren't so far up. Still, my light-headedness kept me awake. I was overwhelmed by the suspicion that if I stopped thinking about my breath for a single moment, my body, with all its shoddily assembled parts—breasts, belly, beak—would simply forget to take in air and I would die.

So I lay there, staring at the planks above my head, the shallow impression Harriet's body made in the mattress, concentrating on continuing to breathe. I tested my limbs, raising first my arms and then my legs, slowly, quietly, inches above my mattress so no one would see. But everyone else was snoring, knocked out by the thinned air.

Or nearly everyone else. After the lights had been out for hours, I heard a soft tap, fingertips on wood, and then another. Slowly, I turned my head. I could barely see Janet—she climbed down her ladder and landed silently on the floor. Laurel was already standing, holding her shoes. They crept to the dormitory door and, after a moment's fumbling, let themselves out. I tried to watch them go, but I saw only the briefest bright slice of hallway light, and then its opposite, a bruise lingering on the backs of my eyelids. I forgot about my breath entirely as I wondered where they had gone, and why, and if they had been swallowed by the night, or if they were out there somewhere doing the swallowing. I waited up for them as long as I could, but I fell asleep before they returned.

I dreamed of nothing, or of falling.

2

I am a person of binges. I have never understood the phrase "too much of a good thing." Look: it's irrational, impossible. See *fig. 1*: when I was a child, I became obsessed with horses. I know, I know, all little girls are obsessed with horses. But I lived for them. I gorged on them. I begged for them in any incarnation: films, toys, patterns, photographs, posters. Once, I cut the hair off a Barbie and superglued it to the base of my spine. I thrilled to wear my pony tail under my clothes, in secret, my parents knowing nothing, thinking me merely human, but it rubbed off after two days, leaving long blond doll hairs clotting in the corners of the house. My birthday came, and my parents, who were still together then, splurged on an afternoon of horseback riding lessons. When it was time to leave, they found that I had knotted my hair into the horse's mane so elaborately that they had to cut me away from it with a pair of rusted barn shears. I still have the clump of matted girl-and-horse hair hidden in a drawer, though after all the times I put it in my mouth, I admit that it is somewhat the worse for wear.

This is all just to say that in retrospect, I'm not so surprised by what happened that summer. Like everything, it was my own fault.

In the morning, a wild-haired Harriet came crashing down from the bunk above me. She hit the floor in a bra and a pair of boxers, and for the first time I could see that she had a pair of luminous wings tattooed across the pale skin of her back; upon closer inspection, I found that the wings were made of tiny knives. Once she had collected herself, I followed her to the Garudas' shared bathroom, which was outfitted with six showers; four toilets; three sinks; two tiny, too-high mirrors; and one huge claw-foot bathtub that looked like it had simply been dropped into the middle of the room, disrupting the tile pattern. It wasn't clear to me what the original intent for this building had been. Surely not this. What builder could have imagined it? I kept looking up into the tilted rafters, trying to figure it out. *Creamery? Granary? Forge? Hotel? Hospital?* Harriet tripped into one of the stalls; she cursed as she peed. Clearly, those wings were merely decorative: the girl was clumsy. I might have laughed, but I too felt unsteady. I balanced against the doorframe as I went through. We were dizzy, drunk on plain air, high on height.

The day unfolded in a pattern that would become familiar to me over the next weeks. Morning meditation was followed by breakfast—always, always oatmeal, though there was a rotating selection of fresh fruit to go with it—and some kind of assigned activity. That first day the Garudas had ikebana, the ancient art of contemplative flower arranging. It looked simple enough to slot the cut flowers into the barbed half-moon bases they gave us, but I couldn't get my arrangements to look anything like our instructor's perfect curls of stem and stamen. Walking around the room, she praised Laurel's elaborate construction, and nodded at Janet's minimalist restraint, and ignored me completely. She was stamen-like herself, our instructor, a thin woman whose limbs seemed connected to her body by only the barest bits of bone and skin. Though she was very old, and the flesh on her face was loose and frayed, I could tell by the way she moved that she had once been beautiful. I wondered if she was surprised when she looked into the mirror at night. I wondered what, exactly, she saw.

At lunch, I sat with Harriet and her friend Nisha, a pot-obsessed Indian girl from Denver who told me that her adoptive parents had sent her to the Center instead of any other clean-her-up summer program because they thought she could learn about her "heritage." Nisha was a Garuda too: the night before, I had noticed her stuffing fistfuls of wrinkled clothes from her rucksack directly into her cubby, transforming it into a swollen block of multicolored cotton before deciding she needed something from the center and pulling it all out again.

Nisha and Harriet asked me polite questions about my hometown, my favorite films, my preferred flavors. I liked them. Harriet was even funny: a jumble of stories and auburn hair and loud laughter, she was the daughter of some kind of Oregonian lumber baron and kept getting arrested for destruction of property. "Wood is surprisingly delicate," she told me in a goofy stage whisper that made Nisha snort. "And so are my neighbors' feelings." Nisha, on the other hand, was tense and jittery—I could see why she preferred to be high—but she was nice enough, despite her habit of laboriously describing old drug experiences. Apparently, there is nothing in the world *quite* as mind-blowing as driving over a mountain, totally stoned, as the sun comes up and "The King of Carrot Flowers, Parts 2 & 3" plays on the stereo (not Part 1, she was sure to make clear; Part 1 is just a pop song). Even back then, when I more or less believed her, I was bored by stories like these. But which version, Harriet wanted to know, which car, which mountain, which strain?

After lunch, we had rota: our two hours of daily work around the Center. "Essentially, we pay through the nose for the privilege to come and do their chores," Harriet said, raising her pinkie in the air as she took an elaborate slurp from her iced tea.

"But despite the name, there is no actual rotation," Nisha said.

"You'll notice that they always make the really violent girls do the dirty work," Harriet said. She stood and stretched her arms, looking around the room; the knives on her back seemed to bend around the straps of her tank top, like a warning. "I'm not sure it's such a great strategy."

"Sometimes it kind of tires them out," Nisha said. "Usually it just annoys them."

I followed them to the corkboard outside the dining hall where our assignments had been posted, handwritten in ink on thick creamy paper.

"Office again," Harriet groaned. "Kill me dead."

"Laundry room," Nisha said, pointing at her own name. "Boring." She looked at me. "What'd you get?"

I pretended to scan for my name, though of course I had located it immediately. "Garden," I said.

"Garden?" Harriet said. She gripped my arm. "Since when is there rota in the garden?"

The expression on her face alarmed me. "Does that count as dirty work?" I said. If Shastri Dominique thought I was violent, it had to mean that she knew what I had done. It had to mean that my mother had called, maybe that she was coming to get me.

Nisha took a step back and looked me over, as if I'd been in disguise this whole time, and had finally revealed myself. "No," she said. "It definitely does not."

The Center, Harriet and Nisha informed me, sourced much of its food from the large organic garden on the grounds. But the garden itself was not of particular interest to them. The appeal of the garden was the gardener. Luke lived at the Center year-round—though *where* exactly, neither of them knew. Not in the main building, where we slept, and where the rest of the staffers had their beds. Not in a tent. He seemed to sleep nowhere. Everywhere was also an option. He wasn't the only man at the Center that summer—there were a few other male staff members, and some visiting monks who came and went on their own schedules—but for the girls, he may as well have been. Strong digging arms, etc.

"He's kind of a legend," Harriet said.

"He's the most advanced practitioner here," Nisha said. "Even though he's really young."

"He's like a prodigy," Harriet said.

"Our own personal holy man."

"I heard he can actually levitate."

"Meditate under water."

"Fly, even."

"He used to be engaged."

"He's not anymore."

"He does something to the plants."

"No one knows what it is."

"He never lets anyone past the fence."

"Especially girls."

Nisha pointed me in the direction of the garden. "But I guess you'll be the exception," she said.

"Good luck," said Harriet, in that singsong, ironic way she had, but when I looked back, neither girl was smiling.

The garden was just out of sight of the main buildings, down a matted path that curved gently around the side of the mountain. It was the size of a baseball field and, like many actual baseball fields, surrounded by a chain-link fence. Inside, a man was squatting among the plants, half-hidden by leaves but clearly wearing a pair of pink floral gardening gloves. For the briefest of moments, he looked exactly like my father. Then I blinked and shook away the association. He was much too young, for one thing. The shoulders were as wide, but the coloring was all wrong. The hair wasn't right, or the face. And yet, even through the blinking, the shaking: there was something.

"Don't touch the fence," he said without looking up. "It's electric."

I hadn't been planning to touch the fence, but now I found that I very much wanted to.

"Why?" I said.

He stood and wiped the sweat away from his face, leaving a few traces of dirt in his beard. His shirt was open a little. His throat shone like a bird's. I turned my face up to the sky to avoid staring. Was it bluer this far up, or was I imagining it?

"Keeps out the animals," he said. "Girls included."

"They said I had rota here," I said. The fence was tall, at least eight feet high. I thought I could hear it vibrating.

He considered this. "How are you with plants?" he asked.

"I used to help my dad in the garden," I said.

He smiled then, and pointed to a door in the side of the fence that I hadn't seen before. "Come on in," he said.

• • •

My father had been a gardener too, an amateur one. Your garden-variety gardener. When I was young, he cultivated our front yard so that one half was filled with flowers, and the other with vegetables and herbs. When he was in a good mood, I was sometimes allowed to help him weed or plant; both left me filthy and tired, but I liked to lock fingers with the root systems as I pulled them out of the ground. "Imagine the garden as your mind," he would say as we knelt in the dirt. "If you plant seeds, and tend the earth around them, they bear fruit. And just like your mind, the flowers are constantly changing. They rise, they bloom, they decay."

"What's the point, then?" I asked him once. "Why grow things that only die?"

He leaned on his shovel. "Everything is impermanent. Mountains. Flowers. Even us, what we think of as ourselves."

I looked down at my stomach, my knees. I held up my bitten fingernails.

"Let me ask you this," my father said. "Where is the self? Can you point to it? Can you tell me what color it is? No, not your sternum. Not your eye. Your Olivia." I could point to nothing that would satisfy him. "You see," he said, and I nodded as though I did.

It wasn't until much later that I understood that the things he said had anything to do with Buddhism, or that others might not subscribe to his worldview. Most of the girls at my school believed that they had eternal souls, for instance. Most of the girls at my school knew that true love, when they inevitably found it, with eyes and thighs like theirs, would last forever. Most of the girls at my school, if they had ever thought about it, which they had not, would have been confident that they actually existed. From a young age, I suspected these things to be not strictly true. This may or may not have contributed to my essential loneliness.

●   ●   ●

After my father left, the garden grew wild. The two halves, edible and decorative, became indistinguishable. Some plants died, others grew tentacles, and the front yard of what was now my mother's house became a mass of curling vine and leaf and stiff dead stalk. The neighbors scowled when they passed, but my mother said she liked it better this way. "Back to the land!" she shouted happily one morning when she found a litter of foxes fighting in the deep brush, the kits pawing at a small kill their own mother had brought them, smearing its red pulp onto the grass.

Needless to say, I never invited anyone to my house. This may or may not, etc.

To start, Luke had me weed the flowerbeds. "Gardening for beginners," he said. "Just tug and toss." Something else I knew how to do. Luke worked beside me for the whole two-hour period, saying little, occasionally gesturing at a gnarled section I had missed. I stole glances at him whenever it felt safe, but he concentrated on his tasks so fully I felt he wouldn't have noticed me even if I'd taken off my clothes. (Not that I was thinking about that sort of thing, of course. No, I was not.) His cheekbones were high and sharp, which gave him the look of an ancient Greek dignitary, and his skin was brown and smooth under all that hair. I fixated on the soft baby skin in the crook of his elbow: I wanted to pinch it. He had freckles too, which was really unfair of him. He never furrowed his brow, even in the sun, and when he reached his hands into the ground, he closed his eyes completely.

He couldn't have been more than twenty-three, I realize that now—far younger than I am as I write this, an age I now find embarrassing in other people, particularly men. But back then, he seemed timeless, ageless, fixed as a character in a film. As if no matter when I had arrived, that summer or twenty years from that summer, he would have been there, waiting for me, looking just the same. Nothing like my father; exactly like him.

Just when my back was beginning to hurt, Luke stood and squinted at the sun. "Rota's over," he said.

I took off the gardening gloves he'd given me and set them carefully on a bench. He bent and picked a purple flower from one of the beds I had cleared. He looked at it for a moment, twirled it between his fingers, and held it out to me, and all at once I felt exposed. For the first time that day, I had the sense of myself as a girl alone with a man. I took the flower, making sure not to touch his fingers with mine.

"Ah," he said. "Your hands are like the Buddha's."

"Thanks," I said, not knowing what he meant. Later, I would blush over the compliment—my fingers are short and stubby, not at all like the Buddha's graceful tapers. I put the flower behind my ear.

He nodded and disappeared into the garden shed. I let myself out.

On my way back to the main building, I considered throwing the flower into the grass. I was thinking of Nisha's face when she saw my assignment, and the way Harriet had dug her nails into my arm. I was thinking of the bright red of the door of the garden shed, which had obviously been freshly painted, days or weeks ago, though the rest of the wood was weathered and gray. It was vulgar, that shining apple red. It was alluring. There was something wrong with me. But in the end, I couldn't bear to give the flower up. As I approached the lawn, I pressed it for a moment between my palms and slid it into my pocket, so no one would see.

• • •

After rota, we had some free time before dinner, which was typically followed by another period of meditation or an evening activity, and then lights-out. When I got back to the lawn that first day, I looked for Harriet and Nisha. Surely they would want a report, I thought, considering, but I couldn't find them anywhere. They weren't waiting for me. I sat alone on one of the large white rocks and watched the other girls mill around and sunbathe, talking or reading magazines in the grass. One of them kept taking off her top, exposing her breasts to the sun. Each time, a staffer would hurry over and tell her to cover up, but whenever the staffer looked away, the girl would pull her shirt back over her head. Every time she was chastised, she looked surprised. Her breasts were high and round and lovely, nothing like mine. I could understand why she wanted to show them.

Toward the end of the free period, I saw Janet and Laurel emerge from the woods. Laurel wore a bright pink caftan that floated behind her like a sail as they walked toward the main building. She was tall, but she walked with a slight hunch, a kind of hollowing. Janet stomped by her side in ripped black jeans and a black t-shirt. Serena was not with them.

"They're so weird," said someone close by. I didn't turn my head. "Always skulking around in the woods. Last year they disappeared for like a week. When they finally came back, they were completely covered in these small scratches, and no one said a word. I don't understand how they get away with it."

"Laurel's all right," said another.

"You're just saying that because you want to fuck her."

"Well," the girl said, and then she made a humming sound, or maybe an eating sound, and the two of them laughed and wandered away, but not before Laurel turned her head and looked right at them—at us—her eyes narrowed, as if, though she was much too far away, she had heard her name, heard herself be desired.

• • •

Dinner that night was a slurry of quinoa and kale and black beans, delivered in one enormous bowl to each table in the long, loud dining room. On the way in, just past the door, there was a little station with stacks of plates. The plates were mismatched in color and size, probably donated; the one I picked up had an unbearably twee strawberry-and-picket-fence pattern. I turned it slowly in my hands and touched my fingers to the smallest, most delicate strawberry, feeling suddenly tender. Then I was promptly jabbed in the back. When I turned to look at the girl behind me, she only grinned. She might have even looked pleasant, except that her mouth seemed twice as large as it had any right to be, her teeth twice as white.

I smiled weakly back; I felt the urge to run, or at least to slink off to a corner where no one would catch me fingering cute plates in my spare time. But I wasn't here to be the same person I was at home, I reminded myself. I was here for a reason. So, still feeling a tingling in my back where I'd been prodded, I took my dumb little plate over to Janet and Laurel's otherwise empty table, right in the center of the room. I sat down, leaving a few chairs between us for the sake of plausible deniability; they ignored me without effort. Above us, the rafters were wound with hundreds of prayer flags in faded primary colors that looked as though they'd hung there for decades.

There was a basket of fruit on the table. I reached out and palmed a plum, but no—it was plastic. I went to put it back, but stopped when I saw two curved wounds, thin creases in the fake purple skin. Someone else had tried to bite into it. Which meant that someone, weeks or years or minutes ago, had known even less than I did. I turned the plum over in my hand. I rubbed my thumb along the creases. As comforts go, it was a mild one, but still. I placed the plum back in its basket, tooth marks turned in for privacy.

"Always kale," I heard Janet mutter, pressing her bamboo fork aimlessly into the back of her hand. She turned her head, and for the first time I got a good look at her left cheek. It wasn't paint that I'd seen the day before; it was a birthmark, in the shape of a crown tipped on its side. It was a deep eggplant color, the same exact shade as her hair. She must have spent considerable time searching for the dye to match it.

"It's like they think we're rabbits," Laurel said, holding up a big green leaf, drawing out the *a*: *raaaabbits*.

"Eat up, girls," a passing staffer chirped, eyeing the fork still digging into Janet's skin, the leaf Laurel was waving like a flag. "You know what they say: Kale is life!"

"Sure," Janet said. "You chew and you chew and you chew and there's no reward."

"I think our Luke would beg to differ," the staffer said brightly. "It's *organic*."

They both seemed to straighten at the sound of his name. Laurel folded the leaf into her mouth and smiled sweetly at the staffer. Janet put down her fork, as if suddenly disgusted. "I doubt it," she said, but so far under her breath I wasn't sure I'd really heard.

A few days went by. I can't say how many; time bled uncontrollably at the Center, even that early in the summer. The Garudas had contemplative oil painting, calligraphy, more ikebana. We went on nature walks, where we learned and forgot the names of trees. We practiced *oryoki*, a mindful eating technique we did not manage to apply to our regular meals, and Kyūdō, a kind of Zen archery at which Janet alone excelled. We meditated for long periods. My dizziness slowly drained away, but I didn't sleep much better. Instead, I listened to Janet and Laurel sneak out at night. Tap, tap. Not every night, but often enough. I didn't sit at their table again—my nerve proving temporary—but I continued to watch them. Sometimes I got close enough to hear something of their constant whispers, each fragment unbearable: *glimpse, gagged, gouge, that kind of girl*. It wasn't enough. Sometimes I couldn't find them at all—they would disappear for hours, with no explanation—and while other girls were punished for breaking rules (within a week Harriet, who could never manage to hide her cigarette butts from Magda, became quite adept at hand-buffing the shrine room floor), when it was the two of them the staffers seemed not to notice, or at least not to mind. I always noticed. I always minded. Serena herself appeared only rarely, and then usually at a distance—I would see her traipsing away across the grounds in a thin white dress, like a will-o'-the-wisp, while the rest of us filed into dinner, or into bed. She was almost never at meals. She was almost never at activities. She was almost never at anything, unless she was, and when she was, she spoke to no one but her friends, the chosen two.

The chosen two: well, they made a strange pair. Most days, Janet woke before the rest of us to go running, coming back to the dormitory drenched and red. She often did push-ups in the grass, sometimes with Laurel sitting on her back, legs crossed, looking performatively at her nails. But she was nothing like the jocks I had known in my former life. For one thing, unless you count the hair, I never saw her wear any other color than black. For another, she never, ever smiled.

"Teeth are for digestion," she said one morning to Shastri Dominique, who had told her that if she'd just *smile*, even if she had to force her muscles to comply, her body would respond with positive feelings, a Pavlovian response to the performance of happiness. "Why would I want to show my digestive organs in public?" Janet said. "Why would you even want to see them? Don't be disgusting."

Dominique only exhaled through her nose, rolled her eyes, and moved toward Nisha, who had managed to fall asleep again, sitting up and dreaming.

• • •

On the other hand: one particularly hot day, the Garudas were gathered for some outdoor activity, waiting for the relevant staffer to appear, and skinny little Jamie—a fragile, friendless girl whose fingers and toes were always blue from lack of circulation—raised one arm above her head, turned white, and crumpled to the ground. Everyone stared. Someone laughed. No one moved to help her except Janet, who in a single motion scooped her up and carried her off to the infirmary, whispering into her ear the whole time. Everyone else had merely puffed out her lips or pursed them, rolled her eyes or narrowed them, and edged away from the girl on the ground. Yes, even me. You should not, under any circumstances, expect me to be the hero of this story.

Once, when no one else was in the dormitory, I snuck over to Laurel's bed to get a closer look at the photographs she'd tacked up around her pillow. They were mostly dreamy, half-cast in sepia, or else oversaturated and hypnotic. In one, she reclined on the floor of a walk-in closet, fabric hanging down around her, a faded t-shirt stretched violently across her breasts—it read BETTY'S HOT VINYL—and bit her lip at whoever was holding the camera. In another, she and a dark-haired boy shared a single cone of pink ice cream in front of a yellow brick wall. Two pretty girls wearing sequins in the forest. Three boys holding up beers that had been duct-taped to their soft, tanned hands. One photograph had clearly been taken on the dance floor: someone in a red and blue dress blurred her way toward someone in a green jacket, a halo of watery light emanating from her head like she was the second coming, a girl Christ on the ascendant, her vodka-soda-lime raised triumphant and ready above the crowd.

I reached out to touch the girl on the dance floor. My finger left a smudge on her dress. The girls in these photographs were the kind that people wrote songs about. This was the kind of life that American teenagers were meant to live. *Park that car. Drop that phone. Sleep on the floor. Dream about me.* No part of my life was so photogenic. Even if it were, no one would have been there to capture it.

Now I know, of course, how easily photographs can lie. Or maybe that's not quite right. It's not that they lie, exactly: it's that they invent their own realities.

There was one more photograph of Laurel, lying on her side on a canopied bed in a pink silk nightgown, the same one I saw her wear most nights at the Center. Soft-bodied, long-legged Laurel, always sleeping in until the last possible moment. When I think of her now, so many years later, this is the image to which I return—the photograph, not the girl. Just looking at it you could tell how smooth she would be, how amenable to your touch. Just looking at it you could see how cozy her flesh, how easily punctured.

In those early days, Harriet and Nisha pestered me about Luke, but I didn't have much to tell them. All he did was point out my tasks when I arrived, then work beside me until rota was over. When I asked him why there had never been rota in the garden before, he opened his palms to the sky. "I've never needed help before," he said. "I must be getting old." When I reported this to Harriet and Nisha, a thrown bone, they shrieked with displeasure. Old? Old? Old? Not hardly. Not a little. Old?

Of course, I told them nothing about how good he smelled, like wood and sweat and burnt sugar, and something else familiar I couldn't name but that tugged at the back of my throat like a swallowed lure. I told them nothing about his soft inner-elbow skin, or how intensely I wanted to touch him, to climb onto his back, to have him swing me through his legs the way my father had when I was small. He could have managed it: he was almost exactly as tall as my father. I had measured this by standing very close to him and noting where my nose hit his shoulder. This measurement was not at all related to the shape of his mouth, except in the ways that it was.

Once, after two hours with the spade, I stood up, shaking out my wrists, and Luke grabbed my hand, just as Magda had. Clearly, Buddhists are not shy about this sort of thing. (It's only the physical body, after all.) I tried to pull away, but he only smiled and pulled on my middle finger, hard, and I heard my knuckle pop. He popped them all, one by one. I closed my eyes to focus on the sensation of my bones shifting beneath my skin. Had any man ever touched my hands before? Only my father, and Luke's hands were much rougher than his, and much dirtier too. My father's hands were always clean, even in the garden. That is one thing I remember about him.

That day, during free hours, I went looking for Shastri Dominique's office. It wasn't difficult to find: the main building was smaller than it looked from the outside, and though there was no map or directory, each of its doors was marked with a small handwritten sign framed in blond wood, indicating its use. When I found the door with Dominique's name on it, I knocked, and could hear her sigh from the hall. "Yes?" she said.

The office was plain, much plainer than I had expected after the shrine room's gilded drama. The walls were white, their only adornment a series of identical-looking framed photographs that ringed the room. The only real color came from the window frame, which was painted red—the same saturated shade as the door of the garden shed.

Dominique herself was sitting at a white desk flanked by large metal filing cabinets. She looked tired—or perhaps that day she just looked her age.

"What can I do for you?" she said.

"I was hoping you could help me," I said, hating the whine

creeping into my voice but unable to stop it. "I'm looking for someone who was here at the Center last year."

Dominique frowned. Her fingers were long but unpainted. They looked like lit candles. "I'm afraid I can't give out any information about program participants," she said. "We have a strict confidentiality policy. It's to protect you girls more than anything."

"It's not a girl," I said. "It's my father."

She hesitated, and seemed to look at me a little harder, as if she might be able to guess whose child I was on resemblance alone.

"Even so," she said.

The coolness of her tone startled me. I looked away from her and noticed that one of the photographs on the wall showed a small group of men standing in front of the Center's main doors. At the bottom of the photograph, a piece of yellowing tape read *Darshan Family 1982*. I looked at the photo to its right. *1983*. Dominique cleared her throat; I ignored her, and followed the photographs around the room until I came to the last one—but no, it was two years old. There was no sign of my father in it. I did see Luke, looking young and clean, his hair short, one arm around Dominique's waist, the other around the shoulders of a woman I didn't recognize, all three thin and grinning. I put my hand against the wall where the next year's photograph should have hung. It felt strangely warm.

"If that's all," Dominique said. "You'd better get ready for dinner."

I didn't ask Harriet and Nisha about my father. Instead, I asked them about Serena, but they only knew what everyone did, which was everything.

• • •

What was known about Serena: that she had been to the Center every summer since her birth, sixteen years ago. That she'd been born there. That she was part Tibetan, and was in fact related to the monk who had founded the place, and that's why she always got the best tent. That's why she was never required to do any of the required activities. That no, obviously she was the heiress of a fat, cigar-sucking oil tycoon, and had more money to her name than any of us could imagine, a number there isn't even a number for, and *that's* why she was never required to do any of the required activities. That actually she was a gypsy princess, and her father was a pirate king, and he'd left her on the Center's doorstep in a basket when she was a squalling hot-faced baby and the kind-hearted Buddhists took her in and in all her years she had never left its boundaries. That no, she had left its boundaries many times, and had in fact been kicked out of thirteen boarding schools, seven of them military. That she had a sister who wasn't really her sister, but her daughter—that old slog. That she'd slept with a movie star. That she'd slept with a teacher. That she was a virgin. That she was a witch. That, virgin or witch or virgin witch, she could fly, and that she would zip around at night, stark naked, and catch birds and rabbits with her hands, and rip out their throats with her teeth, and that their blood would run down her bare breasts in the moonlight. That she was no witch, but a werewolf, and about that moonlight, well—just wait until the fat moon, girls. Then you'll see something! That it wasn't thirteen boarding schools, but thirty, and that they hadn't been boarding schools, but mental hospitals. That she could convince you of anything, anything at all, by looking directly into your eyes and telling you it was true.

And that might have been the end. I might have merely watched Serena and her friends all summer, bingeing on recycled ru-mors, working silently in the garden, confusing Luke with my father and also with the lover I thought I might have someday, or maybe sooner rather than later, why not, and forgotten why I was there, and what I wanted, and then gone back to my mother's house without having changed a thing and let myself grow up just like her, logical and harsh and unbelieving. And maybe that would have been better, all things considered. In fact, I'm sure it would have been. But one afternoon, during free hours, I wandered toward the east side of the main building and came upon a group of visiting monks in maroon robes, huddled on their knees before the Center's elaborate front entrance, building a bright sand mandala on the stones.

At first glance, the mandala seemed to be glowing, but soon I saw that it was only the richness of the colors, reds and golds and ultramarines that had been coaxed into lotus flowers and knots of eternity, spoked wheels and conch shells and tiny Buddhas. It occurred to me that all this careful artistry would soon be destroyed. The half-finished mandala was spread across what was likely the single most trafficked spot on the mountain. Once the monks stood and dusted themselves off, it wouldn't be long before their work was scattered across the road.

"They've been at it since dawn," someone said.

And there she was: Serena, standing next to me, looking down at the mandala. It was as if she had simply materialized there, close enough to touch. She was wearing that white dress again. Up close, it looked slightly wrong on her, as though it had been carefully handmade for someone else. I'll say it now: she was beautiful.

"It'll be ruined there," I said.

"Everything is impermanent," she said.

My stomach turned over at the echo. "It seems sad," I said without thinking.

She reached out and touched my arm. Her fingers were cool against my skin, and I remembered something I had read: how at extreme altitudes, your heart can explode, without warning.

"There's nothing sad about destruction," she said. "Or oblivion." She let go of my arm and took something out of her pocket—a mirror. She looked into it, turned it over a few times in her hands, looked into it again. Both of her wrists were ringed with red threads, like the tatters of fabric handcuffs. She lifted the mirror into the air, caught the sun in it, made it wink. Woolly continents of green polish floated in the centers of her fingernails.

"Impermanence is neither negative nor positive," she said. "It is simply a fact." She held the mirror out to me and twisted around to look at my reflection instead of my face, so that soon it became our reflection, her small shoulder pushing into mine. I saw myself blush.

Consider Narcissus, kneeling at the pond: *While he desires to quench his thirst, a different thirst is created. While he drinks, he is seized by the vision of his reflected form. He loves a bodiless dream.* Or consider the girl standing in front of the mirror, raising a hand. First the mirror-self obediently raises a hand back, but then she smirks, revolts. The horror of the self not quite reflected, the imprint with its own agenda, the created, imperfect double off to throttle its maker—well. It gets us every time.

"Who are you?" Serena asked my reflection.

"Where is the self?" I said. "What color is it?"

Her eyes widened a little. "Oh," she said. "You're one of us."

I said nothing. How could I have, then? It was as if she had seen through me at once, put her finger on the tenderest place, the reason I was there, the reason I already loved her. How badly I wanted to be one of them, yes, one of anyone, but especially this, a believer, a Buddhist, yes, like her, like my father. Even if I wasn't sure I knew what that meant. Did it mean anything at all? My mother's voice was still in my head. Here was Serena, offering it to me anyway, like a crown, assuming it was already mine: behold the easy generosity of the truly secure.

She closed one eye, then the other. She slipped the mirror

back into her pocket. "You're also the girl who's doing rota in the garden," she said. I nodded, but it hadn't been a question. One of the monks tutted softly under his breath. Another murmured in response. I wondered if they were listening to us. What drifted through their minds as they crafted their pristine monument to nothingness? It could have been anything. It could, of course, have been nothing.

Without warning, Serena took a step forward and kissed one of them on the very top of his bare head. He looked up at her and smiled. "Thank you," he said. I was startled at his lack of an accent, and then ashamed.

"Bye," she said, like she was leaving me at the mall.

"Wait," I said, but she had already walked away, and if she heard me, she didn't turn her head. I stood there, watching the monks work, vaguely hoping she might change her mind and come back for me, until I heard the blow of the conch shell that summoned us all to dinner.

That night, I heard Laurel tap, and Janet tap. As usual, I turned my face toward the door, waiting for that slice of light to open against the ceiling. But instead, after a few seconds, I felt a hand prod my shoulder.

"Get up." It was Laurel. "Get your shoes."

I sat up so quickly I nearly hit my head on the overhead beam. Harriet shifted above me.

"Come on, Olivia," Janet said, her voice flat but not unkind. "Come with us. Carpe PM."

Laurel snorted. I hesitated, wondering how it was that a girl who never smiled found it within herself to make a pun. Then I pulled on my sneakers and followed them out of the dormitory. They paused in the doorway, only long enough for each of their tongues to appear, dark wet shapes in the dim light, thrust toward Magda, who was snoring in her single bed, her night guard already spat onto the pillow next to her face. I kept my own tongue in my mouth, not ready, after all, to pledge my allegiance just yet.

They led me across the dark grounds in silence, until we finally turned into what I could barely identify as one of the canopied trailheads Magda had pointed out on the first day. Janet and Laurel stalked upward while I tripped over rock and root, dirtying my palms, scraping my knees. Neither of them stopped to help when I stumbled. After I cried out for the third time, Janet paused and lit a flashlight, a little mercy. It bobbed against her hip, and the circle of light it left on the ground widened and tightened, widened and tightened, as if breathing.

"Where are we going?" I asked.

"You'll find out," Laurel said, her voice dim and disembodied.

But of course, I already knew.

When I think about Serena's tent, I remember it as bigger than the others. Though I know that memory is false, or perhaps implanted. In reality, it must have been a utilitarian, one-person triangle like all the rest of the tents on the mountain. Inside, there would have been a thin mattress on top of a narrow wooden pallet, a small clapboard bookcase, and a single flashlight that expanded into a weak yellow lamp, all of it tinged green by the nylon sheeting, all of it smelling of bug spray. The expansiveness I remember must have been Serena herself, or the fact that, as I was about to discover, she had brought pillows and blankets and candles and a gold Moroccan ottoman and sheepskins and silks to throw over everything, like layers of luscious fat draped over cold gray bones.

Janet whistled as we approached, and when we heard an answering cough, Laurel unzipped the tent from the outside. I stepped in after them to find Serena sitting cross-legged at the head of her cot in a red silk kimono, a large book open in her lap and a box of ladyfingers, almost as large, on the pillow by her side.

"Oh good," she said, without looking up. "You're here. Listen to this description of Maya, will you? 'Her hair is soft, clean, and sweetly scented, black like the excellent bee and arranged in braids.'" She raised her head. "Black, like the excellent bee!" Her mouth looked like it opened on fishhooks; she had a joker smile. Her teeth were a little disorganized, I noticed. This did not detract from her overall appeal.

Janet settled cross-legged on the ottoman in the corner. "What's that now?" she asked.

"*Lalitavistara Sūtra*," Serena said. "'Her eyes are like lotus petals, her teeth are like stars in the sky, her thighs and calves are like the trunk of an elephant, and her knees have a shapely form. Surely she can only be a divine maiden.'"

"Shapely knees indicate divinity," said Janet. "Noted."

"It does make sense," said Serena.

"I have ugly knees," said Laurel mournfully. She lay down on the foot of Serena's bed and stretched both legs into the air. Her knees looked normal to me, but I didn't say anything.

"Well, no one's making any particular claims about your divinity," Janet said. "Besides, *you're* no maiden." Laurel sat up and threw a pillow at her. Janet ducked, and it hit the side of the tent, sending a shiver through it. "Let me have one of those?"

"She sounds rather ghoulish, is all I'm saying," Serena said, passing her the box of ladyfingers. "Eyes like lotus petals? Teeth like stars? Elephant trunk calves?"

"There's really no logic in what people find attractive," Janet said. She held up one of the spongy biscuits.

"There is too logic," Laurel said. "It's actually *extremely* simple. Just maybe not in fourth-century Tibet or whatever."

"Third century," Serena said. "And probably India. Though

I think the *Lalitavistara* is actually a compilation of several sources, so it's hard to say."

"Why is she still standing?" Laurel said.

They all looked up at me. I hadn't realized that I was. I sat instantly on the cold floor of the tent. Serena closed the book, slipping a leaf between the pages to mark her place. Her kimono shimmered with her every movement. I became uncomfortably aware of my pajama pants. My pajama pants had popsicles on them. The popsicles had faces. I think the faces had their tongues sticking out, but I may be self-flagellating now.

"Olivia," Serena said. "Thanks for coming." She motioned for Janet to pass me the ladyfingers. "Have you three met?"

I nodded slowly, taking a cookie. There had been introductions among the Garudas, but I knew that wasn't really what Serena meant. "She's friends with Harriet," Laurel said, prodding one knee with a finger.

"Well, that can be corrected," Serena said. She slid over to replace her book on the shelf, her movements so fluid it seemed the world itself shifted to accommodate each of her intentions.

"Laurel," she said, "let Olivia sit on the bed."

Laurel looked appalled.

"She's our guest. Guests should be given the best seat." When Laurel didn't move, Serena frowned at her. "You can have it back next time," she said. "If you're here, I mean." Laurel glared at me and pushed herself onto the floor. I hesitated, but Serena gestured impatiently, so I took Laurel's place at the foot of the bed. It was still a little warm, and I had to keep myself from kicking Laurel in the back of the head for good measure. You might as well learn this now: even the tiniest bit of power turns me instantly immoral.

"For what it's worth, I *like* Harriet," Janet said.

"You would," Laurel said.

"I just said I did," Janet said. "Are you quite slow?"

"So," Serena said, turning to me. "How's Luke treating you?"

The full force of her attention in that enclosed space was almost shocking. I thought of Maya, whoever she was: those lotus-
petal eyes, enormous, white, and searching. "Fine," I said. "He
doesn't say much. Just sort of hands me things and wanders away."

"That sounds like him," she said. "But would you say he
likes you?"

I didn't understand where this line of questioning was leading. "He gave me a flower," I blurted.

"Did he," Serena said. She and Laurel exchanged a swift
glance.

"I still don't understand why they gave the garden rota to a
new girl," Laurel said.

"Well, they're not stupid," Janet said.

"They *are*, though."

I could feel Serena watching me. I looked down at the popsicles: they had turned evil and leering in the half-light of the
tent. "My dear Olivia," she said at last. "I was hoping you'd join
us tonight for the feeling."

"For what?" I said.

"The Feeling," she said, as if that clarified anything at all.

We followed her out of the tent and away from the clearing,
along an almost imperceptible path that eventually sloped upward to a small platform made of rock, flat and open like a
palm. An overhang loomed on one side, creating a sort of shallow cave, but the rest was wholly exposed, like a bald spot the
mountain was failing to conceal. Serena unfolded her flashlight
into a lantern. Janet spread a blanket on the rock, and Laurel
dropped a large bag onto it.

I felt a little dizzy again. I had no idea how high up we were.
I took a few exploratory steps toward the dark perimeter, but
Serena caught my arm. "Stay away from the edge," she said.
"Trust me, you wouldn't want to fall from here." I stopped and

searched the striated darkness, but it was impossible to see the place where rock became air. The edge could have been anywhere. She pulled me toward what I hoped was the center of the platform and we sat.

Janet called it *sounds that feel good*. Laurel called it *a brain-gasm*. *We are what we think*, Serena said, and the other girls closed their eyes. I pretended to close mine too, but really I watched as Janet drummed her fingers softly along the edge of a wooden box. Laurel rubbed a small piece of fabric between her fingers. Serena dragged her thumbnail along an old wooden comb, creating a neutral xylophonic clicking. I sat. I listened. For a while I felt nothing. But when I closed my eyes at last and focused hard on the sound coming from Serena's comb, something started climbing up my back.

How can I explain this? It will never make sense to you unless you've felt it. But here: it was as though there were strings connecting my ears to my tailbone in a giant V, strings that had always been there but that I had never noticed before, and then the strings lit up, ting, ting, ting, and grew denser, then brighter, and sour somehow, and then something was knitting itself between the strings like a web, snick, snick, something feathery, sneaky, warm. It wasn't sexual, nor was it wholly unsexual. It felt like the shiver you get when someone massages your scalp with too light a touch and you're both enjoying it and desperately reaching out with your very skin and hair for *more*—except distended and stretched, filling your head with the feeling of an itch being scratched, or almost scratched, an itch you didn't even know you had there, there on the hot red underside of your scalp.

Years later, I found out that the Feeling is a documented phenomenon, and was not, as I had thought, a magic specific to us—look how quick I am to say *us*, foolish thing—alone. The official term for it is ASMR (autonomous sensory meridian response), and the little alternative versions of us who practice it these days get their Feelings via YouTube clips, watching some wispy woman with a soft voice apply makeup to her face, or click her long fingernails together, or name everything in the room in a frantic whisper. In one video, a slim-nosed blonde with a German accent fits a wig onto her camera so she can give the viewer a haircut. She combs the limp bangs that hang across the lens. She snips at them with a pair of sewing scissors. *Can you feel it?* she asks. *Can you feel what I'm doing right now? It may seem like you can't, but just see if you can. There. There. You feel it, don't you? Yes, yes, yes, doesn't that feel good?*

I watch it and think: we are all so desperately lonely.

Serena told me once that giving herself the Feeling was the only way she could have dreams.

"Without the Feeling it's only blackness," she said. "Not just nothingness, not just going to sleep and waking up. It's like I'm dreaming the blackness."

"What's the blackness like?" I asked.

But she wouldn't answer.

After it was over, Serena reached into the pocket of her kimono and pulled out a silver box. From this she extracted a slim cigarette, placed it between her lips, and lit it with a little silver lighter. She didn't offer one to me or to anyone else.

"Those things will kill you, you know," Janet said.

"Don't be boring, Janet," Serena said, leaning back on her elbows and exhaling with exaggerated relish. "Anyway, what was it Shantideva said? *Life is a party thrown by an executioner.*" She looked at me. "So, did you get it?" she asked.

"I think so," I said.

"If you don't *know*," Laurel said, "you didn't." She glowered prettily, and I remembered a cartoon I'd seen as a child: a singing goldfish, plump and shiny, made sexy with long eyelashes and purple eye shadow and a coquettish pout, its gossamer tail flicking suggestively around the screen. That was the earliest shadow of a sexual impulse I can remember—from a place near the base of my spine I wanted all of this: to possess it, to become it, and to squeeze it unmercifully in my hands until it died.

"I got it," I said.

"Good," Serena said. "Because the Feeling is only the first step."

"Oh." Laurel sighed. "Don't."

"The first step to what?" I asked. I wanted to kick her again.

"We've been discussing it," Serena said. She exhaled another stream of smoke at the sky. "And we're going to learn to levitate this summer." Her voice was flat, matter-of-fact, as if she were telling me that they were going to the beach this summer, or planning to perfect their bocce game, or finally master the French subjunctive. "Since we're here," she said. "At the Levitation Center." She spread her arms. She had the glint of a zealot.

"Since we're always here," said Janet.

"It's what this place is *for*, after all," said Serena.

"I'm sure you've heard the rumors," said Laurel.

Yes, I had heard the rumors, but which rumors did she mean? The small scratches, the movie star, the mental hospitals, the geological phenomenon? "I thought only certain people could do it," I said. "The chosen ones, or whatever."

"We're going to choose ourselves," said Serena.

"Since no one else ever would," said Janet, tugging at a little plant that had risen between the rocks.

"Speak for yourself, darling," said Laurel.

"It's dangerous," said Serena. "It will be difficult. Do you want to?"

Did I feel a sense of foreboding in this moment? Did I have

any idea, any inkling, of what might happen to us? Did I think what she was offering me was truly dangerous, or even remotely possible? Of course not. Don't be ridiculous. I wasn't even thinking about levitation. I wasn't even thinking about my father, although later I would, later I would tell myself that levitation was the key to truly knowing him at last, the key to his love, and to my own belief—to everything I thought I wanted. But at that moment I was thinking of nothing except for the girl in front of me with the dark hair and the dark smile and the dark eyes sunk deep into her head and her two dark friends, who were waiting for me to answer.

"I want to," I said.

"Good," she said. "We're going to get *everything* we want this summer." She looked into my eyes. "I promise."

And why not? Even before I understood what Serena was really after, the appeal of levitation was obvious to me. Every girl wants more from the world. Every girl wants magic, to transcend the mundanity of her life. Every girl wants power, and Serena more than most. I had felt that about her immediately. Of course levitation, as a power, has a relatively limited phenomenal scope. But it is more than merely lifting into the air. It is a symbol of freedom (all little children dream of flight). It is a symbol of control (ditto). As in so many cases, the blurring of the sign and the signified simply cannot be helped.

For instance, the first thing TV witches learn to do is levitate objects. Pencils, mainly. This often serves as the first indication that they are irreversibly unlike other girls. (Girls love to be unlike other girls, because of the lies we are told about what other girls are like.) Powerful mystical items are frequently found floating over their pedestals. When someone becomes infused with a sudden energy, whether internal or external, mystical or common—rage, love, nuclear radiation—they are likely to be raised up into the air by the force of it. Storm, etc. *I've gotta crow. Spread beneath my willow tree.* The films of Tarkovsky. And so on. This is only in the kind of stories where the rules of physics are malleable, of course. Though one could argue that the rules of physics are always malleable, just like anything else, if you press hard enough, if you use the right instrument.

The monks continued working on the mandala for the next three days. Whenever I could, I would go and admire the way they mapped out the symbols and signs I was beginning to recognize, the way they stepped around the circle like surgeons, never disturbing a grain. When the mandala was finished, it was roped off for a few hours. Photographs were taken, oohs and ahhs uttered, and then, after a small ceremony, the ropes came down. As soon as the monks bowed away, Serena slipped from the gathered crowd. She ran her hands through her hair, adjusted her dress, and stepped forward to be the first one to slide her bare feet through all its articulate arteries.

3

Stop me if you've heard this one before: the story of the Buddha begins in a dream. Like any worthwhile fairy tale, it has a prince, and a crone, and a guide, and three journeys. There is, however, no happily ever after. Buddhists don't believe in that sort of thing. Happily, I mean, or ever after.

Long ago, Prince Siddhartha Gautama was born to the king and queen of the Śākya clan in the ancient Indian kingdom of Kapilvastu. On the night of Siddhartha's conception, his mother, Queen Maya (there she is, starry teeth and all), dreamed that an enormous white elephant, resplendent with six tusks, had entered her body on the right side. The priests who interpreted this dream told her that it meant her son would be exceptional, either as a great king or as a wandering ascetic. So as Siddhartha grew, his father—who, like most kings, rather preferred kingliness to asceticism—worked hard to make Siddhartha's life perfect, so he would never think of leaving it. Thus, the young Siddhartha experienced no strife of any kind. He witnessed no decay, no pain. If an attendant fell ill, she was removed from the palace immediately. If a gardener's hair grew gray, he was replaced.

Imperfect flowers were cut at the root before the prince could happen upon them. Siddhartha lived in a world of endless health and beauty and joy. But he was not allowed to go outside the palace walls, and as he grew older, he also grew curious. Finally, he convinced his father to let him see the land they governed.

The king was nervous. He instructed Siddhartha's driver, Channa, to show his son only beauty. So, Siddhartha saw mountains and rivers, he saw sky deep as ocean. But on the way home, Siddhartha saw something else on the side of the road: a peasant doubled over in pain, his body thin and covered with sores. What's wrong with that man? Siddhartha asked. He is sick, said Channa. His body is diseased and weak. Siddhartha, confused, was silent until they reached the palace gates. But soon he begged to be allowed out again, and this time, despite the pains Channa took to avoid it, Siddhartha saw an old crone hobbling along the road. What has happened to this woman? Siddhartha asked. Why does she walk this way? Channa lowered his eyes. She is old, he said. She has lived a long time, and her body has been very nearly used up. Upset, Siddhartha asked to be taken home immediately. But after a time, they ventured out once more, and on this trip, Siddhartha saw something he found more troubling than ever before: a body lying cold and still on a stretcher. Channa told him the body was dead, and that it would not rise again. Will I die also? asked Siddhartha. My wife? My son? You know Channa's answer.

Siddhartha went back to the palace very depressed. He began to obsess about these things—sickness, old age, and death—that he could not control. His father forbade him from leaving the palace and ordered the guards to stop him when he tried. But one night, after a feast, everyone in the palace except the prince fell into a deep sleep, and Siddhartha saw his chance. He kissed his slumbering wife and son, looked around one last time, and snuck out into the world of suffering.

He wandered for a long time, thinking, learning, studying

with different teachers, acquiring followers and losing them. He fasted for six years. He meditated for more. Finally, feeling himself close to the understanding he sought, he sat beneath a tree—an ancient fig at Bodh Gaya, which grew only perfect, heart-shaped leaves—to consider the nature of human suffering. Mara, lord of desire, appeared with an army, but their arrows turned to flowers that fell harmlessly around the meditating prince. In a rage, Mara sent his three beautiful daughters to tempt the prince from his seat, but Siddhartha was not swayed. Finally, Mara demanded that Siddhartha prove that he was worthy of enlightenment. Siddhartha simply reached down and touched the ground.

The next morning, as the sun rose, Siddhartha cut the last veils of ignorance from his mind. He realized that all concepts were impermanent, empty and without inherent existence. He realized that human suffering came from clinging to false ideas—self, happiness, continuity—and that it could be overcome only by waking up to them. He realized the true nature of reality. It was through these realizations that Siddhartha achieved enlightenment and became the Awakened One: the Buddha.

"Or, maybe," my father said, sitting on the edge of my childhood bed the night after my very first meditation lesson. "Who knows exactly what Siddhartha realized, and in what order, and at which moment. But these things became the backbone of his teachings. The Four Noble Truths." He ticked them off on his fingers. "Life is suffering. Suffering is caused by clinging to things. But there is a way out, and the way out is the Eightfold Path. Which I will also explain someday, if you want me to." Then he stood, said good night, and left, lingering in the doorway for a moment before shutting the door quietly behind him. That night, I barely slept. How could I, considering the depth and breadth of human suffering? How could I, considering the metaphysical teachings of the smooth-skinned

Indian prince? How could I, considering the sounds now coming from my parents' bedroom, and the feeling of these clean,
untucked, untouched sheets sliding soft against my tender legs?

In the morning, I rose slowly from my bunk and dragged myself
into one of the open showers; I leaned my forehead against the
chipped yellow tile as the water ran. I was not used to staying
up all night. I might have even fallen asleep that way, naked and
leaning in my cheap shower shoes, had it not been for the girl
singing atonally in the stall next to mine. (Poor cat, quite stran-
gled.) When I emerged, my towel carefully organized to cover as
much of my body as possible, most of the Garudas were still in
the dormitory, getting ready or resisting the same. Nisha was giving Harriet an extravagant cat eye. Jamie was still curled in bed,
her covers tight to her chin, her eyes open. A girl named Evie
was methodically winding her blond dreadlocks into a pile on
top of her skull; when she was finished, she looked as though she
were wearing a second, expressionless head, the exact same size
and color as her own. Janet and Laurel were not there. Janet's bed
was neatly made: hospital corners. Laurel's was a nest of blankets.

I got dressed and tried to shake off the feeling I had, sudden
but acute, that they'd disappeared, not just from the room, but
from the world—or worse, that they'd never been there at all.
Despite Laurel's pictures still tacked above her stirred sheets,
despite Janet's damp running shoes at the foot of the bed, I was
half-convinced I had imagined them, simply desired them into
being. It was the obvious explanation. Girls like them, a girl like
me. *We are what we think.* Whom did I imagine I was fooling?

But when I entered the main shrine room, there they were,
corporeal and everything, seated in their usual corner. No one
else had arrived yet, not even Shastri Dominique, and the room

looked large and mouthlike. I hesitated. Janet waved me over and patted the cushion beside her.

"We like to get to meditation early," she said as I approached.

"We are very particular about our cushions," said Laurel.

I looked down at her cushion and found it to be indistinguishable from the others.

"Just wait until the sun clears the northeast peak," Janet said. The other girls were filing in now. Shastri Dominique bowed low at the door, found her place at the front, and struck the bowl.

After a few minutes, I turned my head to look out the window and noticed that Harriet was staring at me, her brow knit. I felt a flicker of pride, sour and dumb, like the sensation of stealing something small from someone deserving of theft. I flashed her what I imagined was a winning smile and focused my attention back on the front of the room. I didn't understand Harriet's problem. These girls seemed all right to me. Especially when, fifteen minutes later, our cushions were drenched in a yolky light, a light that left my limbs warm and loose for hours.

If I had known what was going to happen that summer, maybe I would have paid more attention to Harriet. Maybe I would have left these strange girls alone, no matter what they knew, no matter how pretty the light on their cushions. If I had left them alone, maybe none of it would have even happened.

No, here's the truth: I would never have left them alone, even if I had known what was going to happen. Never. There are some things I simply cannot resist.

Later that morning, the danger of fainting more or less behind us, the Garudas went on a hike. We assembled after breakfast at the flagpole on the east side of the lawn, and a nearly neckless white guy introduced himself as Colin and pointed up at the flag. This was called the dream flag, he said, so named because it had come to an important teacher in a dream: blue and yellow twisted together as if each were crashing on the shore of the other. He explained that yellow was the earth, and blue the sky, and the curl of the wave was the Buddhadharma penetrating them both. Janet reached over and poked Laurel at the word *penetrating*, and Laurel pinched her back, but they both nodded at Colin's explanation, as if they already knew much more than he was saying. (The use of *penetrate* to mean "insert into" dates back to the 1520s, but the connotation of affecting one's feelings dates only to the 1630s: a hundred years of being touched but untouched.)

According to Colin, the trip up the mountain would *really* get our blood flowing, and all that blood flow was *totally* going to help us in our quest for ultimate warriorhood. Body and soul, you guys. Like, yeah, etc. Colin looked barely past his teenage years himself—that morning he wore a ratty t-shirt that read BUDDHIST FIST above, imaginatively, a picture of a dark blue fist designed to look as though it were emerging triumphant from his solar plexus. Janet routinely gave him the finger when he turned his back. When I asked if Serena was coming, the other two exchanged a look.

"Serena doesn't like Colin," Laurel said.

"Or exerting herself," Janet said. She jumped up onto a rock. "Laurel likes Colin, though." She gave him the finger again.

"I don't," Laurel said. But then Colin clapped his hands once to call us to attention and she turned her face immediately toward his.

Janet caught my eye. *See*, she mouthed. It was hard to tell how she meant it, since she never smiled. Everything could have been a joke. Everything could have been serious.

"Girls, girls, girls," Colin said. "Let's, like, get started?" He produced a coil of bright ropes from somewhere, and swiftly hooked Nisha and Harriet together, looping one end around each girl's waist and then clipping it to itself, like a snake eating its tail, and also its head.

"The ropes are to remind you that we are all connected," Colin said. "You are like, simply not possible without anyone else?" He clipped Samantha, a pretty petty thief and the only person I had ever met with a tongue ring, to Jamie, who that day looked nearly translucent, like a raw shrimp. Double-headed Evie was clipped to Paola, a girl who suffered from eternal baby voice, but was never mocked for it, on account of her cache of desirable pills and powders. Colin approached Janet and Laurel with a rope—then at the last second, he clipped Janet to me instead. Laurel he attached to Margaret, a broad-shouldered girl whose septum piercing made her look downright bovine.

"Gross," said Laurel.

"Tell me about it," said Margaret. She jiggled the rope. "There's a reason I never had a Barbie." But what that reason was, we were not to discover, because Colin clapped his hands again and we started up the trail.

The mountain, Shastri Dominique had warned us, was full of cracks. Big cracks, smaller ones. Gorges, craters, chasms, crevasses, fissures, abysses both literal and figurative. A girl could easily fall down. A girl could easily be lost. Some cracks had water at their bottoms, some rock. There were cliffsides too, and holes, and ghastly animals with gnashing teeth, ready to pull you into their hidden caves, suck you into their jagged mouths. This in addition to the many twisting, interlocking trails that were thrown over the mountain like a knotted net, a skullcap sewn by a madman, enough to busy any wanderer for years. The mountain had a thousand ways to keep you, Shastri Dominique had said. This was why we were only to be in the woods when accompanied by a staff member. The staff members knew the mountain. They would protect us.

What a ridiculous idea. Girls like us cannot be protected, we swore into one another's palms and shoulder blades. Girls like us cannot be saved. It's the mistake everyone makes.

We climbed. At first, the trail was wide and gradual, sloping upward. I liked this: the birds' layered song, Janet's smooth breathing at my side. The filtered light made the wildflowers that grew along the side of the trail look somehow brighter. We take flowers for granted, though they are absurd things: little sex-crazed jewel boxes. *The reason for a flower is to make another flower*, my mother used to say.

The trail may not have been particularly demanding, but Janet walked fast, and soon I was struggling to keep up. She had insisted we be at the front. I had the impression she liked to be first at most things. The rope bobbed between us. I slapped a mosquito off my arm, leaving a small red smear.

"This is a nonsense interpretation of the notion of interconnectedness," Janet said. "Don't tell Serena. She'll have a field day." She wrapped her fingers around the rope.

"It seems like Serena knows a lot about Buddhism," I managed.

"She's been coming here every summer since she was a kid," Janet said. "At this point, she's probably read every book in the place. She's been to about a thousand lectures, too."

"She doesn't come to activities very much," I said.

"It is difficult to get Serena to do anything she doesn't want to do," Janet said mildly.

"What about you?" I asked her.

"I like the activities."

"I meant—do you believe in all of this? Interconnected-ness?" I hesitated. "Levitation?"

The path was getting steeper, but Janet didn't slow down. I was breathing hard now; I felt both annoyed and relieved that she didn't seem to notice. "I think most of it is bullshit," she said. "In the way that most of everything is bullshit." She kicked a rock out of our way, and it tore a hole in the bushes on the side of the trail. "But also, Serena walked up to me on my very first day here, all of twelve years old, and told me hello and that she liked my face and that she had decided she was going to change my life forever. It wasn't entirely false advertising."

"What do you mean?" I said.

"You have to admit, it would be pretty interesting." She squinted upward. "And it's not like we have anything else to do."

There was a crash behind us. Paola had pushed Evie into the bushes and then, inevitably, been pulled in with her. This was followed by a period of elaborate cursing. Colin, who was somewhat out of breath himself, ran over to haul them out and untangle their rope and lecture them again on the whole inter-connectedness thing.

I took advantage of the commotion to rest my legs, until, after only a few moments, Janet tugged me forward again. "What about you?" she said. "How'd you wind up here, of all places?"

"My dad's into Buddhism," I said. When that didn't seem like enough, I said: "And I don't get along with my mother." I don't know why I didn't simply tell her that my father had aban-doned me without a word, or that I had—let's admit it—run away from my mother's house, if you can really call it running away when you leave plain tracks and credit card receipts and no one bothers to come after you. Janet would have understood perfectly, I know that now, but at the time it all seemed raw and terrible, a wound too new to let breathe.

"What about Laurel?" I asked.

"Isn't it obvious?"

It wasn't, or not to me, but I nodded anyway.

Janet was from New York City, a place I could only imagine as an endless series of sharp edges and hard surfaces. Her mother had left her father when she was six, and now lived in Cincinnati with an accountant and a set of twins, half siblings Janet had never met. Her father worked long hours, and she had more or less raised her two younger brothers in their small Brooklyn apartment.

When I told her that my parents were divorced too, she shrugged. "It's very popular," she said, but after that I thought her movements were a little looser around me.

Janet couldn't afford the price of the program. It was an aunt who financed her stays at the Center every summer, she said, a mostly estranged sister of her mother's with herds of cats, an addiction to incense, and a hefty inheritance (courtesy of not one but two suspiciously deceased husbands), who had visited her family's apartment in the city once and had sent her a registration notice and a plane ticket that summer and every summer since. But she'd never visited again, and when Janet called one night to ask if she could come live with her, her aunt pretended she didn't know who was calling. Janet did a very funny impression of this. She was almost able to keep the bitterness out of it.

We stopped after an hour in a grassy clearing flanked by two oblong boulders. Most of the other girls immediately sat down, taking off their shoes or splaying themselves theatrically on the ground. I was desperate to splay along with them, to explore what I was sure was an epic series of new blisters, but Janet showed no signs of fatigue; she just stood there, at the edge of the clearing, as if waiting for instructions, so I stood too. Samantha began poking her finger through a hole in the bottom of her sneaker, steadily widening it but apparently unable to stop. Paola spat repeatedly into a bush, while Evie patted her shoulder absently, looking up into the branches, their squabble at least temporarily forgotten. Harriet had been carrying Nisha on her back, their connective tissue unrelated to the physical rope; now they leaned against each other to stretch. Margaret and Laurel were sitting under two separate trees, their own physical rope a trip wire between them.

This was as high as we would go—any higher and the paths became murky, the ground less stable, Colin explained. As we unclipped, he began taking peanut butter and jelly sandwiches from his button-covered backpack and passing them around.

"Oh," said Laurel. "Luke's jam is like magic." Breathlessness suited her, I thought.

"Or like chemistry, even," Janet said.

"Why is everyone so obsessed with him?" I said, too loudly. I was sure I knew the answer, but I couldn't help myself. I wanted to hear them say it.

Laurel curled her lip. "You know, Janet, I think this one's dumb," she said. She licked some jam off the side of her wrist. "Why is she so dumb?" Cruelty suited her too. But before either Janet or I could say anything, Laurel shifted her attention over Janet's shoulder. "Harriet!" she called, smiling widely. "Hi. Did you want something?"

I turned to look. Harriet had her mouth set. She shook her head.

"We haven't even *talked* yet," Laurel said. "How was your year?"

All of the other girls suddenly seemed to be watching us. "Pretty good," she said.

"Good," Laurel said, slinging one arm around Janet's shoulders and coiling the other tight around my waist. "Now mind your own fucking business."

• • •

Laurel was from Virginia. Her house, Janet informed me, had wings. Her father was some kind of financier, and her mother was an ex-socialite heiress who spent most of her time at various teas. They first sent Laurel to the Center while her mother was on an Eastern medicine kick, and even after she'd kicked her kick—the guru had turned out to be a fraud, the turmeric hadn't agreed with her stomach—they kept sending her.

"I thought I was going to hate it, the first year," Laurel said. "But turns out the girls here are *very* amusing." She reached out and managed to pinch Janet's arm before she could pull it away. "Anyway, my parents still think it's good for me."

"Shows what they know," I said, and at this, she threw back her head and laughed, and I was almost shocked by the warmth that spread through my body. Laurel had a quality about her that I've noticed in well-liked people my entire life, but have never been able to emulate: when she focused on you, she made you feel like you were the most attractive, interesting person in the room. She pleased by making others feel pleasurable. Of course, it didn't hurt that she was attractive. Of course, it didn't hurt that she radiated wealth. You could see the wealth in her cheeks, clear as anything. Day. Crystal. Vodka. My own parents managed, but things were harder for all of us after the separation. Corners and coupons were cut. Laurel was going to be a debutante in the fall.

"They're even making me perform at the ceremony," she said.

"Perform what?" I wanted to know.

"My parents gave me a choice when I was a kid," she said. "Piano or violin. I, of course, crossed my arms and said *harp*." She stuck out her bottom lip, now and, presumably, then. She got a harp. The orchestra at her school didn't know what to do with her. They kept giving her piano parts, and no one ever heard her angelic glissandos over the chorus of slammed keys. Not wanting to waste their investment, her parents signed her up for a nearby harpists' ensemble. Harpists are strange people,

Laurel informed us. One woman in the group was in her fifties and had never once cut her hair; she looped it around her waist when she played. "Her *ends*," Laurel said, throwing a hand over her eyes. "They haunt me." There was only one man in the group. He had a kind face, nearly handsome, and he wore old-fashioned wire glasses and vintage three-piece suits. He was Laurel's favorite, and she liked to sit beside him and watch him play.

"I used to dream about him," she said. "He had the most magnificent harp I've ever seen. And he played so delicately with those large hands. But he never once even looked at me." She closed her eyes, picturing—what? His hands, his harp, his ability, his inattention? Whatever it was made her hum two low notes to herself.

Such small obsessions, I would find, were typical of Laurel, who was delighted by beauty in all its forms and abhorred ugliness, especially when it constituted, as she put it, a "missed opportunity." Why would anyone ever choose to have her world be ugly, she wondered aloud once. Because ugliness is the truth, said Janet. Because beauty costs more, I said. Neither ugliness nor beauty exists on an absolute level, said Serena. At this, Laurel flung her legs out in front of her, traced her fingers along her smooth calves. If we're all living in a constructed, illusory reality, that's fine, she said. Mine's going to have a chandelier. And cake. Easy for her to say, I thought. Her house already had a chandelier.

My mother would have agreed with Laurel, for what it's worth. She always refused to watch horror movies or documentaries, arguing that paying good money for bad feelings was the absolute height of insanity. I once found her position silly, irresponsible, even. But now I agree with her. Now it's plodding historical romances or old episodes of *Buffy the Vampire Slayer* or nothing. I don't want to feel anything anymore. I want only comfort. I want only to forget what we did.

When everyone had finished eating, Colin stood, cleared his throat, and pointed at the rock face opposite the place where we were standing. The mountains were so close together we could count the individual branches on the trees on the other side, but it would have taken hours to climb down and around to touch them. Two smooth furrows sloped down the rock, maintaining a parallel stance until they disappeared into the brush.

"The Sweet Sorrows," he said. He cleared his throat again. It was an annoying tic he had. "As the story goes, long ago a handsome boy and a beautiful girl from a settlement at the bottom of this mountain fell in love, but each was betrothed to another." (He really said it like that. *Betrothed to another*. He had completely dropped his displaced surfer-dude style for a sweeping storytelling voice. Janet groaned and gave him the finger again when he said it, even though he could see her, but he only winked.)

"They would climb the mountain to meet every night, right in those very bushes, but as their respective weddings approached, their families became suspicious. Finally, the night before the wedding, the girl broke off her engagement, unable to face life without her one true love. The scandal was incredible. She was ostracized from her family, driven out of town for her disobedience, and left to survive on her own in the woods. The boy, seeing his lover's punishment, quickly married the girl to whom he had been promised. They say his lover, thusly spurned"—(ibid.)—"stood alone at the top of the mountain, waiting for him in their old meeting place, sobbing uncontrollably until her tears grew so large and numerous that they carved those two tracks in the stone. Even then she kept crying, harder and harder, hoping he would come to her, and after some time her body twisted and spread, her unmoving feet grew into the ground and her untouched, unloved skin crusted over and she became an enormous tree. You can see her from here, girls: the weeping willow that still hangs over the cliff's edge."

"Look at the way it's positioned," Harriet said, off to my right. "Someday soon, that willow's going to fall."

"But will it make a sound?" Nisha asked.

"Is it just me," Janet said, "or does it seem like an inordinate number of the world's geological features were supposedly created by crying women?"

"Crying women, dying women," Laurel said. "I'd have eaten that treacherous little bastard alive."

In Māori legend, a woman's tears, shed over a lover's death, once froze into a giant glacier. You can, if so inclined, hike it today. They say the Weeping Rock at the peak of Turkey's Mount Sipylus was once a woman named Niobe, who bragged about her virile husband and her many children in front of the wrong infertile goddess, and woke to find them all murdered, her legendary pride quashed under the weight of their bloody bodies. That'll teach her not to be so full of herself, the townswomen said. She cried for so long that the gods took pity on her and turned her into an unfeeling stone. But soon, even the cold stone began to leak, and it sits to this day atop the mountain, crying rainwater over its dead men for all eternity. There is of course Daphne, who may or may not have been crying but was certainly on the verge of being grabbed and raped and perhaps murdered along the way, these things happen (*What was she wearing?* they'll all want to know), when she was transformed into a tree, and so ask yourself. Or ask the Egyptians why the Nile overflows each year. (Or ask me: it's because Isis cried so hard over Osiris that her tears made the great river rise.) They call it the Night of the Drop.

• • •

That afternoon, as I worked beside Luke in the garden, still exhausted from the hike, I kept thinking of those forbidden lovers.
I could easily imagine Luke waiting in the forest, hands in his
pockets; in my fantasy the girl for whom he waited was both me
and not me. Today, a blue vein was visible in that creamy elbow
skin, as though his wiring were showing. He wore a thin white
t-shirt that read, in peeling iron-on letters, NOTHING HAPPENS.
It was slightly yellow under the arms, but there was a small hole
in it that I wanted to put my finger through.

"You know," I said, "everyone talks about you." Only the
day before, Harriet and Nisha had been waxing ecstatic about
the angle of his chin. The day before that, a Lion named Svetlana had asked me to slip Luke a note I could smell from where
she held it in her hand, and I had told her I would do it, because
Svetlana was the kind of girl who becomes instantly violent
when refused. Instead, I had taken the note into the shower
with me and held it under the water until it disintegrated, and
peed down the drain after it for good measure. Even Jamie
seemed to grow whiter and thinner whenever his name was
mentioned, if such a thing were possible.

He turned, squatting back on his heels. "What do they say?"
he asked. He shook a clot of dirt off his glove. He peered at the
fence over my head. He was performing disinterest admirably,
but he wanted to know—even I could see that, even then.

"They say you can levitate," I said. "For one thing."

"Oh, that." He turned his attention back to the plant he was
coaxing into the ground.

"Is it true?"

He squinted at me. I could see a few strands of chest hair
through the hole in his shirt. "Is that all they say?" he said.

"They all want to marry you," I said. I knew I was being
childish, but I couldn't help myself.

He laughed.

"Yes, it's very silly," I said.

He raised an eyebrow. "You don't want to marry me, I take it?"

"I don't believe in marriage," I said. That, at least, was true. "No offense."

"You're a very interesting girl," he said, in a voice that made me want to take back what I had said. He reached out and encircled my ankle with two of his fingers. He squeezed it tight, then released it, and returned to his work. Afterward, I kept catching him smiling.

Now, with many men behind me, I can recognize this for what it was: an intimacy too easy to be real. The flower he gave me on the very first day, the probing questions, all those gentle, innocent touches. He knew what he was doing. I did not. This is the way plenty of stories go, of course. But this one will end a little differently.

That night, the four of us returned to the rock palm. We had decided to start with the basics. Light as a feather, stiff as a board, that kind of thing. Ten million slumber partiers couldn't be wrong, or at least not completely, Janet said. But Serena was distracted that night, dissociated even. She was often distant. You could map her by this prefix pattern, from the Latin, meaning *apart, asunder, away*, or even *utterly*, or signifying reversal, negation, lack, release, or, sometimes, intense force. She often looked as though the world weren't real to her, as though she had to swim through it like salt water.

So: Light as a feather. Stiff as a board. Serena's kimono slipping. My fingers on her hot skin. Her body in the air between us.

"This isn't enough," she said.

Serena stood in the center of the thick wool blanket, and Laurel and Janet and I each took a corner, and then we backed away until it pulled taut under her feet.

"More," she said. We refastened our grips. I took half the blanket under my arm and leaned back, my toes lifting. Laurel was panting, she was pulling so hard, and for a few seconds, Serena rose up—the blanket, with enough force applied, had become as stiff as floor. She raised her arms. She jumped. The blanket jolted and we all fell in a confused jumble on the ground. My cheek landed against a soft patch of moss, my knee bruised against the rock. Twigs cracked like bird bones beneath our bodies. I laughed.

But Serena had fallen hard. She rubbed at her hip with a palm. "This is serious," she said. "Every year, thousands of people come up here, to the *Levitation Center*, hoping to do this. But everybody, everybody fails."

"Almost everybody," Laurel said.

"Exactly," Serena said. "Let's try again." We tried again, pulling and pulling until the blanket burned our fingers.

The magic carpet: a dream almost as old as the dream of human flight. That you might find an old, everyday object and use it to elevate your old, everyday self. Except that old, everyday objects tend to do old, everyday things.

"This is kid stuff," Serena said at last. "We're better than this."

We were, as it turned out. But not that night.

4

I don't remember when I realized that my father wasn't like other fathers. I don't have a specific moment to point to. The feeling was simply there, like a skin. Soap, sneaker, suitcase: everyday. As a child, I snuck into his shrine room, turned the objects I found there around in my hands, guessed at their names. The little bell, the little scepter, the peacock fan. No other father I knew of had any of these. At school, I told my classmates that I was a Buddhist—how my mother would have raged, had she known—but I couldn't tell them exactly what that meant. *But what do you actually* do? they asked, obedient churchgoers all. *We meditate*, I said. *So it's just sitting around*, they said. *No*, I said, *no*, but I wasn't sure. I couldn't explain.

Here's something you may not know about Buddhism, something Serena explained to me that my father never did: contrary to popular American mythology, Buddhism is not actually about gentleness, or kindness—though the Buddha did promote compassion for all creatures, and though basic goodness, which means exactly what you think and also more, is something many Buddhists cultivate. "*Wisdom* is the primary concern of a Buddhist," Dzongsar Jamyang Khyentse Rinpoche wrote. "Morals and ethics are secondary." The ultimate aim of Buddhist practice is not inner peace (om, namaste, etc.) but rather to end human suffering. Turns out that the way to do this is not to be kind to your neighbor, but instead to become fully awake to the truth of the universe. Well, sure. Why not?

My mother dragged me out of my father's shrine room whenever she found me in there alone. She forbade him from talking to me about religion. "Some things you can't help but pass on to your children," she told me once. "But I want you to have every possible choice about this."

"I choose Dad's religion," I said. "You don't even have one."

"Your brain isn't fully developed yet," she said. "You can't pick anything as important as religion until it is." When I asked her when my brain would be developed, she seemed to consider it, staring hard at the place between my eyes. "Not until you're married," she said at last, and laughed at her own joke, and tucked her long black hair behind her ears like a girl, which I see only now that she still so essentially was.

My mother was too kinetic for meditation, of course. She was too loud for church, too large for any temple. My mother found the idea of basic goodness unsavory, if not downright insane. My mother believed in nothing.

Nothing, of course, for Shakespeare = *nothing*, as in nothing, also as in *noting*, as in gossip, and *noting* as in overhearing, and *noting* as in overhearing gossip, and *no thing*, as in what a woman has between her legs. My mother believed in all of these nothings. Nothing was sacred. Noting was sacred. No thing was sacred.

Well, opposites attract. We are told this. Paula Abdul has seared this into our brains. My parents were attracted, that much is clear. But they were repelled too, and just as forcefully. I don't know what that means. Magnetization was not the only force at work, I suppose.

After breakfast the next morning, we found Serena waiting for us on one of the Center's whitewashed boulders, immersed in her copy of the *Dhammapada*, a verse collection of the Buddha's essential teachings, a picnic basket on the ground between her feet. It was the first truly hot day since we'd arrived, and everything was oversaturated and filmy. I could already feel the sweat beading on my lower back, dampening my t-shirt. Even Janet looked a little deflated, but Serena radiated perfect nonchalance, stretching one leg and then the other as she read. Now I see what a firm grip she had, how rigidly she composed every scene, the life of *tableaux vivants* she built up around herself. Now I imagine the way she must have propped herself up just so, waiting for us. But that day, she seemed to have sprung from the ground, as much a part of the landscape as the rock beneath her thighs, as unconcerned and constant as the punishing heat itself.

Serena hopped off the boulder, and the three of them linked arms automatically, and somehow the linking didn't limit their movement but freed it. Janet picked up the basket, Laurel took the book, and they all began to walk. I didn't mind the exclusion as much as you'd think: I still loved them as a set. Their movements and conversations were like an expertly dealt deck of cards, every exchange quick and sure and easy. Muscle memory. I can't help but remind you, here, that the heart is also a muscle.

So even if I hadn't worshipped their collective beauty, or their declarative freedom, or their easy belief in my father's religion, I would have worshipped this: their flagrant, defiant *belonging* to one another. I worship it a little even now. Yes, despite everything—no, because of it. I am perverse, you see. Please note that I never pretended otherwise.

You should also note that Buddhism, as a mode of thought, has little use for worship, and none for idolatry. The Buddha told his followers to trust their own experience. He instructed them not to accept anything blindly, even if it came from him. If what I offer is helpful to you, please use it, he said. If not, throw it away.

Girls, on the other hand, are master idolaters. They are like Catholics in that way, or Satanists—all gilded shrine and ceremony, all theme and ritual and symbol. They hunger for the gaudy trappings of faith.

I took a few quick steps to catch up with them. "We only have a couple of minutes until our morning activity," I said. Today it was some kind of team-building obstacle course the staffers had arranged on the lawn. I could see them milling around, wiping their foreheads and admiring their work. One section was constructed of patterned sheets stretched over the ground, like a child's fort. Tires made a lacy pattern in the grass.

"Isn't she sweet," said Laurel.

We kept walking. I asked no questions. Gift horse, etc.

The path to the rock palm was easier in the light. Laurel sang a little as we hiked, a song I'd never heard before, something about turquoise dragons and tiger's lightning. Her voice was pretty, lower than I'd thought it would be, and not breathless at all. Janet and Serena joined in at the bit about the fearless warriors. When we'd almost reached the tents, I noticed a sleek gray cat sitting in the grass by the side of the path. She turned toward us as we passed, and I saw that there was only a slit where her left eye should have been, like an empty buttonhole, with something milk white and unmoving behind it. I must have made a sound, because Serena looked back. "That's Ava," she said.

"Ava?"

"Avalokiteśvara," she said. "Named after the bodhisattva, the personification of perfect compassion."

"What happened to her eye?" I asked.

"Just lucky, I guess," Serena said. "Ki ki! So so!" she shouted, and Ava disappeared into the bushes.

In the daylight, I could see that the rock palm was flat and clean and almost entirely edged by forest, except for the plane that jutted out over the drop, coming to a sharp point, as if accusing the horizon of something. I inched over; we weren't at the summit by any means, but it was still dizzying to stand at the edge. I could see, across the valley, the weeping willow that once was a girl. I could see the ground too, far away, sharp yellow rocks and tangled bushes. It made me feel sick to look at it. I looked up instead; the sky was cloudless.

From behind a tree coated with minty lichen, Laurel pulled out three lawn chairs, their spongy plastic cracked and faded.

"Sorry, Olivia," she said, setting them up in a row. "There isn't one for you."

"She can have mine," Janet said.

"No," Serena said. "You sit in yours." She settled herself in the center chair, the blue one, pulled her sunglasses down from her head and stretched out her legs. The plastic squeaked against her skin. "Olivia will come sit with me," she said. She opened the picnic basket and took out an enormous bag of Jordan almonds. I went over and sat at her feet.

Janet sat in the yellow chair and Laurel reclined in the red one. Laurel rolled up her shirt, and I was briefly transfixed by the impossible smoothness of her stomach, that soft, unbroken plane, her navel ring a little crown jewel. I wanted it to stay inviolate and clean forever, like a blank page. I also wanted to slash a jagged hole through its center, the way you can't help but disturb a still pond you find in the forest, make it gulp your heavy rock.

Related: not long ago I read that our impulse to bite cute things is simply a product of cognitive overloading. Our brains are chemically confused by too much cuteness. This is so cute it *hurts*, we say. In fact, it does hurt: our brains interpret confusion as a threat, and a threat as pain. So an emergency neural signal is sent out: *destroy destroy destroy*. I'll eat you up I love you so, etc. Mouths open, jaws and fingers flex, but societal norms generally prevent us from ripping the soft downy heads off other people's babies, no matter how unbearable they smell, and so we nip and nibble only, hold little toes to mouths, make exclamations of edibleness. This is how we trick our brains into believing the threat has been disabled.

Serena put her hands on my head, and I steeled myself a little. My mother used to make me sit this way when she French-braided my hair, which she used to like to do every Sunday, despite my furious protests. The braiding hurt, because she pulled so hard, because she was not a gentle person, but the braids were soft and smooth, and afterward, admiring myself in the mirror, I was always sorry I had fought her. This fact did not keep us from the same argument a week later, of course. But Serena did not try to braid my hair. She just ran her fingers over my scalp, passed bunches of hair between her hands, making fresh and tingling parts where they had never been before. Even in the heat, her hands were cool. I leaned my head back between her legs, and the yellow fabric of her dress surrounded me, making the bright day even brighter.

I thought of how we must look from the outside: four girls sunning themselves on a ledge high above the earth. I imagined the photograph we would have made, had someone been there to take it—Laurel's head tilted back in laughter; Janet scowling and strict, her purple hair like a glare on the film; Serena staring down the camera, her face inscrutable; Olivia at her feet, still unsure, probably caught blinking. We were so young. We weren't so young. I wanted to collect it, that hour, that day, and stuff it still breathing beneath my bed with everything else I'd loved and thought I'd never forget the shape of. Even while it was happening, I knew I wanted it to last forever. I couldn't have known it would last almost no time at all. I couldn't have known that by the end of that summer, one of us would be erased completely, blacked out, as though something had spilled over the photograph, was already spilling that sunny, lazy day, already creeping, thick and dark, up to the developed edge.

"I'm going to tell you a story," Serena said. She pressed her fingertips into my scalp and I wanted to cry out for how good it felt. (Not many girls had ever touched me either, unless you count my mother, and you shouldn't.) In Serena's story, she was eleven. It was her third summer at the Center and she had wandered away from her parents to pick flowers in her favorite flower-picking place. Clouds passed overhead, changing the light so quickly it disoriented her, sent her careening dizzily across the grounds. She found herself near the garden. The new assistant gardener was there, and warmth came off his body in waves, so clearly and forcefully it made her take a step back. He looked at her as she approached, and then, with no ceremony at all, he began to float up, like a balloon. She didn't scream. She didn't run. She watched him rise to look over the top of the electric fence and then float back down. He didn't say anything to her after. She watched him tend the garden until her father came, took her hand, and brought her in to dinner.

"But how did he do it?" I asked. *Oh, that,* he had said, the liar.

"If we knew, we wouldn't be having this conversation," Laurel said.

"I've been trying to do it on my own ever since. And there are a few more things I've read about that we can try together, to get closer," said Serena. "But all the books say that once you do get close, you need a teacher."

"I seriously doubt he'll agree to teach us," Janet said. "Even if he does know how."

"He does," Serena said. "And he will."

"He never has before," Janet said.

"You've asked him?" I said.

"Of course I've *asked* him. But I'm serious this year," Serena said. "I've been preparing for this for a long time. This is the summer we're finally going to do it. We just have to convince him first." She pulled my hair tight against my scalp. "And now we have an inside man, which can't hurt."

There was a sour edge to the pride I felt at this. Was this the only reason they had chosen me? "How are we going to convince him?" I said.

"Just ask yourself," Laurel said. "What do we have that he wants?"

"He doesn't want anything," I said.

Laurel laughed, throwing her head back against the plastic. "Of course he does," she said. She pushed the waistband of her shorts a little lower. I closed my eyes, concentrating on quelling the prickling in my throat.

"In case it's not clear, Laurel would like Serena to prostitute herself," Janet said.

"In case it's not clear, it's a win-win," Laurel said. "Sleep with an extremely hot guy. Learn to *literally* fly. Where's the bad?"

"Where do I start," Janet said.

"Obviously *you* wouldn't understand," Laurel said, and I leaned forward, because this was a partial answer to something I had been wondering, something important that couldn't be asked directly. Laurel had obviously had sex. She had told us already about screwing the pastor's son under the high school's bleachers after church one Sunday that spring, the way his crucifix kept hitting her in the eye as he pumped and strained, until she caught it and ripped it off. Fake silver on a cheap chain. He followed her around for weeks afterward, laden with flowers and misspelled poems ("I miss your sweat body / I miss your sweat face"), but she wouldn't suffer a repeat performance. He kept saying the same stupid thing to her: *You look like an angel.*

In truth, I felt that I would have known this about Laurel even if she hadn't talked about it openly. It was something in the way she held herself. But her jab meant that Janet was, like me, well, *unversed in the ways of men*, as my mother would have put it.

fig. 1: the closest I had ever gotten to sex was the time I built myself a bedmate. I stuffed a matching set of pajamas with dirty clothes and topped it with an old pillow printed with Mickey Mouse's insane grinning head. I'd seen the movies, or some of them. I was desperate to know what it would feel like. I nestled into my soft monster's armpit at night. I reached into the fly of the pajama pants and pulled out a handful of stuffing. I climbed up onto him, rubbed against the little semi-soft cone. I did more. I acted out the things I'd seen, heard of. Needless to say, this illuminated almost nothing.

• • •

"I'm not going to sleep with him," Serena said. "But I am willing to suggest that I *might*, if he tells me what I want to know."

"There's no denying it's a classic strategy," Janet said.

"My way's much more direct," Laurel said. "Sex makes men talk."

"Your way is complicated. Sloppy."

"There's nothing wrong with sloppy," said Laurel. "How about this, I'll go for it instead—with those arms I bet he'd take me halfway to transcendence in one go."

"Stop," Serena said. Her voice was suddenly icy, and the smirk melted off Laurel's face. "You won't touch him. I don't want you to even *think* about him that way, Laurel. It could ruin everything we're trying to do."

"Why?" I said quietly. My popped knuckles were burning.

"We are trying to transcend our physical reality, not surrender to it," she said. "*Understand that the body is merely the foam of a wave, the shadow of a shadow*, the Buddha said. *Snap the flower arrows of desire and then, unseen, escape the king of death*." It sounded good, though later I would try to pull it apart and find nothing there. It wasn't until the end of the summer, after everything, that I would finally understand what she meant.

"Sex is actually allowed in Buddhism," Laurel said. "In fact, there is some direct connection between tantric practices and levitation. Didn't Padmasambhava achieve it after spending a month in a cave doing nothing but fucking his consort?"

"Aren't you the expert now," Janet said.

"We all have our areas of interest," Laurel said.

"It's not about allowed," Serena said. "And we're not Padmasambhava. This is exactly why I don't want you getting involved in this part. You're not advanced enough."

"Well, if you don't need us at all," Laurel said, "just say so."

"I need you, dummy," Serena said. "Everything I've read suggests a group is more powerful than a single practitioner. Just not for this part."

"And what if your plan doesn't work?" Janet said.

"Then I'll make another," Serena said. "I've prepared for multiple scenarios."

"Desire is the root of all suffering, the Buddha taught," Janet said.

"Desire is the root of all pleasure, too," Laurel said. She was sullen now. She knew she had lost.

"Pleasure is also suffering," Serena said. "Because it goes away. You know that. That's why you're here. Now, do we have an agreement?"

We had an agreement.

For the record, I had no idea whether Serena had ever had sex. I wasn't even sure if Laurel and Janet knew, and I didn't ask them. It seemed contrary to the spirit of things. Serena said very little about herself, as a rule. Conflicting rumors aside, I knew nothing of her life outside the Center. This too was part of her appeal. Now I'm reminded of Sappho's poetic fragments, or some of the salvaged figures from the Acropolis, the pyramids—curved half-moon faces, carved-out bodices, headless women, armless women, hairless women, disembodied hands still holding on to their precious baubles, having lost everything else, two legs and a shoulder riding an eyeless, hoofless horse. *Fragment with the head of a goddess.* What's there is beautiful, but the real ecstasy (from the ancient Greek *ekstasis*, signifying displacement or trance, literally "standing elsewhere") comes from the violation of the form— from the empty space. *He loves a bodiless dream.* The holes into which you can imagine the missing parts, more appealing in the mind than they could ever be in marble, or in flesh. The holes into which you can imagine yourself. The sacred is always obscure. This is a trick we never tire of playing on ourselves.

5

My father, when he was young, was handsome, and not just in the way all girls think their daddies are handsome. He wore blue-tinted contacts over his blue eyes; women would stop him on the street to marvel at the blueness. My mother was not one of these women.

He was a dentist, and his waiting room was always full. He was popular, my mother told me, because of his reputation for silence. That is, he never asked you questions while his fingers were in your mouth. When he had his surgical mask on, and his nose and mouth were erased, the blueness was blinding.

I didn't like being taken to his office as a child. The metal of it all disturbed me. People with their faces covered.

My mother was handsome too. Not even Paula would extend the theory of opposites so far as to expect otherwise. But her dark hair and dark eyes and loamy olive skin made a stark contrast against my father's blue-and-blondness. Unlike him, she had been born far away, to a woman who had made the voyage to America quite pregnant, dragging a child in each hand (my mother was one of these children) while her husband played cards belowdecks. And she was tall, my mother. Six feet at least, with an ovoid face and stretched limbs, but it was her long, thick hair that seemed to take up all the space in the room. (She never braided her own hair, or in fact tried to control it in any way.) The only thing that took up as much space as her hair was her voice. I could hear her from anywhere in the house. I sometimes felt that I could hear her from anywhere on our street, anywhere in our city, anywhere in the world.

Speaking of opposites: I almost never heard my father raise his voice. Instead, he responded to any quarrel or difficulty by softening his consonants, gentling his sentences, as if strife had only to be coddled, held close and licked clean. When my mother and I argued, my father would look at her and say, "Be soft." And then he would look at me and say, "Be soft." It's no coincidence that it was he who was able to disappear.

I look nothing like my mother, alas. I look like my father's mother, the wife of a dairy farmer, with fat low breasts and wide hips and a heart for a face. In college, a boy trying to unzip my jeans would gesture at the reclining nude fixed unevenly to his wall, Blu Tack bleeding at the corners, and intone in my ear: *You look like a Modigliani.* I would look up and see a painting of my mother. I would laugh into the boy's sour mouth. He would turn out to be the kind of boy for whom this ruined the mood. Well, bullet dodged, I suppose.

(An angel, a Modigliani, a model, a slut. Men are always comparing naked women to other things, as if our exposed flesh is too bright to be experienced without simile. As if bare breasts won't blind you if they're cans, cantaloupes.)

• • •

When I was young, my mother made Italian wedding soups and gnocchi and polenta with slabs of butter folded into the center. She fixed the porch steps and repainted the house and repotted the plants and sang in the evenings. She built a fire pit in the back-yard, and killed spiders, and rescued sparrows, being careful not to touch their wings. (I have, at times, been jealous of birds.) When I had the hiccups, she made me drink a glass of water with a knife in it, blade angled toward my eye. Hurry, she said, clapping her hands. She was always changing her mind, moving the furniture.

She worked at an advertising firm, but if you asked her what she did, she would tell you that she was an artist. At home, in the two-carless garage she used as a studio, she built enormous figures of women out of clay, their bodies obese and towering, earth-and-water flesh pooling and mounding over rebar bones, their faces sagging and distended, the opposite of her own. She called them the Mournful Fatties.

On warm Saturday nights, she would invite all of her friends over, a wild array of people from buttoned-up businessmen to frizzy schoolteachers to pink-haired, nose-ringed comedians, and someone would have a full band in their back pocket (bass, guitar, drums, trumpet), and they would dance around the fire pit, stage belt-sander races across the yard, and play hide-and-seek among the Fatties, or dress them up in old clothes my mother kept in a trunk for this purpose, as sea captains or fairy princesses or accountants, all while drinking bottles and bottles of wine so red it was almost black, their voices reaching me in my bedroom like bells.

The dancing was my mother's favorite part. She would dance as long as she could get anyone to dance with her, and she could always get someone to dance with her. Men or women, though mostly men. She would pull their bodies close, wrap her legs and arms around them, grind her hips into theirs as they ran their hands along her thighs. She loved to be dipped, swung, and twirled. She loved to be touched, anywhere, by anyone.

During these evenings, my father would usually stay in the house. I could hear him turning the pages of his book, or not turning the pages. There were hours and hours of not turning the pages.

After her last guest had left, shoes worn through for his wife to wonder at in the morning, my mother would come in and kiss my father on the forehead. "Come to bed," she would say.

"I'll be up soon," he would say. And she would set her wine glass down gently beside him and go upstairs alone, and he would turn the page.

Still: my parents, I always thought, loved each other as much as they were supposed to. No, that's not right—for a long time I simply never thought about it at all. I assumed they loved each other because that's what parents did. Mommy loves Daddy. Daddy loves Mommy. That's how you got here, you know. (It is, more than likely, not.) Whatever silence, whatever argument, whatever smooth white china dishes thrown methodically down the staircase, one by one, spraying thick shards like arrows into the carpet, whatever standing and watching with folded hands, whatever curses—I figured that must be simply how it goes with Mommies, simply the nature of Daddies.

Except no, that's still not true, because I must have known something was wrong. I was only twelve when I entered the kitchen on a calm morning, looked at my mother drinking coffee at the table, my father washing dishes at the sink, and informed them that since I was almost a teenager now it would be perfectly all right for them to get divorced. I wouldn't be traumatized, I said. I understood these things. I didn't want to hold them back. They laughed at me, but less than a year later they separated, as if my permission had meant something to them after all. I do not remember feeling any kind of awe at myself, or any amount of pride. I felt only relief, a cooling sensation in my extremities.

Desire is the root of all suffering. I moved stiffly through my tasks that afternoon in the garden, willing myself to say nothing, to ignore Luke's face and that milky elbow crook.

"What's up with you?" he said.

I was plucking steadily at the basil plant, its supply of leaves apparently endless. He poked me in the ribs, and all of my nerve endings turned toward that spot. "Ow," I said. There's no explaining some things, like the smell of basil, or what happens between people.

"You look like someone died," he said.

"People are dying all the time."

"Well then," he said, laughing, "you may as well be nice to me."

"I'm being nice," I said. He poked me again, and I held my hand over the spot.

"Tell me a story," he said. There was a slight whine in his voice that surprised me. We had spent so many hours in the garden in silence; it had never bothered him before. It was as if someone had given him a tip that I was going to try not to love him, and he had decided that he'd really rather I did. He tilted his head, exquisite. He squinted at me, exquisite. He scratched at his beard, exquisite. Disappointing Luke was the root of all suffering. So I told him a story. That is, I told him all the usual stories a girl tells a man about herself, and also more. Binges, etc.

For instance, I found myself explaining how my father's new house was small and clean. How it was so new it seemed somehow fake. It was the kind of house you could build in a factory and cart off to any suburb in America, my mother had said, but my father assured me this was not so, that it had been built where it stood, as if this were something I cared about. It was the exact opposite of the house I had grown up in, which was old and rambling, with a nonsensical floor plan and creaky stairs and one wooden panel that, if you pushed on it, slid upward to reveal a secret compartment in the wall. But there was nothing inside the compartment when I discovered it, and no matter what I hid away in there—food, money, a letter—no ghost girl or wall sprite came to collect it and leave me a bit of power or a mortal bargain in its place. It was just a hole in the wall, and I was the only one who ever looked into it.

Then I found myself telling him about the day I was standing with my bicycle on the corner, down the street from my house, and a boy came up and pushed me down, stole my bike, and pedaled away laughing. This was not long after my father had left. I ran home and told my mother, who called the police. I spent the rest of the afternoon in the back of a squad car. For a while, every time we passed a black boy, the cop would grip the wheel and ask, *That him?* though the boy hadn't been black, and though I had described him carefully, twice. But soon the cop stopped asking, and his shoulders grew soft, and he began to talk, and to laugh loudly at things my mother said. She was wearing a floral sundress that day, one I liked, with buttons down the front. I could see her bare knees from the back seat. I had to stop liking the dress after that.

Later, in the car on the way to my father's house, she said she was sorry about what had happened, sorry about my bike, glad I hadn't been hurt. "Better to learn earlier rather than later that there are bad people in the world," she said. "Maybe if your father understood that concept we wouldn't have to live in this neighborhood." We stopped, and her face was bathed in red light; she looked boiled. When we arrived, she didn't get out of the car. "Pay attention to her tonight," she told my father through the window. "If you can manage it."

My father and I sat on the porch and watched her back out of his driveway. She ran over a bit of his lawn in the process. I kept crossing and recrossing my arms. He asked me what had happened with the bicycle and the boy. I told him the story. "Hmm," he said. His hands were on the porch railing. It creaked under his weight. Lying to him felt intolerable.

"I mean, that's what I told Mom," I said.

He nodded, as if he had known all along. But he didn't look at me, and so after a moment I told him the true story. The true story began like this: I was standing with my bicycle on the corner, down the street from my house, and a boy approached me and said, "I like your tits."

"Oh," I said, looking down at them, new swollen things. "Thanks." I did not yet know not to be flattered in these scenarios. The boy wasn't ugly, but he wasn't handsome either.

"Do you know what a pussy is?" he asked. (I blushed as I reported this, both to my father and again, years later, to Luke, but it felt like an important part of the story.)

"Yes," I said. I was thirteen, after all. Back then I knew everything.

"It's this," he said, and pressed two fingers between my legs, right there on the sidewalk, in the middle of the day. I took a step backward.

"Excuse me," I said.

"Nice bike," he said, shifting his attention easily, my pussy and my ten-speed being of about equal interest to him. He asked if he could ride it around the block.

"Just once?" I said. Just once, he assured me. My heart was beating fast. I handed it over and he hopped on and pedaled away. Shocking twist: he did not come back. I waited for a long time, and eventually stomped home to tell my mother that I had been pushed, yes, pushed off my bike, through absolutely no fault or stupidity of my own.

"You lied to the police?" my father asked at the end.

"Yes," I said, miserably. I waited; he didn't say anything, and after a minute or two he eased himself up off the railing and went into the house. I was sure I would hear him lock the door, because I was a criminal now, a deviant to be barred from all decent homes, but he left it open. I could hear him walking around behind those thin transportable walls. Soon he came back outside and sat beside me. He pressed a small jade figurine into my hand.

"I was going to wait and give this to you on your birthday," he said. "But I think you should have it now."

It was a young woman, naked from the waist up, her bare breasts covered by a thoughtfully arranged string of beads. She had one leg tucked in, and the other was beginning to wander off her lotus-ringed platform. She wore an elaborate crown, and the tiny look on her tiny face was one of serenity.

(Here, I caught myself, embarrassed again. The description of the jade breasts was somewhat less important to the story. But Luke was smiling. "Tara," he said.)

"This is Tara," my father said. "One of her major forms, at least. Green Tara."

I rubbed my thumb over her face. I did not think of my mother.

"Tara is a great bodhisattva, a benevolent protector goddess, and the personal favorite deity of many Tibetans. Buddhist stories are full of Tara springing into action to save her devotees from certain death, snatching them away from the edge at the last moment, pulling their feet from the fire. She is the ultimate compassionate warrior. But the most important thing she protects you from is fear of *fear*. When you call on Tara, you're asking to be freed of the delusions that keep you from seeing the world as it is. You can recite Tara's mantra whenever you need her: *om tare tuttare ture soha*."

I repeated it until I had it memorized, and two days later, when I returned to my mother's house, I hid the figurine inside the secret wall compartment. I wanted to put it on the dresser in my bedroom, with all of my other tiny things. It might even have gotten lost there, I realize now, amid the bracelets and matchbooks and the many delicate glass animals that had once belonged to the grandmother I had never met, the one who had brought my mother here. I might have forgotten all about her, the Green Tara. But I was afraid that my mother would see her, and so I hid her, and because I hid her, I looked at her all the time.

"Not many American girls get gifts of Green Tara," Luke said.

"My father is a Buddhist," I said. I hesitated. Shastri Dominique had dismissed me. Luke wouldn't. I knew he wouldn't, from the way he was looking at me. There are some things you can tell no matter how old you are. "He was here last year. John Ellis? About as tall as you. Blond hair, blue eyes?" I could feel my heart beating in my ankles.

He made the face people always make when remembering on cue: squinting upward as if his experiences were being projected on an invisible screen two feet above his head. As if that helps. "Rings a bell," he said at last. "He came for a *dathün*?"

"I don't know." I was already memorizing it. *Dathün.*

"It's a month of silent meditation. Lots of people stick around for a while after. If you only do a week, it's torture. But if you do the full month, it's like you can't get enough."

"Do you know where he went?" I said. "After the after, I mean."

He laughed. "That's not the sort of question I ask people," he said.

"He didn't come home," I said. My eyelids burned. I looked at the sky to keep from crying; the clouds that day were fat and fluffy, smug as aftermaths.

For a minute, nothing happened. One cloud moved slowly

toward another. Then I felt Luke pull me against his chest, wrap his heavy arms around me. I shuddered, sure for one wild instant that I was going to be electrocuted by his touch—but that was the fence, not his body. I knew the difference. "It's all right," he said. He hugged me tight. "It's not your fault." I could feel his heart beating. I could feel my neck beginning to sweat. "What can I do?" he said.

I closed my eyes and saw Serena. Her fingers in my hair, her raised eyebrow, her crowded grin. I didn't think about the blurred logic of her plan, or what it could mean. I thought only that I could get something for her, something that the other girls couldn't. *He never lets anyone past the fence.*

I took a deep breath and felt my body expand against his. "I know you can levitate," I said into his shoulder. "Can you teach me?"

Did his heart begin to beat a little faster, or was I imagining it? "Levitation is not something you should be trying to learn," he said after a moment. "Who have you been talking to?"

"Please," I said. I turned my face up toward his. Maybe Serena wouldn't have to promise him anything after all. Maybe he would tell me now, and I could give her exactly what she wanted, and she would be grateful, so grateful she would never leave me.

He hesitated, looking down at me. He sighed. "Close your eyes," he said at last. I closed them, and he held me a little tighter. "Imagine yourself as a feather, floating upward," he said. I could not imagine myself as anything. I could only feel the dampness of his shirt against my cheek, two soft things. "Imagine yourself as a bird, hollow-boned and small."

I tried. He adjusted his arms a little. One hand slipped onto the bare skin of my back, between my shirt and shorts. He left it there, and after a few seconds, began to move his thumb up and down, almost imperceptibly, against my skin. It felt like a little animal there, curious and rough and rubbing.

"Imagine the distance between yourself and the ground growing, growing, growing. Imagine you are lightness itself, nothing but lightness and air." His thumb kept moving against my skin. What did it mean? I wished he would spread his palm against my back, run it up my spine, clutch at my vertebrae, scream into my face. Something.

But instead, he stepped away from me. "You can open," he said.

"What was that?" I said. I scanned his face for some clue as to what had just happened. Was it possible I had imagined the thumb? I knew he had held on to me for much too long. My skin was buzzing, as if he had some electricity in him after all.

"It's a visualization some practitioners have found useful," he said. "Let's call it the first step toward what you seek."

"Thank you," I said.

"Good girl," he said. "There's the smile I was looking for."

I hadn't realized I was smiling. "Rota's over," I said.

That evening, the Garudas and Dragons had what the staffers called Transcendent Yogic Exploration. This was essentially a yoga class, led by Dominique in a large meeting room whose chief feature was an enormous slab of rock pushing in from the mountain like an inserted tongue. To my surprise, right before the class began, Serena slipped into the room. She didn't come straight for us, but instead made a lazy lap, looking around, dragging her fingers along the stippled rock, like Niobe reformed. She seemed to make the other girls nervous. The Dragons were whispering furiously among themselves. Look, look: the virgin witch gypsy werewolf slut in the flesh. Don't startle it, no sudden movements, you don't know what might happen.

"What's their problem?" I asked Janet, to cover the fact that Serena's appearance had unsettled me too. The hug, the thumb: what would Serena think, and had I done something to invite it, and either way had it left any signs?

"Some people find Serena unsettling," Janet said, with approval. "She is a bit strange."

"These girls just aren't used to encountering anyone with purpose," she said. I thought this was not at all what made Serena strange, but didn't say so. Anyway, by then she had sat down beside us, and was looking up at Dominique.

In her brown leggings and tight black tank top, Dominique seemed halfway a tree already; the gods would have made short work of her. That day, her hair was collected into one thick braid, which hung straight and shiny down her back, like a coal-black spine. When she hopped up into a handstand at the front of the room, the braid flopped to the side, and we saw one wide-open eye tattooed at the base of her hairline. We all stopped looking at the eye when she raised one arm out to the side and then rose to the fingertips of the other, her only connection to the earth the barest bits of skin and nail.

"We are working here to become more spacious," she said, her voice thick from all the blood running into her head. "In both mind and body. The more spacious you can become, the lighter you will feel."

The back of my neck prickled. I felt Serena's hand on my arm, and when I looked up, I saw that her other hand was on Laurel's knee, and that Laurel and Janet were holding hands. We let go only when Dominique began to lead us through the steps that might, someday, allow us to do what she had done. We kicked and struggled against the wall, lifting our legs, slamming and sweating, thrusting and slipping, trying to become spacious. Trying to become light.

I want to say this: there was so much brazen touching between us that summer. You may have noticed it: Serena's fingers on my scalp, Laurel's elbows digging into Janet's tight shoulders, all of us lifting, pulling, pushing into one another's hair and skin and muscles. It wasn't only our small circle either. I had noticed that Harriet loved to pick up Nisha, literally pick her up as though she were a child, and carry her around, Nisha always performing a protest but grinning sleepily. Samantha and Paola often slept in the same bed, twinned and curled like ears, though this might have been something else, a different kind of need fulfilled. Even the staff members thought nothing of touching us: remember the way Magda took my hand, the way Luke tugged on my fingertips. I had no experience being touched in that way, not so casually, with such easy affection. At first, I found it disconcerting, invasive even—but soon I grew to crave it.

Now I see violence in all that touching. Now I see it as a prophecy. Mine, mine, mine, we said. Your body is a toy, a prop, a proof. Give it here, let me put my hands on it. Let me scratch deep into that first layer, catch flesh underneath my fingernails. The change I make will be irrevocable. The change I make will be a declaration. My spit and sweat will mark you mine. There's nothing casual about it.

This doesn't mean I crave it any less.

Yes, even now.

That night, we didn't meet, for the Feeling or otherwise. I lay in bed, whispering the bird visualization to myself, over and over again, so I would remember it. (Another man, another mantra.) I had learned something; I told myself that was all that had happened. Before I fell asleep, I thought I heard Janet slip out into the darkness on her own. By the morning, I had forgotten, and it wasn't until the next night, when we were hiking up to the rock palm together, that I even thought to wonder where she had gone.

But I soon stopped wondering, or even thinking about Janet, because as we hiked, Laurel entertained us with a running stream of what she called *Important Information* about the other girls at the Center. Harriet, she told us, had failed the eighth grade; she was older than us. Paola's mother was in jail. Samantha had been in love with her cousin for years, and kept a photo of him under her pillow. We could look for ourselves if we didn't believe her, it might as well be a picture of Samantha herself with short hair, *so* egotistical. Margaret was once so desperate for sex that she let her dog lick her between the legs. "And no one knows anything about Jamie," Laurel said, "except that apparently she has a phobia of changing in front of other people. I wouldn't be surprised if she's covered in scales."

When I asked her how she knew all of this, it was Janet who answered. "Laurel knows everything about everybody," she said. "She's like an idiot savant for secrets."

"I simply happen to have an excellent memory," Laurel said. "Unlike some people whose names I could mention." She tilted her head. "Janet's basically a goldfish."

"Why would I bother to remember someone's sordid past or complex series of illicit lovers or gross thing with their dog if I know you're going to do it for me?"

"What I'm hearing right now is that you can't live without me," Laurel said.

"It's really much too early in the summer for suicide pacts," Janet said.

I didn't think so, I wanted to tell them. I was ready for a pact. But I didn't say anything. I didn't want to give myself away.

On the rock palm, Serena produced a small bottle of whiskey and four plastic cups. I never knew where she got any of this stuff—the cups, the whiskey, the Jordan almonds—but needless to say, it only enhanced her magic. "We are what we think," she said again, standing above us where we sat on the blanket, rickety chairs eschewed. (The chairs were only for daytime, I'd been told. Another one of their rules, equal parts arbitrary and strict. Theme and ritual and symbol.)

"We are what we think," we echoed. I had never had any hard liquor before this. I took a deep swallow and then nearly gagged and spat it out.

"You're going to have to work on that," Serena said.

"What's that toast," I managed. She reached into her bag and tossed me her copy of the *Dhammapada*. I opened it. *We are what we think*. It was the very first line in the book, the very first saying of the Buddha that someone thought they should write down.

"The Buddha wrote thousands of sutras," Serena said. "They say any one of them can take you all the way." She held up the bottle. "But there are also . . . other strategies. Alcohol is one way to access a different plane of experience. Maybe it's not the purest ecstatic state, but I'm willing to try. There's a reason lots of famous Buddhists died of cirrhosis. It does *something*."

I took another sip and grimaced.

"Don't you have anything for her to mix it with?" Laurel said. She had already drunk half of her pour.

"Mixers are the girl's way out," Serena said.

"We actually are girls, you know," Janet said.

"Which is better than the alternative," I said.

Serena bent down to grab my chin with her free hand. "No," she said. "Don't be stupid." She shifted her hand and drove her fingers into my cheeks, and suddenly I became aware of my jaw as a system of bone and teeth. I thought of skulls I had seen, not human ones, but canine: enormous eye sockets above jawlines populated by sharp, ill-fitting molars. Just as it began to hurt, she let go and patted me on the head.

I've said Serena was beautiful, but actually, that's not quite right. Laurel was the real—or at least the conventional—beauty among the three: she looked like the women on magazine covers, the ones that the rest of us periodically reassure one another do not exist without Photoshop. No, there was something about Serena that kept her from being truly beautiful—something too arch about her mouth, too sharp about her eyes, maybe. Something cold or flat. Too narrow or too wide. Those teeth. I can't quite explain it. Sometimes, like now, she looked hard, frighteningly hard. But still: her face was coercive, compulsory. It was hard to look away from her. And what else is beauty, after all?

I took another sip. "Luke showed me something," I said.

"Was it something hot?" Laurel asked. "Or long?" Janet pushed her over, and Laurel fell expertly, without spilling her drink.

I repeated the bird visualization for them, leaving out the part about the embrace. "It's probably nothing," I said. "But at least it's a start."

"You know," Serena said, watching me, "we've tried new girls before. But you're the only one we've kept."

"How come?" I said.

"We like you," Janet said.

"Just in case," Laurel said, at the same time, so that the sentiments were tangled.

"We can smell our own," Serena said.

I thought this was the nicest thing anyone had ever said to me.

As we drank, Serena read to us from her biography of Milarepa, the famous Tibetan yogi. Once he achieved enlightenment, we learned, he could not only levitate but fly around at will. Of course, before that, he had to live in a cave alone for years on nothing but nettle soup, until he was barely more than bones and covered in a light green fur. Of course, before that, he had to labor for many years in intense spiritual practice. Of course, before that, he had to murder thirty-five people at a party with black magic, an act of vengeance against the slobbering aunt and uncle who had cast him out into the cold. He summoned a hailstorm to bring down the roof. He reveled in the chaos, the destruction, the bloodshed. He danced on their blackened graves. We liked Milarepa. Even if he ultimately reformed.

Of course, Serena explained, her finger in the book, levitation has never been limited to Buddhism, or Hinduism, or any of those arcane, far-off religions that most of the world practices. She reminded us of Saint Joseph of Cupertino, of Thomas Aquinas, of the ascension of Christ. She told us about Saint Teresa of Ávila, who was so shaken by her levitations that when she felt her body begin to rise, she'd call for the nuns to hold her down, as she begged her God with all her might to relieve her of the gift.

Saint Teresa wrote of the experience: "It seemed to me, when I tried to make some resistance, as if a great force beneath my feet lifted me up. I know of nothing with which to compare it; but it was much more violent than other spiritual visitations, and I was therefore as one ground to pieces." *As one ground to pieces.* Her face, in painting and in sculpture, is a sublime vision of ecstasy, her mouth opened, her eyes lifted, elevated by God and blood and something, something else.

We drank the whole bottle. Rather, Serena and Laurel drank the whole bottle, while I choked down a few cups and Janet mostly held hers against her breastbone.

"Why aren't you drinking?" I asked her. A few cups had been enough: the night had become warmer, closer; I felt as though a blanket had been thrown over us, the world outside erased. Out of sight, out of existence. I wanted to stroke Janet's hair. I wanted to put my fingers in Laurel's mouth. I had never been drunk before, either.

"She's a lightweight," Laurel said. She pulled out her button and put it in her mouth. That summer, Laurel carried a large coat button on a piece of string in her pocket; periodically, she would slip the button into the space between her teeth and lips and tug on the string. It was a lip-strengthening tool, she told us. A dentist had prescribed the button when she was a child, after he noticed her mouth hanging open in the waiting room, and she'd kept using it. (*For fun and profit*, she said. *Orally fixated*, said Janet.) Laurel pulled on the button until it came away from her mouth with a little pop.

"I've just seen what an asshole it can make you," Janet said.

"You don't have to be drunk to be an asshole," Laurel said. Button, pop.

"True," Janet said. "Most people operate in the red on that spectrum every day."

Serena poured the last of the whiskey into her cup. She held the empty bottle above her head and then, without warning, she let it go. I gasped instinctively, but the bottle just bounced on the stone. "How do you feel?" she asked us.

I felt warm, sunk, unseparated; like I was part of the rock and part of them and part of the velvety black. I couldn't figure out quite how to express this, though, so I said nothing.

"Not like levitating," Laurel said. She wiggled on the blanket. "More like kissing."

"Too bad," Serena said. She nudged the empty bottle with her toe. "What did you think this was for?"

"For fun?" Laurel said. She stuck out her bottom lip. "Fun is something pretty girls like us are supposed to have at summer camp."

"This is in no way summer camp," Serena said.

"Would we call us pretty?" said Janet. "As a group, I mean."

"You have to admit there's archery," I said.

"Zen archery," said Serena.

"Arts and crafts, hiking, yoga," Janet said. I smiled at her.

"You know who can really levitate," Laurel said. "Planes.

Planes!" She was drawing out her words again: *Plaaaaaanes*. She tried to stand and tipped over instead. She scrabbled around on her hands and knees, as if looking for something.

"How did you get so drunk?" Serena said. I knew how—I'd seen her drink almost half the bottle. But Serena had drunk almost as much, and she seemed only enhanced, herself and more. Laurel had flipped onto her back, legs and arms splayed.

"Maybe we should do it another night," said Janet.

"How do they get up there?" Laurel said. "No, actually. Who thought of that? I mean, listen, I know who. I may be extremely attractive but I'm not stupid, Janet. But I mean, what was the step after the propeller?"

Serena made a disgusted sound. "Janet," she said evenly, "take her back down, will you? It's pointless for you anyway." She gestured at Janet's full cup.

Janet stood and pulled Laurel to her feet. Serena reached up and squeezed Janet's hand. They exchanged a look that I couldn't quite parse.

"Janet, Janet, Janet," Laurel sang. "Let's make out, okay? Just this once."

"Behave, you," Janet said, with obvious affection. She pulled her toward the path. Neither of them looked back at us before they disappeared.

Serena held up her hand until the sound of Laurel's voice had dissolved.

"Finally," she said. She pulled out her little wooden comb, the one I'd seen her use that first night, and scraped her thumb along its tines. This sound, she had told me, was the only one that ever truly gave her the Feeling. Even other, similar combs didn't do the trick. This one had been her mother's. I closed my eyes, but the hollow music of the comb sounded far away, overwhelmed by the crackling of the forest.

"It's no use," she said after a few minutes. "I don't feel it any-more." I opened my eyes. She had pulled out her silver cigarette

box. "I'm tipsy, of course, but I don't feel *it*, just normal drunk."
She held out the box. I shook my head. She put one in her mouth
and snapped the lid closed. I didn't ask her what *it* was.

There was a long silence. I realized that I had never been
alone with her before. I looked down at my hands, and they
seemed to me completely foreign, like someone else's hands, like
they had no relation to me whatsoever. I curled and uncurled my
fingers.

"Come lie down," she said. "I want to try something." She
moved backward and I obeyed. The rock was cold against my
spine. She took my head into her lap and rested two fingers on
each of my temples.

"Have you ever had sex?" she asked. So she had been wondering this too. I hesitated, too long. "I didn't think so," she
said. "Don't worry, it means I can trust you." She began to rub
my temples in small, slow circles. "You're lying on a beach," she
said. "A beautiful, white sand beach. With palm trees. All of a
sudden, four men come up to you, wearing deep blue robes that
cover their faces and hands and shoulders, everything."

Her fingers bored into my temples like awls.

"You don't move. Then they slit open your arm." Suddenly,
Serena slid her finger from my shoulder to my wrist, hard and
fast enough that I released a little breath. "And they start filling
it with black sand." She drummed her fingers along the length
of my arm. "More sand, more, more," she said. She switched to
the other arm and opened and filled that one before running her
finger lengthwise across my collarbone. "Pounds and pounds of
it." She slid one perfect nail between my breasts and I had to
bite my own tongue to keep from crying out. "They pour and
pour until all the blood and muscles in your body are replaced
with black sand. The men say: *You're a beautiful girl, Olivia. That's
why we have to do this.* You say nothing, because your mouth is
filled with black sand."

Then she rolled up my shirt and cut my stomach open in a

cross, slice, slice, before filling it with her fingertips. Her hair brushed over my body as she leaned to fill my legs, her fingers finding my hip points under my cotton shorts and tracing downward, then upward again. By the time she reached my head, I was void of anything but the drumming of her fingertips and the tingling of my skin and the vague image of the men in blue, pouring burlap sack after burlap sack of coarse black crystals into my body.

"Now that you're full," she said, "they stitch you back up." She ran her nails over all the open wounds as if closing a zipper, and then skimmed the pads of her fingers across the same places as a salve. "They take you out into their boat. You're so heavy that the boat hangs low in the glassy water. There are no boats anywhere else on the water, or anywhere else in the world. They take you to the middle of the ocean, and then they drop you overboard." She was rubbing my temples again. Her voice seemed deeper than before. "And then you go down, down, down, down, down. You go down forever. Your body rests at the bottom of the ocean, in the dark." She pressed her hand against my forehead, hard. Then she leaned her forearms into my chest, and my stomach, legs, feet, pressing down. "It's heavy down there, so heavy. There's nothing but the dark dark dark, and the sand, and the heaviness." She got up and lay on top of me, nestled her forehead against my own. I didn't move. I didn't breathe. Her pubic bone bore into mine.

"But one day, you wake up, and you're back on the beach." She rolled off. "And you open your eyes."

I opened my eyes.

"The waters have pushed you back, pushed you up from the bottom at last. You try to move, but you can't. Because all of your insides have been replaced by black sand and seawater." And for a moment, it was true. My organs were ossified, my limbs pinned. I tried to raise my arms and my body resisted, only for a beat, just enough for doubt, enough to set my heart, which had been so still a moment before, to a quick double beat. Then my fingers creaked to life and I sat up, feeling as stiff as if I had been asleep for centuries, hemmed in by brambles and dust. The trees swam around my head. Serena looked at me seriously. "That's how it is," she said. "But lightness is the antidote."

She reached again for her cigarettes; this time, I accepted one. "Like this," she said. I copied the way she held her hand, her mouth. I took a drag and erupted into coughs. She offered me no encouragement. She was looking out into the woods, as if she'd heard something moving there.

"When did you start smoking?" I asked when my throat had cleared.

"I've always smoked. I smoked in the womb."

"Your poor mother," I said.

"Yes," she said. She took another drag and looked me over. "My poor mother was obsessed with levitation, you know."

"Really?"

"She was devout, you might say. A devotee. My father indulged her. We used to come here together, the three of us, every year. My mother was a follower of this one particular teacher, who taught that the practices used for cultivating levitation also happened to be the fastest path to enlightenment. He taught that the two are uniquely connected. If you can achieve one, you'll achieve the other. He's part of why this place is so famous. He said that if you can learn to become light, *truly* learn, then you will also become enlightened." She snapped her fingers and laughed, but it sounded hollow, hungry. "It's right there in the word. And then you'll be able to do anything. The world will be utterly open to you." She stabbed out her cigarette, half-smoked, and lit another. "Every year, my mother came to study with him. Luke was there, too, at the end. They must have received the same teachings, only Luke was a quicker study, I guess. I remember how much she wanted it, how hard she tried. She was always with him, always trying to learn, get extra lessons, an overachiever, like my Janet. But anyway, that teacher died. And the next year, my mother killed herself. She hanged herself. Here, at the Center."

My mind went blank—no, blank and racing, like a television tuned to static. Does that even happen anymore? Does anyone else think about the fact that static is anything but static?

Serena leaned back onto the ground. "It's sort of a Brutalist solution to levitation, but she got what she wanted, I guess. Her teacher always said that the last things she would see before her enlightenment were her own feet lifted above the earth."

"I'm so sorry," I said, too late and too lame.

"It was a long time ago," she said. "It gets longer all the time. I wasn't even the one to find her, though I do have this image in my mind: blue ankles, knocking together. They're probably not even hers, though. They're probably from TV. Someone else's ankles are all I have of her." She looked down at her lap. "That and all these dresses, which aren't exactly my style. But otherwise they'd just be in a box somewhere." The one she wore that night was a saturated ocher, like a late-September leaf.

"They suit you," I said.

"They don't," she said.

I wondered what she wore the rest of the year. I found that I couldn't imagine her in winter, or in school. "The very worst part," she said after a few moments, "is what my father said. I wasn't supposed to hear, of course. He was on the phone. He thought I was in my room. *She was a sucker,* that's what he said. *It was her own stupidity that killed her.*" She blew out a stream of smoke.

"What an asshole," I said, finding my voice again. But secretly, I thought: Serena's father and my mother would almost certainly get along. I thought: Maybe they could meet. I thought: Maybe they could meet and fall in love over their devotion to nothing, their refusal to be suckers, and then they could get married after a whirlwind romance, and Serena could move into my house, no, my room, my bed, and be mine forever, tangled in my sheets, blowing smoke at the ceiling. Unless of course my mother rejected him, and wouldn't that be just like her, to ruin this for me.

"Doesn't matter," she said. "He's gone too. I live with my grandmother now, in this old defunct creamery she inherited and won't leave. She fixed up one of the milk barrels with a little bed and a light, and that's where I sleep."

"You're joking," I said. "You sleep in a barrel?"

"I dream of milk," she said. "My grandmother says one day I'll grow too much in my sleep and be trapped in my room forever. High levels of calcium in the air, or something. But I'll be gone long before that happens." She laid a hand on my leg. "I never told my mother about seeing Luke, you know," she said. "I hoarded it. Sometimes I think that if she had known levitation was possible even without her teacher, or that Luke could teach her too, she wouldn't have done it. Sometimes I think it's my fault."

"No," I said.

"It was the same summer," she said. "I saw him. She died." I couldn't find anything to say to that. She shifted a little on the rock. "But I want you to know up front that I would person-ally never kill myself," she said. "I'm telling you that now. No matter what. I wouldn't want to have to start everything over."

"Okay," I said.

She took a deep breath. "Good," she said. "Tell me your secret now."

"What secret?" I said, but she only looked at me and waited, and so in the end I did tell her: about my missing father, at least, and about the year of nothing, but not about my mother, and what I had done to her, and not about Luke.

Unlike Luke, Serena did not touch me. Unlike Dominique, she looked thoughtful. "No daddies allowed at Buddhist camp," she said.

"I know."

"It's part of the charm, really."

I said nothing. There was something feral about her, I decided, underneath that still-lake exterior.

"What's his name?" she said after a minute, and I told her. "I'll make some inquiries," she said. "Dominique is full of shit. I'm sure I can find out where he's gone." She stroked my cheek. "Just wait until he finds out you can levitate," she said. "That's obviously how you're going to win him back. That'll show him what kind of girl he abandoned." She looked so fierce then, so sure, and I believed her, and it was like something breaking open. Yes, of course: if I learned this, my father would realize he'd made a mistake. It would be the ultimate proof of my worth, of my belonging to him and not to my mother: I would surpass him at his own obsession. I imagined myself floating in his living room, and his gasp of awe, his rush to wrap me in his arms.

"Don't tell the others," I said.

"Don't worry," she said. "Those two wouldn't understand anyway. They both think they know the world so well. Despite the fact that they've reached totally opposite conclusions." She was scrutinizing the ground. As I watched, she collected the ends of our cigarettes, held them loosely in her left hand. She never left anything behind. I noticed again the soft red strings that circled her wrists.

"Protection cords," she told me, when I asked. "Whenever an advanced teacher comes to the Center, they make a few of them. They tie a knot, and say a mantra into it."

"They're pretty," I said.

"They serve a purpose," she said. "There's a difference."

Here, this may help. Six teachers on the nature of enlightenment:

Dōgen: "Like the moon reflected on the water."

Chögyam Trungpa: "Ego's ultimate disappointment."

Osho: "You are, but the mind is utterly empty."

Krishnamurti: "A state of negation."

Bodhidharma: "Lots of space, nothing holy."

Suzuki Roshi: "What do you want to know for? You may not like it."

When we separated that night, Serena to return to her tent, me to go down the mountain, she squeezed my hand. "I'm glad you came," she said. "I think I've been waiting for you." The sky was a scrub of stars, the kind of wide-open sky that only hangs above wilderness. But it didn't make me feel small. I felt enormous. I felt that every star in that whole vast nothingness had pushed aside the drapes, opened her bedroom door, and turned her wide white face to look right at me.

I didn't pull her comb out of my pocket until I was safely back in the dormitory. I hadn't stolen it, I reasoned, I had simply picked it up from the blanket when she wasn't looking. *Borrowed*, that was the word. I would give it back, if she asked. A few long black hairs were wound around the wooden tines. I crawled under the covers and held it to my heart like a talisman.

6

Often, when I was a child, I would sneak into my mother's studio to commune with the Mournful Fatties. No part of their bodies, of course, was left to the ecstatic imagination. My mother found her ecstasy in overflow, not obscuration. This is an essential thing to understand about her.

My favorite Fatty was an old one, whom I couldn't remember my mother making; she had always just been there. She was the ugliest of the bunch, her face like an imploding planet, her large breasts hanging almost to her crotch, her hands gnarled and monstrous, her kneecaps misaligned. I named her Beth, and when I was very young I would sit on the garage floor between those massive feet and tell her stories, bring her tiny treasures I'd found. Shells, beads, Jolly Rancher wrappers. Beth liked that sort of thing. Later, I tucked one of my favorite plastic ponies—the palomino, dearly beloved—between two rolls of Beth's cold cracked flesh, a gift. Beth was my first refuge when my parents would argue, my mother's voice rising like steam into my bedroom, my father's an imperceptible murmur, or when I was home alone and afraid, seeing eyes in all the corners. I liked to rub Beth's flabby butt; you can probably still see the small circle I wore down with my rubbing. I liked to see how much of my face I could fit into her massive hand. But when I began to become aware of my body and the ways it should and should not look, I stopped going into the garage. I became afraid of the Fatties, as if their grotesquerie might somehow be contagious. I thought that if I loved Beth, there was some chance I would become her. This is a logical fallacy to which I have willingly subscribed for many years.

Does beauty, in the end, hurt us? my mother used to ask, idly, as she smoothed the contours of a bulbous face, or packed a massive clay hump onto a shoulder or groin. I admit: until that summer, I never considered the answer.

Studies have shown that the act of looking at something attractive—a person, a product, some honest-to-goodness nature—triggers an involuntary series of synapse firings in the motor cerebellum. As it turns out, this is the exact same neural sequence that causes us to reach out a hand. Beauty, then, literally moves us. We all know this: beauty can easily force a hand. But will we ever shake the pressing delusion, as Tolstoy put it, that beauty is the same as goodness? After all, how often does *goodness* truly force a hand? More likely it stays it, and even then, barely, and even then, only for a time.

Here's a story I told Luke, some hot day in the garden: once, my father took me with him on one of his trips. I don't remember the drive or the monastery or the exact purpose of the ceremony we attended, but I do remember that it too was high up in the mountains, maybe even higher than the Center. My mother was out of town, or I'd never have been invited along.

I wasn't supposed to be choosing, after all. My unformed brain, etc. "Our secret," my father said, and I bloomed.

There were hundreds of people in attendance that day: faded colors, loose pants, faces turned up to an enormous statue of a meditating Buddha. The very last step in the ceremony was to paint in the eyes of the Buddha, and here the attendees were invited to participate. Two monks on two ladders held two paintbrushes in front of the Buddha's two eyes, and hundreds of silk ribbons, in red and gold, were attached to the handle of each brush. The ends of the ribbons were distributed through the crowd, to connect us to the painter, the brush, the eye, the Buddha, the infinite. A boy with brown eyes and dreadlocks gave me a ribbon, and so I held it, but as the artists lifted their brushes and the attendees raised their arms, I began to feel unsteady. My vision popped and sparkled, and then began to fade, edges first. I tugged on my ribbon, which had turned wet and dark in my palm.

"Daddy," I said. "I can't see."

I felt, rather than saw, his face turn to mine. Or perhaps that's not exact. I could see the outline of his head clearly, his hair and ears glowing and distinct in a halo of afternoon light— but between them, where his features should have been, my dimming vision registered only a kind of bottomless pulsing blackness.

The empty-faced shape knelt beside me, holy, unknowable, wholly unknowable. "You need water," it said.

It was at that moment that I fainted. I didn't see what kind of scene I caused: maybe no scene at all. Everyone's eyes were focused upward, and not at the girl on the ground. Isn't that always the way?

When I woke, I was propped up on my father's knee. I could see his face again, right where it was supposed to be, between his ears, and above him, I could see the looming face of the statue, its drying eyes clear and unconcerned.

"You gave your sight to the Buddha," he said. He patted my sweaty forehead. "Very generous of you."

Later, he bought me an ice cream sundae and a t-shirt from the monastery gift shop to commemorate the miraculous occasion. As an afterthought, he also bought me a small canteen, to remind me to hydrate properly in high places. He told everyone we met what had happened, squeezing my small shoulders, beaming down at me. They all thought it was amazing, simply amazing. I even received a bouquet of wildflowers and a kiss on the cheek from the dreadlocked boy. He had a large gap between his two front teeth, the kind that made you want to put something in there.

Luke liked this story, as I knew he would. He pressed me for details. He agreed that it was generous. He agreed that it was amazing. "There's something special about you," he said. "That much is clear." He hugged me again, slipping his hand under my t-shirt in a way that might have been utterly unintentional and might have been a declaration. When he let go, I scanned his face for the answer, but he showed no sign, or the sign was too obscure, or I had invented it entirely.

I didn't tell Luke that the fight my parents had after we returned from that trip was worse than any before. I remember it like this: I lost consciousness, and when I regained it, my father moved out. There must have been time between the two, but in my memory, he doesn't even unpack. We drive away from the lap of the giant Buddha, and when we get to our house, he simply drops me off and keeps going. Still, I had thought that trip was the start of something, as well as the end. *Our secret.* I thought there was something we shared. But he never invited me along again.

• • •

Related, perhaps: once, I found my mother lying in her bed, fully clothed, alone, the sheets black with her hair. When I asked her what she was doing, she raised an arm into the air. "Your father," she said, "is a beautiful vessel." I waited. After a while, she raised the other arm, as if hoping to be lifted from the sheets by an enormous mother of her own. "But there's a hole in the bottom," she said.

The days were getting hotter. I felt roasted, as on a spit, eight thousand feet high. We continued to meet at night, to give ourselves the Feeling, to play at lightness, but during the day, Serena said that it was too hot, too hot to do anything that mattered. We spent hours on the rock palm, eating peanut butter and honey sandwiches and popcorn and the small frosted cakes Serena liked and never seemed to run out of, drinking warm, sweet lemonade that grew warmer and sweeter as the day went on. Laurel plucked everyone's eyebrows, even mine, into perfect comets. One afternoon, Janet taught me to do a cartwheel, which no one could believe I didn't already know how to do, while Serena and Laurel sat back and gave us grades on form (very poor, in my case), writing numbers on their palms in eyeliner and holding them up. Janet taught us all to play poker; we made bets with small stones. Serena said it was purer that way. The fact that Janet won every game might have also been a factor. But most of all, I remember space. I remember doing nothing, but doing it together, which made it something after all. Now when I put a dish in the microwave for thirty seconds I am paralyzed by the discomfort of unorganized time. Is thirty seconds enough to read something? Check the weather? Pee? I reach for anything to occupy me, but now I've spent all of my time wondering how I should spend it, and the machine beeps, and I have purpose again.

• • •

"What do you know about emptiness?" Serena said on one of these days, draped over a rock, her fingertips in the grass.

"Nothing," I said.

"Good answer," Janet said, and the other two laughed.

I thought, before, that emptiness meant nothingness. But that's not it, or not quite. Serena explained it: Emptiness doesn't mean that nothing *exists*, but rather that nothing has a fixed identity or importance. While the objects and people and phenomena that populate our experience are *there*, in a relative way, they have no inherent nature, no ultimate existence. Rather they are in constant flux, acting and acted upon, utterly subjective and unstable.

"You think that the things around you are real," Serena said. "You think that they mean something, and that you—that is, the impermanent, illusory construct that you call *you*—can somehow possess them. But if you realize that you can't, then you will begin to lose the pain that comes with attachment. You will shed the agony of clinging to solid concepts. Like the earth, for one. Like your body. Even your thoughts." Everything she was saying felt new and familiar at once. It was as if I'd lived with a set of books on my shelves for years, walked past their spines every day, and had only just now taken one down to read it.

"Which means that suffering doesn't exist," Janet said. "Not on an ultimate level. Neither does happiness, of course." Serena laid her head on Janet's shoulder, and Janet kissed it. Laurel dropped her head into Janet's lap. They glowed in the late afternoon sun.

"The more we realize our own emptiness, the lighter we will become," Serena said. "Until eventually—pop." She smiled and pointed at the sky.

They were so sure. They believed without question. Serena sounded just like my father. I wanted nothing more than to believe along with them. And sometimes I felt that I did. Sometimes, buoyed by Serena's depth of knowledge, Laurel's easy acceptance, Janet's utter contempt for everything else, I did. But no matter how much we meditated, or how much we talked, my mother's voice never entirely left my head.

From the Heart Sutra: *Form is emptiness, emptiness is form. Emptiness is not separate from form, form is not separate from emptiness. Whatever is form is emptiness, whatever is emptiness is form.*

Or you know, as Schrödinger said: we're all just atoms in the void. Not that it helps.

His trapped cat, too, seems relevant here. Or not, as it were.

Anyway, we may all just be atoms in the void, but according to quantum mechanics, no objects objectively exist at all, in the void or otherwise. Particles have no inherent values, only probabilities, and they only materialize when they are measured— which means that on a quantum level, reality simply isn't there unless we're looking directly at it. If a tree falls in the forest and no one is there to hear it, there is no tree, and no forest. (Is it any different if that tree was once a girl? I think it is not.) The world does not exist independently of us, theoretical physicists say. All perception relies on our own subjective consciousness. We call the world into being with our attention. Or put it this way: we are continually hallucinating our own realities, including the realities of our selves. Quantum physics, as you can see, is extremely Buddhist. Again, not that it helps.

"Emptiness is what makes levitation possible," Serena said. "When you understand the illusory nature of phenomenal experience, you can easily manipulate it." Milarepa, it is said, could climb inside a conch shell without making his body any smaller or the conch shell any bigger.

"So why can't we do it?" Janet said. "We all understand that consciousness is an illusion."

"There's a difference between intellectual comprehension and true understanding," Serena said. "That's why we need Luke."

"Speaking of Luke," Laurel said, raising her arms in the air.

Janet had begun to dig a little trench in the ground with her heel. Laurel looked at the trench, and then at Janet, and then dropped her arms to her sides as if in exhaustion.

Serena was looking at the trench too. "I'm working on it," she said.

In the garden that afternoon, I bent over to pluck a trio of tiny ripe tomatoes from the vine, and when I straightened, Luke was staring at me. I smiled at him; he didn't respond. I could feel his gaze on my skin like a touch. I felt the urge to bolt but only stood there, caught in the force of his attention. Deer, head-lights. After what seemed like minutes, he spoke. "Oh good, the tomatoes," he said, as if emerging from a trance. Was it a trance I had caused? I brought the basket to him, and that night I stood in front of the mirror, trying to re-create the way I had held my body, to catalogue whatever organization of limbs had caught his eye, had silenced him so completely, so that I might use it again and again, until Laurel pushed me out of the way to rub cream on her face and I remembered who I really was.

Later, we snuck into the kitchen in search of the steaks the head chef, Tenzin, had hidden for herself in the kitchen's walk-in freezer. Tenzin was a jolly Tibetan woman who'd been at the Center as long as anyone could remember. "Tenzin can't go three days without red meat," Janet had said. "Never mind three months." (Tibetan Buddhists, unlike some other varieties, tend not to be vegetarians, despite the usual prohibitions against killing living beings. *It's too cold there*, Serena told me. *You can't survive a Tibetan winter eating only plants.*) Laurel, who did rota in the kitchen, had the keys, and after half an hour of searching, just as I was beginning to shiver, we found the steaks under an unmarked box in the far back corner of the freezer. Janet cooked four of them in a kitchen lit only by moonlight and the fire of the gas stove. Laurel produced two bottles of champagne she had found somewhere, but Serena refused them.

"That's not what we're doing right now," she said. Another rule: she never drank outside ritual. Alcohol was only useful for levitation. So instead, we accompanied our steaks with cold glasses of creamy organic milk, though I was almost certain I saw Laurel sneak something into hers. Afterward, we sat around eating strawberries from an enormous clay bowl.

"Strawberries are the sexiest fruit," Laurel said. "Look: they force your mouth into the kissing position."

"Just what you need," said Janet. "More kissing." I still wonder what Luke did to those strawberries. I've never had redder, or sweeter.

"Everyone could use more kissing," Laurel said. "Well, *almost* everyone."

Serena hopped off the counter where she'd been perched and approached the mirror that hung by the door. She faced her reflection and stuck a strawberry in her mouth, green end first. It looked like a tongue, protruding there, and I thought of the first night I had followed Janet and Laurel out of our dormitory, their own real tongues silhouetted in the dark.

She gestured for us to join her, and soon we were all sticking out our red tongues at the mirror, the seeds of the strawberries melting into taste buds, the shine of the ripe fruit into spit. Laurel posed, tossing her hair, winking. Janet stared herself down, suddenly serious. Serena found a sharp pair of kitchen shears. She held them in front of her face, blades open wide. She looked herself in the eye. Then, with one swift movement, she cut off the tip of her tongue. It landed, half a strawberry, on the floor. She handed over the scissors.

It was hard to go through with it, much harder than you'd think. My hand fought me. I had to push my real tongue back and forth against the strawberry's leaves, create a little physical distinction between what I saw and what I knew to be true, in order to snip off the end. Our eyes are liars; the best.

I'd have a similar feeling years later, when trying to jump off a high ledge into the ocean. I'd seen countless people do it before me; I knew it was safe. But when I approached the edge, it didn't matter what I knew. Again and again, my body forced me back. (Though I suppose I should be grateful for my physical cowardice. After all, it is the only reason I am here to tell you this story.)

Janet, of course, sliced through her strawberry without hesitation. She knew what was real and what wasn't. Laurel dropped the scissors twice and had to turn on the light before she could make herself close the blades.

"We're fighting the snake brain," Serena said. "Intellect versus instinct. When you have power over the snake, you can do anything. *We are what we think.*" We ate all the remaining strawberries, except for the ones we had cut. These, Serena buried deep in the trash. "Just in case," she said.

This is all to say: I had never had friends like these.

Friends like these: Janet had accepted my companionship easily, but it was clear that Laurel still had her reservations. She treated me like a small but irritating nuisance: the flatulent cat your neighbors leave with you for a month while they're in Bermuda, the baby screaming upstairs, the weird lump on your leg that you can't identify and won't go to the doctor about, which might be cancer or a colony of spiders or nothing. I noticed she didn't like being alone with me; it was only when the choice was between that and solitude that she'd sometimes settle for my company.

She had a point, of course. What right did I have, entering their perfect trinity? The square is infinitely weaker: all those parallel lines warp and bend under too much weight.

And there were still some secrets that weren't shared with me. Sometimes I would wake in the night, and either Janet or Laurel would be gone from her bed, and when asked about it in the morning they'd look at me blankly, or suggest I'd been mistaken, or simply change the subject. Once, I came into the dormitory to find Laurel red-eyed and furious and Janet sitting straight as a poker on her top bunk, staring at the ceiling.

"I don't care what you do," Laurel said, before she'd noticed me.

"You obviously do care," Janet said.

When I asked them what had happened, they both ignored me. They'd clearly been fighting for some time; we all went to dinner and they refused to speak a word to me or to each other, even when a Tiger came and sat beside us and began to tell us all about her band, Death Plum, which featured no instruments, its members preferring to use whatever was around to create their songs. "We call it *world music*," she said, drumming her hands on the table, pinging her fork against her water glass. Something about the texture of her leather jacket made it impossible to forget that it had once been another creature's skin. Janet stared at a beam above her head. Laurel bit all the lipstick off her lips. But neither of them said anything, and so I asked her to play us a song, because I could, to punish them.

Harriet and Nisha, sitting at the other end of the table and listening, laughed silently into their soup. When Janet and Laurel were looking the other direction, they flashed me a thumbs-up each. I smiled back, feeling traitorous to the core.

That night, there were no taps. But I heard Janet get up, slip on her shoes, and leave. An hour later, I heard Laurel leave too. I knew without being told that they were headed in opposite directions.

In the morning, everything was normal again. They didn't mention the fight, and so I didn't either, but later, I asked Serena what had happened. She narrowed her eyes; she didn't know anything about it. "But I will," she said. "I'll find out."

Sometimes the four of us would walk down to the pond at the edge of the Center grounds, where the temperature always felt a few degrees cooler. I loved that oblong pool of water: it was dark and green, like a hole in the world, surrounded by stalks of unknown plants and greasy aquatic bushes. It struck me as somehow accidental, or temporary, the kind of pond that moved from place to place when no one was paying attention. The first time they took me there, Jamie was already sitting on the hand-carved bench, her arms wrapped around her body. She turned as we approached and scattered, rabbitish.

"Was it something we said?" Laurel wanted to know.

"She's actually a pretty fast runner," said Janet, watching her. "Interesting."

I knelt at the pond's edge. There was movement beneath the surface, something bright filtered by murk. Without thinking, I reached in and sank my arms to the elbows. The water was cool and thick, and I felt an oily brush against my fingers. A fish swam close to the surface. I saw the extravagant mustache dangling from its prehistoric snout before it turned up its white belly and rolled away. *Koi*, I knew from somewhere. I wondered if I could catch one and squeeze it.

"Legend has it," Serena said, "that if you drink enough of the water, you can cure yourself of anything."

"How much is enough?" I asked.

"No one knows," Serena said. "No one's ever had enough. You might have to die of it first."

"You'd certainly have to kill all the koi," said Janet.

"*Koi*," Serena said, "means *love* in Japanese."

In the garden, Luke continued to cajole me into telling him stories about myself. He seemed to brighten with every bit of information, like a plant after watering. But slowly, he told me things about himself, too. He told me that he was from California; he missed the ocean, the tight feeling of salt on his skin. He told me that he'd had a little sister, but she'd died suddenly when they were both young. He wouldn't say any more about that. He'd started college nearby, and first came to the Center after seeing a flyer for a free meditation class. After that he began visiting every weekend, and eventually befriended the gardener, an old man who couldn't carry the bags of mulch anymore, and he'd taken up the job less than a year later, when the man retired. He'd dropped out of school to do it. He said it was the best decision he'd ever made in his life. The Center gave him lodging, meals, a small salary. The Center gave him purpose. He was grateful to earn his own way in life with physical labor, he said. It meant something to him to be beholden only to himself. He attended all of the Center's lectures and programs, met every visiting teacher and monk. He was even learning Tibetan.

"I think without the dharma, I'd be a monster," he said once. I suppose I should have asked him what he meant by this, but I couldn't focus. I was sure he was no monster. How could he be? (Somewhere in the ether, Tolstoy rolls his eyes.) When he spread the mulch, he did it so tenderly, with his fingers, as if tucking each flower into bed. I still couldn't identify that famil-

iar smell. Soil and chocolate. Cinnamon and fern. Pomegran-
ate baseball honeycomb leaf. Who knows what anything smells
like? Things only smell like feelings.

The first time Serena came to the garden, I had no warning. She
simply appeared outside the fence one afternoon while I was
pinching the mums. I heard a cleared throat, and there she was,
on the other side of the fence, in a long goldenrod shift I could
see her legs through. She raised a hand in greeting.

"Don't touch the fence," Luke said.

"I know," Serena said. "It's electric." Her voice sounded different to me: higher, maybe. Sweeter. Luke turned back to what
he'd been doing, washing some clothes and sheets by hand in a
big blue basin. I tried to catch Serena's eye, but she was focused
on the back of his head.

"Luke," she said. "We need your help."

He didn't turn around. "Is that so?" he said. His voice was
stern, but I could see part of his face: he was grinning.

"We're getting close," she said. "But we need a teacher."

"I think I heard something about this," he said.

Serena caught my eye. "As expected," she said.

"You of all people should know how foolish this is," he said.

"You of all people should know I'm not foolish," she said.
"Come to my tent tonight."

He finally looked at her, the smile gone. "You know I can't
do that," he said.

Serena took a few steps forward, until her face was inches
from the wire. Luke came to meet her. She raised her hand again,
and without hesitation, pressed it full and flat against the electric fence. Nothing happened. They stood there for what seemed
like minutes, looking at each other, their bodies almost touching
through the wires. I thought of Houdini's wife at the Hippo-
drome, passing him the key to his restraints with a passionate kiss.

It had been hidden beneath her tongue: a perfect place for a little key. Kisses, as you know, are often keys. They have been known to unlock sleeping damsels. They are adept at breaking curses. By their very nature they open mouths, and also arms, and often legs. Of course, kisses can also be locks: *sealed with a kiss, kiss the bride, the kiss of death, kiss the gunner's daughter.*

But it seems important to say, here, that Sleeping Beauty was never really woken by a kiss. In the original version of the story, published in 1634 by Giambattista Basile, after SB (here named Talia) pricks her finger and falls into stillness, her father, thinking her dead, leaves her body to rot, splayed uncovered on a velvet bier in one of his country mansions. It is there that another king on a hunting trip eventually stumbles across her. For some reason, he understands that she is asleep, not dead. (For the disparity in the two kings' comprehension there is no explanation.) He tries to wake this beautiful maiden, calling out to her, but she will not wake. So he rapes her, and then he leaves.

(The translation I have read puts it this way: "Crying aloud, he beheld her charms and felt his blood course hotly through his veins. He lifted her in his arms, and carried her to a bed, where he gathered the first fruits of love. Leaving her on the bed, he returned to his own kingdom, where, in the pressing business of his realm, he for a time thought no more about this incident.")

Nine months later, Talia delivers twins (apparently a couple of fairies appear to cut the cord and, I don't know, tip ice chips into her unconscious mouth) but does not wake until her daughter, rooting around for a nipple, finds the pink tip of her mother's lifeless finger and, voila, sucks out the offending flax splinter. Later, the rapist king shows up for another round, and finds a little family, all three awake. On the one hand, he is overjoyed.

On the other hand, he is married. And soon, because she is no fool, nor a woman asleep, the queen discovers all. She sends her best servant to fetch her husband's misbegotten children, and orders them killed and cooked and served to him on silver platters. Then she summons Talia to the castle and tries to throw her in a large fire. What betrayed woman would wish for less? But alas, the cook takes pity on the children and serves lamb instead; the king catches his wife fireside and immolates *her* instead, and then he begins to plan a fancy wedding for himself and Talia. All the principals are saved! If being saved means getting married to your rapist.

The story ends with this proverb: *Those whom fortune favors / Find good luck even in their sleep.*

Again, if good luck means, etc.

When Serena finally looked over at me again, she was smiling. "Electric," she said, "my ass."

Then she turned on her heel, and it was only once she was out of sight that Luke moved away from the fence. "Finish up, will you," he said, to me, I suppose. Then he went into the garden shed and closed the door and didn't come out again, even when I called his name. So I finished washing his shirts and drop cloths, and before I left, I hung them all to dry on the fence I now knew couldn't hurt me, ignoring the clothesline, feeling both stupid and proud.

But look. Have I explained him properly? Do you understand it yet? That piled hair, like a mystic. The way his t-shirts pulled against his ropy muscles, but not too tightly, not like he wanted you to look, only when he moved the right way. The little round sunglasses he sometimes wore, like John Lennon, and how you could see yourself in them, only a smoothed version of yourself, and how easy it was to believe that was the way he saw you, too. How silent he was, some days. How you had to earn his attention. How sometimes he gave it when you weren't expecting anything. How he would never laugh at something unless he found it funny, would not entertain conversations that did not interest him. How I would try topic after topic, each one greeted with polite disinterest, a holy man's serenity, until I struck upon something he fancied. Then he'd turn to look at me, delighted—that radiant smile, that rare laugh. His face would change. "Well," he would say. "Tell me more about that."

Now I see it all for what it was, of course. Or, mostly.

As for her, I won't even try to explain. Like the Feeling, you'll never understand unless you've felt it.

That night began like any other—tap, tap, shoes, tongues, the dark, the path—except that when we reached the rock palm, it was deserted. Someone had obviously been there, though, and had dragged an old futon onto the smooth rock. There was a large rip in the center of the upholstery, and through the wound I could see a sliver of the futon's insides: sad wet foam, the color of burnt sugar. There was a lantern hanging on a branch, swinging slightly, emitting a feeble squeak.

"This seems normal," said Janet.

"I hope we're not supposed to sit on this thing," said Laurel.

I could see Janet gearing up to push her down onto it, but then we heard footsteps, and Serena appeared, coming from the direction of the tents.

"Hello," she said. "I've brought us something." She paused for effect, and then beckoned toward the darkness, and after a few seconds Luke came up the path behind her, beaming around at us all. I'd rarely seen him outside the garden before;

he looked wrong here, in our place. He was too tall. His head was much too big.

"How did you get him to come?" I asked. I felt strangely betrayed, though I couldn't have explained exactly how.

She thought about it for a second. "I went back," she said, and both of them smiled.

"For the record," he said, "I don't agree with what you're doing."

"Then why are you here?" Janet said. She had taken a few steps away from them. Her hands were in fists at her sides.

"Serena told me what she was planning, and I thought it would be safer to have someone here to keep an eye on things. Since there doesn't seem to be a way of dissuading her."

"We don't need supervision," Janet said.

Serena walked over to her, wrapped her arms around her neck, and whispered something in her ear. Janet's face didn't change, but her hands relaxed slightly.

We sat in a circle, and Luke began to lead us through the bird visualization he had taught me in the garden. Sweat gathered in the small of my back. I couldn't look at him. "Imagine yourself as a feather, floating upward," he said.

"Imagine yourself as a bird, hollow-boned and small," Serena said, to show him that she already knew. Luke did not look at me. He only smiled at her again.

As soon as it was over, Serena began giving us instructions. Janet positioned herself at the edge of the futon and squatted down with her head between her legs. She breathed deeply as Laurel counted to a nervous twenty. Then Janet straightened, put her thumb in her mouth, and Serena pushed, hard, on her solar plexus, and Janet crumpled as if dead onto the futon. I held back a gasp at the whites of her eyes. But after only a moment or two, she shook her head and blinked up at us.

"How long was I out?" she asked.

"Just a second," Laurel said.

"Olivia, you go next," Serena said. I stepped into my place in front of the futon, and finally looked over at Luke, who was leaning against a tree with his hands in his pockets, as if he were watching the most mundane performance: a lawn being mowed, an animal being born.

"Did you know," Luke said, "in Ireland they call this game the American Dream."

There is a moment right before you lose consciousness, when you're still aware of the world around you, but feel a profound dissociation from it, as though you're merely a witness to a space you have no part in. Then comes the rush of euphoria and heart-beat, the lightening, the blackening. I had done this before, of course. On a mountain very much like this one. But back then I hadn't understood what lightness meant. Maybe this was what my father had been looking for, I thought as I fell, maybe this was what I had missed.

Now I know that the American Dream can leave you in a coma or even kill you. But of course, we knew that back then too. It wouldn't have been any fun otherwise.

When I opened my eyes, hours or minutes or years later, I saw, peering over me, the enormous head of the Buddha. But no, it was only my father, smiling, his hair long again, his eyes some-how dark. Then of course it was Serena pulling me upward, and I shook my head clear. I kept hold of her hand for a few extra moments, to make sure she was no imposter. I didn't look at Luke, though I could feel him there, like a heat flare, burning.

Next it was Laurel's turn. Her eyes rolling, her sigh like cut flowers as she fell.

"I was dead longer," she said when she opened her eyes. "Wasn't I? I was dead longer than both of you." We nodded. She had been unconscious for nearly half a minute. It meant nothing to me, but I saw Janet lick her lips. Even at this she hated to lose.

Serena went last. She squatted down, hyperventilated, and stood, blowing on her thumb. Janet pushed her in the right place, but Serena only took a step back.

She frowned, wiped her thumb on her dress, and then looked at it, as if there were some possibility it was faulty.

"Did you do it wrong?" Janet asked.

"No," Serena said.

They tried again: nothing.

"Maybe it just doesn't work for you," Janet said. She looked over at Luke for the first time all night. I couldn't read her expression.

Laurel, who had dropped to the ground in exhaustion, her hair and legs spread, drew a lazy circle in the fallen pine needles with a finger. "It wouldn't mean anything," she said. "If you couldn't do it."

Janet cleared her throat.

"Come here, Olivia," Serena said. I stood in front of her and she took my hands. "You're going to help me." She placed my hands around her neck and reached around to tuck a strand of hair behind my ear. She stroked my cheek with a finger. Then she lowered her hand again to touch my thumbs where they now rested against her windpipe, like an old woman absent-mindedly fingering a brooch. I was old enough then, perhaps, to think of Plath: *If the moon smiled, she would resemble you / You leave the same impression / Of something beautiful, but annihilating.*

If I wasn't, I'm thinking of her now.

"You're going to choke me," she said. I tried to move my hands away, but she gripped my wrists. Then she lifted one arm in front of my eyes to remind me of her countless protection cords, which I thought looked in danger of disintegrating at any moment. "I'll be safe," she said. "Just press down until I start to fall."

"Girls," said Luke, but he didn't move to stop us. He'd taken his hands out of his pockets and was watching us with interest.

"I can't," I said. So she waited, and we stood like that, staring at each other, her skin sweating slightly beneath my fingertips, until after a while I did begin to choke her, a little at first, my thumbs exploring the ridges of her throat, and then harder, squeezing, thinking of that swirling, sexy, plump little goldfish, its eyelashes not unlike Serena's, so long and so dark, begging to be touched, to be handled with rough, unyielding hands, to be undone, unmade, until suddenly she was falling backward away from me.

She missed the futon. Her body jerked and twisted and she hit her head hard on the rock and then I saw it: a thin gyre of bright red blood that spooled upward from her temple and hung suspended and shining in the air above her face, hung there for a moment, like a smoke ring, before dissolving back down into the blackness.

In Hindu tantric tradition, the goddess Chinnamasta is represented as a naked, full-breasted sixteen-year-old girl, her body the color of the hibiscus flower, which is also the color of blood. Traditionally, she stands above a couple in coitus, and has just a moment ago sliced off her own head. She holds her still-dripping scimitar in one hand and her own severed head in the other. Her long black hair hangs loose. She is inclined toward lust. From her neck erupt three shooting fountains of blood, two of which are caught in the mouths of her two female attendants, and the last of which makes its arc into the mouth of her own severed head. All three mouths suck greedily at the blood of the goddess. All three bodies wear garlands of skulls around their necks. A snake often slips among the garlands. Chinnamasta is revered for her sexual power, her fury, her self-sacrifice, and for her embodied reminder that life, death, and sex are inseparable, forever wound (*wound*: the word's multiple meanings do not escape me in this moment). She is sometimes interpreted as being a symbol of sexual restraint and sometimes interpreted as a symbol of sexual energy. She represents death as well as immortality, self-destruction as well as self-renewal. She is a reminder that life feeds on death. She is a reminder that death requires life. She is not widely worshipped. She is considered to be too dangerous to approach, even in supplication.

The three of us stood, staring at Serena crumpled on the ground. Her face was pale. I felt a black cavern opening up underneath me. My limbs felt heavy and immobile, filled with black sand. *You're a beautiful girl, Olivia.* I looked at Luke, and he too was frozen. Serena had been right. This had something to do with him, with his presence here, his body filling the space that until tonight had been only ours. Janet and Laurel were deviations in the darkness somewhere in my peripheral vision. We stood. We stared.

Finally, one of us—it was Laurel—screamed.

We lurched forward as one body, arms outstretched. But Luke got there first. He moved Serena onto the futon, cradled her head in his large hands, and I felt a pang wholly unrelated to her safety. He brushed her hair out of her face and she opened her eyes.

"That was incredible," she said. She sat up, pushing Luke away and rubbing her head. I looked for the hole that had let out so much blood and saw only a little cut, the tiniest sliver, near her hairline. She pressed on it, closing her eyes.

"I felt it. I was so close," she said. She arched her back, rolling her head on her neck. The toes on her left foot spread apart. The toes on her right foot stayed pressed together.

"Did you see it?" I said.

I could feel my heart in my throat, as if it too had levitated, up out of my chest cavity, straining to sacrifice itself against my teeth. Laurel reached out and took my hand, her eyes fixed on Serena's temple. I laced my fingers with hers, a little miracle in that.

"You saw it?" Janet whispered.

"What?" Serena said. "Saw what?"

"Your blood," Laurel said quietly. "Just a little bit of blood."

"Blood from your head," Janet said.

"What?" Serena said. She was looking at me, and so I had to answer.

"It floated," I told her. And then she wasn't looking at me anymore. Then she only had eyes for Luke.

7

The four of us played the fainting game every night for a week, but we couldn't re-create the results we'd had with Luke. Even when Serena cut open her own hand with a knife before we started, she only ruined her dress. We fell and fell and fell: that was all. We tried new things, whatever we could dredge up, hoping something would catch: I thought the most promising of these was yogic flying, sworn levitation tactic of Transcendental Meditators, though Serena called this practice "idiot hopping" and so it was. Luke refused to return to the rock palm, no matter how much I begged him during rota, no matter how many times Serena came to stand outside the fence. It was too dangerous, he said. He should never have come at all. He should never have encouraged it. In the garden, I settled into long silences. Luke told me I needed more sleep, and fed me berries out of his palm, but he wouldn't talk about what had happened. He wouldn't even admit that anything had.

I began to question myself. Had Serena's blood really floated? I had seen it so clearly; then again, the strawberries.

(What would my mother have said? But no, I wasn't supposed to be thinking about her anymore.)

Still, we must have been accomplishing something in all those hours at the rock palm, because Dominique helped me into my first handstand during yoga at the end of that week, holding my heavy legs while my face turned red.

"Closer," she murmured, and moved on to press her palms into the small of Nisha's bent back, coax some warmth into Jamie's thin limbs. I had noticed by then that she never touched Serena.

One night during this time, Laurel pulled a small bag of white powder out of her pocket. You must have known this was coming; I admit that I did not.

"I asked Paola," she said by way of explanation.

Serena eyed the bag. "What did you tell her?"

"Only that I wanted to lose my feet. She said this was guaranteed." She shook the little bag. "Which it better be, because her markup is beyond." It was ketamine, she told us, a drug she'd never tried, one famed for its powers of dissociation.

"No," Serena said, and I was ashamed at the relief that spread across my shoulders. I looked over at Janet, but she was absorbed in something else, pressing her fingers into her ankle, as if it pained her.

"You don't have to do it, if you're scared," Laurel said. She opened the bag and poured out a little on the side of her hand, too expertly, I could tell even then. "We'll let you know if it works." For a moment, I thought Serena did look afraid, and then her face cleared and she slapped the bag out of Laurel's hand, sending all the white powder into the dirt, like a magic creature's trail.

"I said no," Serena said. "That's not the right way to do this."

Janet was paying attention now. "What's the difference be-tween this and drinking?" she asked as Laurel sputtered and knelt to salvage what she could.

"You know the difference," Serena said. "Don't ask me any more stupid questions."

The next morning, Serena caught us as we were heading to breakfast. She had a thin blue book under her arm. She had decided that we needed to fast. "I can't believe I didn't think of this before," she said. "All the famous levitators have done it." We wouldn't completely starve ourselves, of course. We'd eat nettles, like Milarepa.

"Didn't Milarepa turn green and furry?" Laurel said. She had not quite forgiven Serena for the night before.

"Yes, but we don't have time for that," Serena said, unmoved by Laurel's bad mood, or the sunglasses she was refusing to re-move. "We'll have to combine it with the things we already know work."

"Or sort of work," Janet said. "Maybe worked, a little bit, one time."

"It can't hurt, anyway," Serena said. "I found a recipe for nettle soup, and tea."

"Buddhist Master Cleanse," Laurel said. "All right, I'm in."

"Shocking," Janet said.

"It's not so you can look hot in a bikini, Laurel," Serena said.

"I already look hot in a bikini, Serena," Laurel snapped.

"Where are we going to find nettles?" I asked.

"We'll just have to start looking."

According to *Cunningham's Encyclopedia of Magical Herbs*, the nettle (*Urtica dioica*), also called stinging nettle, burn weed, and *ortiga ancha*, is a masculine plant, ruled by the planet Mars. It is most powerful in spells connected to exorcism, protection, healing, and lust. It can be used to reflect curses or repel ghosts. Its lusty properties are best invoked in the bath. But of course, fresh nettles must be handled with care. They cannot be eaten raw. Their leaves and stems are covered with tiny hairs called trichomes, which, when touched, detach and plunge themselves into the skin like little needles, depositing painful poisons. We weren't planning to eat them raw, of course. We weren't as dumb as all that.

But it didn't matter how dumb we weren't, because we couldn't find any. We spent the morning walking around in the woods, heads down, until our necks grew sore. Whenever anyone spotted a toothy-looking plant, she called Janet to come touch it. Janet had assured us she didn't mind the prospect of the pain. I think after a while she was looking forward to it. By what would have been lunch, we still hadn't found anything, and we were already exhausted.

"It's almost time for rota," I said.

"That's an excellent idea," said Serena.

When Luke saw the four of us approach the fence, he stood, though not in greeting. Instead, he walked over to the door and locked it from the inside. There was something different about him that day. It took me a few seconds to realize that he wasn't wearing his usual gardening clothes. He looked nice: jeans and a white button-down shirt. He looked clean.

"Luke," Serena said. Her voice was sweet again. "How are you?"

"What do you need?" He seemed incapable of looking directly at Serena for long. He kept flicking his eyes to her, and then away.

"We were wondering where we could find some nettles."

"Now what, I wonder, would you want with those?" he said.

"We've been reading about Milarepa," Laurel said.

"I bet you have," Luke said.

"They're supposed to be really healthy," I said. "There are nutrients."

"Do you grow them in here?" Serena asked. She took a step forward.

"I don't cultivate weeds," he said.

"Help us search, then," Serena said. "You know what they say: a young back is a terrible thing to waste."

Luke snorted, and I let out a breath I hadn't known I was holding. "Nettles grow near water," he said. "Find some water, find some nettles. Good enough?"

In answer, Serena pulled her dress over her head and let it fall to the ground.

She wasn't naked; I would tell myself later that what she'd exposed was little more than what you'd see if you came upon her at the beach. And yet it was more. Her bra was white lace, and when she turned, I could see the brown skin of her proud little breasts and the shadows of her nipples, bigger and darker than I'd imagined them. (I had, yes. Hadn't you?) Her panties were heartbreakingly girlish: pink cotton with white scalloped trim and a little bow in front.

"What are you doing?" Luke said. There was no alarm on his face, or even surprise, but his voice had gone hollow, as though he were at the bottom of a bowl.

"I'm making sure you understand the rules," Serena said. She raised her arms. The shadow of a hawk passed over her like a blessing.

"Put your clothes on," Luke said. Serena only laughed at him. He was following the script, but he wasn't selling it. She did a few twirls, tucking one leg in like my Green Tara, and then, without saying anything, began to walk back up the path.

Laurel scooped up the discarded dress. "Well," she said. "Bye."

I tried to catch Janet's eye, but Laurel had already taken her hand; they followed Serena's retreating form without looking back. I only realized later that Janet hadn't said a word during this entire exchange.

Serena: I wish I could describe her body to you now. But you know it, you've seen it. Anyway, the image I retain isn't of her flesh at all, but of the sun half blotted out by her hip, lighting up the little hairs there, piercing my vision when she moved, so that when she finally disappeared around the bend, I could see the negative imprint of her body in shimmering bruise pink, patterned over and over again against the grass.

Once they were all out of sight, Luke unlocked the door. But instead of stepping back to let me in, he stepped forward, and left the garden without a word, disappearing into the woods, in almost the exact opposite direction that Serena had gone.

Without anything else to do, I sat on the bench in the garden and waited for him to return. After a while, I lit a cigarette. I had been carrying around a pack of Serena's for a few days; they were squashed and loose from my pocket. I didn't mind. I was trying to get addicted to them. I had heard so much about addiction, that furious body craving that had spawned an industry of patches and psychotherapies, but the feeling eluded me. I didn't know what it was to want something that way, in the cells. (Didn't I?) I wanted to want that way, and to satisfy my want, and to want again. I was getting closer: the smell of the smoke made me think of the black sand. I lay back on the bench and closed my eyes.

Serena wanted to escape the role of the slit-open damsel, that was clear. But it wasn't only that. I understood it now, the smoke piling around my face, the nicotine turning my stomach, her body twirling behind my eyelids. She wanted to be the robed men. She wanted to wield the knife, pour the sand. She wanted to say who was a beautiful girl, and what that meant we had to do. Lightness was antidote, perhaps—but it was also the flaming sword.

Serena would not wait, if she were here. Serena would act. I stood and walked around the perimeter of the garden, toe to heel. I touched the red door of the shed, still too shiny. I pushed it open. Inside there was nothing but tools and bags of soil. I touched everything, just to be sure, like checking teeth. Then I went out through the gate and around to the back of the fence, where a little matted path revealed itself. I had seen Luke walking from this direction on days he'd arrived late to rota. I thought he must live somewhere down that path. I had told no one about this, not even Serena, though I'd considered reporting it to Nisha, who still believed he lived "nowhere."

Without really thinking about it, I started walking. Why not? The trees rose up enormous around me almost immediately, and after only a few minutes, I might have been in the middle of an ancient forest, nowhere near a clearing of any kind, never mind a whole meditation center crawling with teenage girls. The change in temperature was almost shocking, like jumping off a pier. But I was not afraid. My body did not resist. I kept walking, and eventually, a small cabin materialized before me. It was the kind of structure that told you nothing at all about a person: simple, wooden, the inside hidden by old floral curtains that might have been hanging in the windows for decades. An ax leaned against the side of the house. Faded prayer flags fluttered from the eaves.

I knocked.

When, pray tell, has any little girl ever found anything good in a cabin in the woods? Who inhabits such places? Cannibalistic gingerbread fetishists, cross-dressing wolves, recently eaten grandmothers, polyamorous dwarves in the market for a cleaning lady, loamy, malevolent erl-kings, acorn-toothed vegetation gods, vine-spitting green men, hungry old ladies with iron teeth and mortars and pestles parked askew in the driveway, headless, deathless, deal-cutting, green-skinned knights & aging final girls & witches & hags & crones & chain saw enthusiasts & hillbilly horrors & bad scientists & cult leaders & the possessed, by demons or drugs or dreams.

And here I was with no cape nor girdle nor fat tasty brother to protect me. Alone and unguarded, like the stupidest woodsman or princess.

I knocked again.

Luke opened the door. He looked as though he had been expecting me.

"No rota today?" I said, as sweetly as I could manage. If I closed my eyes, I could still see the rind of Serena's hip.

"In fact, no," he said. "I have an appointment today. I came to tell you, but . . ." He trailed off and spread his hands. Up close, his cleanliness was distracting. I had only ever seen him sweaty, covered in soil. Now he looked exposed, as though his last protective barrier had been painfully scrubbed away.

He even wore a watch. I noticed because he looked at it. I was waiting for him to say something more about what had just happened, to chastise me or confide in me or commiserate with me, but he did not. "Actually, I've found something that might interest you," he said. "I still have a minute, if you want to come in."

I wanted to come in.

From the inside, Luke's cottage looked a little like a tree house that had fallen out of its tree. It was modest: a single bed covered in a thin pink blanket, a kitchenette, and a low bureau crowned with four toothy towers of books. A table and two chairs were positioned by the window. On the table was a vase of wilting black-eyed Susans.

"Can I offer you something?" he asked, oddly formal now. "Lemonade?"

"Okay," I said. I wandered over to the bureau and drew my fingers across the titles of his books. Some of them I recognized from my father's bookshelves: *The Heart of the Buddha, Catch-22, Siddhartha, The Rings of Saturn*. Not *Lolita*. *Lolita* would really be too much, here.

He set a glass on the table. "I put in a sprig of our lavender," he said. "And here," he said. He handed me a photo album bound in red leather. He smiled at me with half his mouth.

I sat at the table and turned the pages of the album. The sweat on my fingertips made them slip on the plastic sleeves. All of the photographs were from the Center. They looked like they had been taken with disposable cameras and developed imperfectly, at a gas station or similar. There were multiple close-ups of plants with Luke's thumb in the shot for scale. (That thumb—the sight of it made my spine tingle.) There was a photo of the Sweet Sorrows and another of the koi pond. There was a snapshot of a visiting monk, his head brown and smooth as a nut; a tall man I didn't recognize was pushing a big white envelope into his stomach, somewhat missing the monk's helpless hands. There was a whole page of Dominiques, here standing in front of the sunset, here laughing and looking over her shoulder. A few had been taken in the shrine room, meditating girls from summers past; I could pick out a familiar face or two. Not for the first time that summer, I felt a strange bruised tenderness, a nostalgia for the current moment.

Then I saw it. It was a picture of the grounds, of nothing, really: a few scattered adults standing around. But a man I recognized sat on one of the Center's trademark white boulders, his head turned slightly away from the lens. The photograph couldn't have been taken more than a year ago. His hair was the same length it had been on the last day I'd seen him. There was a strange woman standing by his side. Her hand was on his shoulder. His feet were raised off the ground.

"Did you find him?" Luke asked.

I pressed my finger into my father's face. When I took it away, nothing had changed. Father, woman, boulder, feet. I felt the room contract around me.

"I want you to be careful," Luke said. "It wasn't just the nettles that made Milarepa levitate, you know."

"I know," I said. The feet in the photo seemed significant to me. I recognized the boulder he was sitting on. I had sat on it myself. My thighs burned at the thought. It's strange, the importance we assign to handling things our loved ones have touched, or to revisiting historic scenes, of epic battles or first dates. To sleeping in Lizzie Borden's bedroom. These are attempts at folding time, at pinning one piece of fabric to another. But time doesn't work that way, you know. That's why you feel so empty afterward.

"I don't want you to get hurt," he said.

"Who is she?" I asked.

Luke wiped his hands on a towel and came toward me. He reached out as if to tuck my hair behind my ear, then pulled his hand away at the last moment and put it in his pocket.

"The bad news is: you're falling through the air, with nothing to hang on to, and no parachute," he said. "The good news is: there's no ground."

I wanted to scream. My father used to say this exact thing. My father used to sit on the same rock I did. My father had gone to the Levitation Center, but he hadn't come home. All of my life he had been looking for something. But what was it?

I thought of the way Luke had looked at Serena, her body almost naked, barely hidden behind thin swatches of white cotton and lace. I gradually became aware of my stomach, the flesh of my arms, the sweat behind my knees, all of them inferior to hers. It was the way he had looked at her that made me take a step toward him. I knew he loved her, despite the fact that he hadn't yet given her everything. If he loved her, I was safe, and also ruined.

"You smell like cigarettes," he said. He took the empty lemonade glass away from me and set it down on the little table. Our lavender slumped like a worm at the bottom.

"I smoked in the womb," I said. I didn't know what to do with my hands.

"No, you didn't," he said.

My head felt inflated with air. I smelled like cigarettes. My hands were empty. I was alone with Luke. I could see his bed. Where he slept, where he touched himself. I wanted him to touch me. I wanted to be rubbed, stroked, bitten, pinched, smoothed over, and dug into. I wanted to be skinned like a rabbit and stretched between two poles. I wanted to be forced open like an oyster. I wanted to be caught, coded, specimenized, my wings pinned back and stamped. There were too many places on my body that had never been touched, not by anyone, not even by me. I imagined them black with disuse, smoldering in wait. I wanted them exposed, licked. I was tired of being the one to look, to want, to wait. I was tired of being the one to binge. I wanted to be put whole into someone else's mouth. I wanted that person to want me so badly, to fear me so much that they couldn't help but bite down.

I took another step, testing the space between us. He didn't move. He was decent, patient. I was connected to him by something electric, a taut, shimmering string. It pulled, pulled, pulled me forward until I was so close I had to press my hands into his shirt, his clean shirt, that's what happens when you treat the mulch like bedclothes, when the sweat is honeycomb leaf. I gripped the fabric. Luke said nothing; he looked only curious, waiting to see what I would do next, his arms relaxed at his sides. Serena would never understand. She'd never feel this, what I was feeling now. She wouldn't allow it, not with that cold mirrored heart of hers. *Desire is the root of all suffering.* I understood, but I didn't care. I couldn't care. I could only give myself over to this power of not-power, this body requirement. I reached up and wrapped my hands around Luke's neck, but instead of pushing down with my thumbs to choke him, as I should have, oh, I should have, I pulled his head toward mine and kissed him, hard, digging my nails into the back of his neck, pushing my hips into his.

I felt something hot moving in my stomach. No, it was only his tongue in my mouth. I pushed into him, pushing him backward, that large man, a kind of magic in that alone. He made the tiniest sound, not a groan or a complaint, but something like air escaping, and suddenly I felt light-headed. He put his hands on my hips, and then they were lower, and I remembered something I'd seen from the back of the cab on the winding road up to the Center weeks before: a heavy policeman in sunglasses standing on the side of the road, the door of his cruiser open into oncoming traffic, pointing his gun into the ditch; at what, I couldn't tell. He fired two shots in quick succession, but by the second one we were too far past; I pressed my face against the window and saw nothing. The cancerous cabdriver had seemed not to notice. What was it? An exercise? An execution? A mercy kill? It was the first time I had ever been kissed.

Luke pushed me away from his body with stiff arms.

"You don't want this," he said.

"I want it," I said. Just a little more, I thought. A little more and I would be the one to lift into the air. I had felt it, the lightness, I had felt it, and it was Luke, and I would get there first, before all of them, and then I would have everything, he would love me again forever. I leaned forward, but Luke was stronger.

"You're a peach," he said.

There was a knock at the door. "Shit," he said. He looked me over quickly before catching his own eye in the mirror. He ran a hand through his hair and then went to open the door.

It was Dominique, in a pretty brown dress I'd never seen her wear before.

"Oh," she said, seeing me there. I'm sure we were both thinking the same thing.

"I forgot to leave Olivia a note about rota," Luke said. He smiled down at me the way he might at a small dog. "No need to go back to the garden, just take some extra free time now." Dominique nodded, casting her eyes around the room, as if searching for clues. Whatever she saw, or did not see, it was enough. She stepped through the doorway, and we changed places. Over her shoulder, Luke winked at me, but as soon as I had crossed the threshold, I heard the door lock.

I walked back to the empty garden. I had the urge to throw myself against the looming electric fence, to climb it and hang on while the shocks ran through my body. I imagined myself held aloft by its power, my body frozen, limbs akimbo, like one of those cartoon cats who've stuffed their fingers into sockets, my skeleton lighting up and darkening over and over again. Then nothing about me would stay hidden. Then I would not be ignored. Then my outsides would be my insides, everything shot through with light, and everyone, everyone would see.

Then I reminded myself: that fence didn't work. Serena had proved that much. Its power was no match for ours. Luke was wrong. I was not a peach.

8

I couldn't go back to the dormitory. I was trembling, as if I really had become electrified. Everyone else would be in rota for another hour at least, and the empty lawn looked scalped, like a trap. I elected not to be caught, not yet. I started up the mountain, toward Serena. For this instinct, I have no explanation, except to say that I have always felt compelled to carry anything to its logical extreme. I've mentioned the thing with horses. More, more, more, sang my stupid little heart.

Here's a story about my father, one I never could have told Luke: I was twelve when I discovered pornography, on that first edge of things. (Serena's mother was already dead.) I looked for hours that first night, but didn't feel anything flicker in myself until I began clicking on the insistent ads, which, once touched, bloomed into all manner of images, filling the screen with naked bodies slapping against each other or purled and poised, tongues and fingers extended. I suppose I too find my ecstasy in excess. Before this I had only seen the soft-colored sex scenes you find in PG-13 films. I had only recently worn out my gruesome bed-man. I remember the shame afterward, as I closed each window, and each one resisted closure as aggressively as it had before. Except now each blooming felt like an affront, a hydra sprouting new and uglier heads, and by the time the screen was blank I was cold and tired and disgusted.

Of course, I know now that no matter what you can imagine, someone, somewhere, is masturbating to it. Some of these urges have names. *Psychrophilia*: sexual arousal from being cold; *agalmatophilia*: sexual attraction to statues; *nebulophilia*: arousal by fog; *lithophilia*: attraction to stone and/or gravel; *climacophilia*: arousal from falling down stairs; *chasmophilia*: attraction to caverns and valleys. Don't be shocked. Don't laugh. We're all deviants. (Does this mean none of us are?)

(Well—no.)

My father approached me a few days later with a book. "I've noticed you've been looking at some pretty hard-core pornography on the internet," he said.

I could say nothing. I wanted to coil into myself like a pill bug, beginning with the back of my throat. I searched for an explanation, or some kind of denial, but my father just stood there, holding out the book.

"If you're interested in knowing more about the theory and history of porn—why people look at it, why they make it, its place in our society—you could read this." He waggled the book at me. "It offers a little bit of context."

This was unbearable: *porn*, he'd said. I can't remember what I mumbled back, but I know I didn't take the book. I felt worse than I would have if he had punished me.

I wonder now what my mother would have done if she had been the one to discover this early exploration. She wouldn't have given me reading material, of that I am certain. Maybe a slap. Maybe some condoms. Well. She wasn't afraid of sex like he was.

It was beautiful in the woods that day. I haven't said this enough—how beautiful it was at the Center. I felt it the most on that climb to Serena's tent, my mouth swollen, the trees sturdy on either side of me, their leaves glowing bright green in the sun, casting a chiaroscuro of warmth and shade across the verdant ground. The clean smell of pine and rock, the shuddering, singing air, the soothing empty fullness of the mountain. Something almost like the Feeling crept into my limbs.

I had kissed Luke, and he had kissed me back. But now, as I climbed, the thrill began to wear off, and I found that underneath it was that same dull shame. Why, when I had gotten what I could finally admit I had wanted all along? I have my theories now. But that girl there, pressing her palms against her hips to try to reclaim the feeling of the first hands that had ever touched her that way, though not the last, not by far—she doesn't see that she was trying to put her tongue in her father's mouth. She doesn't recognize him in all that makeup. But she feels the falsity all the same.

Desire is the root of all suffering, the Buddha taught.

A memory: once, when I was a child, I saw a beautiful blue backpack covered in little gray ponies in a store window. I wanted it desperately, of course. Horses, etc. I threw myself at my parents' feet in supplication. My father laughed and stepped backward. My mother picked me up by the shoulders, reset me to standing, brushed off my knees. They tugged me away. It was too expensive, and besides, I already had a backpack. I became inconsolable, dragging my small feet, sobbing. The world had ended. I could not live without my pretty pony backpack.

Eventually, my father knelt in front of me. "You're miserable," he said, "because you don't have what you want."

I nodded.

"But yesterday, you had never seen that backpack, and you were happy."

I guessed this was true.

"So what is creating the unhappiness?"

Another: my mother, sitting on the porch swing, drinking a glass of wine. I was in the kitchen, pretending to wash the dishes, watching her watch the sunset. She liked to watch the sunset. I wished I had her eyes, her waist. My father came around from the front garden. He leaned his shovel against the house and climbed the porch steps. My mother was swinging, and the regular scrape of chain against hook made a wheedling music. As my father passed her, he reached out a hand to pat her shoulder. My mother caught his hand with her own and held it tight. He stopped, leashed by his own arm. She pulled his hand down, rubbed it once with her thumb, and then placed it firmly on her left breast. They were still for a few seconds, looking at each other, and then my father carefully extracted himself from her grasp. She turned her face back to the sunset. He kissed her on the head and came inside.

"Hey, kid," he said.

Outside, my mother threw her wine glass into the bushes. I expected a crash, a shatter, a flock of ravens exploding into the air, but it made only the smallest rustle.

• • •

I called out for Serena when I reached the clearing. Nothing. I called again, louder. The empty tents seemed to create their own sound, a sort of negation that drowned out my voice. I peered up into the trees, but could see nothing through the bottoms of the glowing leaves. Cracks of light crossed my eyes.

"Ki ki," she shouted from somewhere above me. "So so!"

Then she landed neatly at my feet, absurd magic thing that she was. She was wearing her dress again, but there was still something unclothed about her.

She took my hand and led me to her tent. Inside, I was surprised to find Janet and Laurel. Between them, on the floor of the tent, was a heap of giant, leafy stalks.

"You're here," I said, stupidly. I don't know what I had been expecting, or not expecting. I hadn't imagined this moment at all.

"Reports of our deaths have been mildly exaggerated," Janet said. The palms of her hands were bright red.

Serena was looking at me intently, as if trying to read my mind. I thought of Luke's mouth on mine, and then I thought, hard, of the opposite of his mouth, just in case. *Ice cube. Sidewalk. Tire iron.* Without meaning to, I also thought of her comb, now hidden in my cubby, tucked into the pocket of a pair of jeans it was much too hot to wear. *Splinter. Apple. Coin.*

"Did something else happen?" she asked.

"What did he say about us?" Laurel wanted to know. I could see her appraising my feet, my fingernails, in much the same way that Dominique had. Well, that much I could tell them.

"He stormed off to his cabin after you left," I said. "Obviously I followed him. But he was meeting Dominique there."

Serena bit her lip. "I thought she was done with him," she said.

"After last year," Janet said. She shifted uncomfortably on her cushion.

"What happened last year?" I asked.

Serena waved her hand. "Long story," she said.

Laurel was still regarding me coolly, as though she knew something had changed, and was trying to figure out exactly what. I felt a stab of fear. I didn't know what Serena would do if she found out I had broken the rules.

But then again, there was no reason she would. I would keep my secret. *Glass door. Pineapple. Hole.* I smiled at them. I shrugged.

We snuck into the kitchen that night to prepare the nettles. Tenzin had printed up a healthy number of signs since the last time we'd been there, and posted them everywhere: THIEVES WILL BE BOILED, they read, above a black-and-white photograph of a steak. Janet drew a smiley face on one of the steaks in purple Sharpie, to throw her off our trail.

We made the soup with Tenzin's immersion blender, mixing water and the cooked nettles with handfuls of sea salt and garlic and lemon. I tried a spoonful, and was surprised by how much I liked it. The tea, which we made by straining the nettle boil-water, tasted good too, somehow both bright and earthy, and though there was no sting, I swear I could feel a resilient tingle in my throat, the barest hint of danger.

"Freud thought the human dream of flying was all about sex," Laurel said afterward, as we cleaned the bowls. "Both being rooted in the same obsession with the unknown."

"Freud also thought that women only want sex so they can pretend to have their own penises," Janet said.

"Typical," Serena said.

"You can't blame him," Laurel said. "All men think sex is about them. It's hardwired. Even the words for sex are all masculocentric, have you noticed? Screwing. Banging. Nailing. Pounding. Smashing. Ramming. Tapping. You'd think they were building a goddamn boat." She poured the nettle tea into a large thermos. We had tucked the soup in the back of the fridge. I had noticed her drinking surreptitiously from a flask again. I wondered where she was hiding it, and what exactly was inside.

"Masculocentric?" I said.

"I told you I'm not fucking stupid," Laurel said. "Look it up."

"*Bumping uglies* is pretty neutral," Janet said.

"I hate that one," Serena said. She looked down, put her hand between her legs. "Anyway, mine's not ugly."

"Well, I think we should say pocketing," Laurel said. "With pocketing, we get the power." She reached an arm into the air, made her hand into a cup, and tapped her fingers together at the top, like *ma che vuoi?* or a cartoon Italian after a bite of his mother's *pasta e fagioli*. She sucked her teeth. "So you say, 'I totally pocketed that guy,' or 'I'm going to pocket the shit out of you.'"

"You *do* want a penis for your very own," I said.

"I *want* to start a new vocabulary," Laurel said.

"I'll suffocate you," Janet said.

"I'll drown you," Laurel said.

"I'll swallow you whole," Serena said.

It was at that moment that the lights turned on. Tenzin stood in the doorway, her hand on the switch. She was not disheveled. Her hair was not in curlers. She looked as though she had been expecting us. It would have been just like her to wait for us to clean up after ourselves, Laurel told us later.

"This is a severe infraction," Tenzin said. Soap leaked slowly from the sponge I was holding, dripping down my forearm. Tenzin looked like a drafter's study in concentric circles. Two round eyes in an almost perfectly round face, a neat round bun perched on top of her head like a scoop of salt-and-pepper ice cream. Below the neck, too, she was round, but somehow not fat—it was as though she'd somehow possessed a large, taut ball of blue silk and was now walking around impersonating it. Even with the gray hair, her age was impossible to discern.

"We couldn't sleep," Serena said. She wiped the scraps of nettle off the counter and into her hand, and casually deposited them in the trash.

"I'm going to have to wake up Shastri Dominique," Tenzin said. "You girls may have a long tether here, for reasons beyond my understanding, but this is my kitchen."

"I don't think that will be necessary," Serena said. Tenzin raised her eyebrows and Serena pushed past her out into the hall. Tenzin sighed and followed. When they returned a few minutes later, Serena looked intensely smug.

"All right, girls," Tenzin said, her face tight. "Go to bed. But don't let me find you here again."

Serena, of course, refused to answer any questions about this. "Don't worry" was all she would say. "I know how to talk to people." Janet and Laurel didn't even bother asking. Either they knew something I didn't, or they knew they didn't want to.

When we got back to the dormitory that night, I fell asleep immediately. I woke only once before the conch shell: in the very early morning, as the light was beginning to line the windows, when I heard Janet climb up into her bunk, returning once again from wherever she'd been.

9

Here's something my father once told me, when I was ten or so and hated, violently and for no reason, a girl in my fifth grade class: that I should feel love and compassion for everyone, no matter who they were, because in the countless past lives and reorganizations of atoms, every single person on earth was at one time or another my mother. It could be in the past or perhaps in the future, but on some existential plane, some other incarnation just as real as this one, everyone was my mother, and had given me life, and fed me, and cared for me, and therefore I owed them my love and gratitude.

"But I hate my mother too," I said. (And why not? She was the one who chastised me, punished me, swore and screamed and pulled my hair when she was supposedly trying to braid it.)

"No, you don't," he said. "But all right, how about this. You can remember that everyone you know, even the worst person you know, even Veronica, was once *me*, or will be me in the future. I'll die, like I have a thousand times, and because everything is connected, at some point, part of me will be Veronica, and part of Veronica will be me."

I'd reached for him then, because the idea of his dissolution, his separation from me into millions of atoms and time and space and other people whom I hated, particularly Veronica, stupid Veronica with her ludicrous shiny unbraidable hair, was too much for me to bear. "I don't want you to be anyone else," I said. "You can't die."

"Death comes without warning," he said. He spread his arms. "This body will be a corpse." Then he took me to get a cinnamon bun. The people at the cinnamon bun place all turned and smiled when we entered, and they all knew my father by name, and remembered his order, and this reassured me. If the cinnamon bun people know your name, I figured, death can't be so near.

Dentists are something like twice as likely as other people to kill themselves, of course. Everyone knows that, especially the daughters of dentists. Some years, more doctors kill themselves than dentists, but since dentists are much likelier to suffer from psychoneurotic disorders, that seems more or less down to luck. It's stress, people say. Stress and access to drugs that'll do the job. Plus, everyone hates going to the dentist. I can see how that would wear on a person. There's no denying that the human mouth is a weird place to work. Teeth can readily alarm.

So when he was a day late returning, when he was a week late, a month late, with no word, the papers piling up—of course I considered it. Death comes without warning. But it can also be planned.

Later, though, we decided against the idea. I said that my father wouldn't kill himself, that he wouldn't do that to us, to me, that he was, essentially, happy. My mother said that if my father were going to kill himself, he'd have done it where everyone could see. It would have been a spectacle; he would have wanted a fuss. He'd have wanted to be cremated too. Buddhists are typically cremated. You can also cremate your pets, whatever their chosen faiths. By the time my father disappeared, I had a row of little tins, each lid adorned with a cheery still life of fruit or field, each one with the dusted bones of a rabbit or finch or guinea pig inside.

Next, I developed a theory that he'd been kidnapped. That someone, someone who was unhappy with his veneers, say, had waited for him after work and jumped into his car and forced him to drive to a secret hideout, where he tied him to a chair and gave him filling after filling. Why not? Everyone hates the dentist.

"Don't be ridiculous," my mother said. "He just ran away." She was drinking coffee at the kitchen table, somehow taking up all the space at once. "Like a little boy. That was always his greatest dream, did you know? To be a little boy again."

"There's nothing wrong with that," I said.

"Remember that thought when your brain is fully developed," she said.

In the morning, the Garudas had Kyūdō. This was Janet's favorite activity at the Center, and we never skipped it. Janet even did her rota with Sarah, the Kyūdō instructor, and apparently had for years, except for last year, when she'd had a broken arm and had to sit in the office with Harriet. You could still see a faint tan line on her arm from the cast. *Bicycle accident*, she said when I asked.

We met Sarah at the Center's simple archery range, which was set in a clearing at the end of a cedar-chip path. Three targets pinned to hay bales sat at the far end of the range, shaded under a green wooden canopy. Sarah went around to the back and came out with an armful of bows.

"Remember, the object is not necessarily to hit the target," Sarah said, passing out the bows. "The object is synchronization of body and mind and the present moment, okay? Hitting the target is just a plus." When she reached Janet, she shuffled the bows in her arms and handed her the one with a faded purple ribbon tied to the tip.

"It is a little like polishing a mirror, only the mirror is your mind," Sarah said. "Make sense?" Everyone laughed, except Janet, who was stretching her shoulders, staring down the range as though it had done something to her. Sarah lined us all up facing the targets, and handed us each a handful of arrows and a special leather glove with only three fingers. She stood in front of us, demonstrating how to put it on. We'd done this before, of course, but something about the glove resisted learning; we had to be shown every time. "You must be like a tree," she said. "Strong and flexible at once."

"You know what else is like a tree," Laurel whispered. "Long and brown and with a bush at one end." I concentrated again on things that weren't Luke: *knife, thermostat, packing peanuts.*

"So what you're saying," Janet whispered, "is that when a man and a woman truly love each other, his penis grows a canopy of thick roots into her body and spreads out and feeds on her nutrients and stays there until it dies of disease or old age or gets chopped down and sliced into pieces and turned into lumber?"

"Exactly," Laurel said.

"Can't wait."

Laurel rolled her eyes and started to say something else, but Janet turned crisply away from us, lifting her bow to her hip, and Laurel, for once, decided to shut up and follow her lead.

It was only here, at the Kyūdō range, that I thought I finally understood Janet. She was a natural with the bow. As she pulled back the string, she seemed to relax rather than tense, and I could see how much she lived in her body—how she thought with it, almost, as if the color in her cheeks were pure mind, hovering there, red and ready underneath her skin. I saw the way the guided steps created space for that connection. And if Kyūdō could do so much, I thought, imagine what levitation could do. The ultimate physical control. The body to heel at last. No wonder she wanted it.

Plus, she was really good. All of our arrows fell like ripe apples from our bows, or if we were lucky, glanced off the sand a few feet ahead of us. Jamie couldn't even really get the glove on. It was too big for her delicate hand. Harriet and Nisha kept collapsing into laughter halfway through the steps. Even the arrow Margaret got off on sheer strength only skidded a few yards. But when I looked up, Janet's was humming in her target's golden pupil.

"Our little toy soldier," Laurel whispered as Janet made the long solitary walk to retrieve her arrow. She pulled her bowstring tight and then let it go, arrowless.

"She went out again last night," I said.

Laurel leaned on her bow. "Here's the thing about Janet," she said. "Her father used to test her all the time. Make her prove herself. I mean, I think at the beginning it was supposed to be good for her. Like, you want an ice cream? Beat your brother to the end of the block. You need new clothes? Win them from me in a card game. You want to go to the doctor today? Fight your brother until one of you hits the floor. You need me to sign something? Hold your hand in the fire for thirty seconds without screaming."

"You can't be serious," I said. But: Janet, who hated to lose at anything. Janet, who was always pushing herself, always better, faster, stronger.

"It's different now," Laurel said. "He can barely hold down a job, much less give her anything she needs. Wet brain, you know." She tapped her temple with one finger. "She's the one keeping that family going. Though honestly I don't know why she even bothers."

"What about her brothers?" I asked. "They must be old enough to help out."

"They're old enough," she said. "But they grew up mean."

I knew she was trying to tell me something, but I couldn't figure out what it was. When I didn't say anything, she rolled her eyes. "She's just doing what she has to do," she said. "Wherever she goes, whatever she does, it's not about you, so don't get in the way."

I leaned my head back, and as I did, I noticed that Harriet was staring at me again, her expression inscrutable, while Nisha inspected her bowstring. I felt a small stab. I did like Harriet, despite the fact that I had ignored her warnings. I did wish, sometimes, that I could stand next to her and laugh at her jokes, and not be concerned with anything else, not levitation or Luke or my father or where my friends secretly snuck away to in the middle of the night. I smiled at her, and as I did, I realized she wasn't looking at me at all. She was looking at Laurel.

Laurel followed my gaze. "Classic," she said, and slipped her fingers around my wrist. I waited for her to say something else, but then Sarah came and stood beside us, and we both turned back to the cleared range. Not, in Laurel's case, without flashing Harriet the brightest of smiles and running her tongue along her red red lips.

Luke wasn't in the garden that day, though I did find Ava, sunning herself on his bench. When I reached to stroke her head, she jumped away, and I saw that she'd been sitting on a folded piece of paper. I snatched it up: it was a note from Luke, but it said nothing, only that he wouldn't be there that day, and which beds to weed and water, and a firm instruction to not come looking for him. His handwriting was loose and elegant, like a girl's. I wondered if he was angry with me. I folded the note carefully and put it into my pocket. I would give it to Serena later, I promised myself. I wouldn't keep it under my pillow and read it at night, tracing the loops with a finger, trying to determine secrets of personality and desire from the slant of consonants. I wouldn't put it in my mouth. What would be the point of that?

I'll say this for fasting: I did feel lighter. In the days that followed, consuming nothing but nettle soup and tea (of which we had plenty, Tenzin having apparently decided to turn a blind eye to our culinary experiments), I would often go into the bathroom and look at myself in the mirror, carefully checking for cheekbones. I didn't find them, but I did find that my stomach felt small and void, and yes, light. I have never in my life been skinny and romantic. For a while, I fancied myself tragic, like a consolation prize. But I had always felt that I was missing some essential experience of youth by never being nubile, thin and limber. By never having long brown legs and a flat, tympanic stomach. I didn't want to grow old and never have had those years of beauty, to have only ever been this moist, lumpy thing. Or worse, to lie to myself and remember an invented pretty youth, just to have something to sigh over when a storm was coming and my knees were bothering me and the folds of my fat were sticking to one another and also to the back of my chair in all the humidity. Because there is something terrible about a girl not neatly zipped into her own skin, or so we are repeatedly told. There is something rude about it, something offensive to all who see her, especially her friends, who would like her to be beautiful, as beautiful as a mirror. While we fasted, I felt worthy of reflection.

$$\cdots$$

But of course, we had other reasons to thin out our bodies. "When lift plus thrust is greater than load plus drag, anything can fly," Sister Bertrille explained. Yes, the Flying Nun. She weighed a mere ninety pounds, I've heard—not counting the cornette, of course. And you see what she accomplished. It's right there in the name.

We knew we were doing the right thing the first time we went up to the rock palm after beginning our fast. Our new emptiness elevated everything. The lack of food made us faint quicker, stay out longer, though I still had to choke Serena to make her fall. It unmoored our meditations, intensified the lightness games. It even made the Feeling more intense—or at least it did for me. Serena had been looking for her comb for days. "Nothing else works," she said. "And I need to dream. The blackness is driving me mad." I helped her turn over her tent, shake out her blankets. I raked my fingers through the grass around places we'd been, the back of my neck growing hotter and hotter. I felt guilty, of course, when the rest of us threw back our heads and Serena only stared, but I told myself it was simply too late. I couldn't say anything now, even if I had been willing to surrender my prize.

Once during this time, I stood next to Laurel in the bathroom, both of us squeezing our stomachs between our hands, turning to the side, then back again. "Smaller," she said. When she spoke, I could smell something clean and high and corrosive.

"Smaller," I agreed. It occurred to me that my body was beginning to look ever so slightly more like my mother's. I wasn't terribly disappointed about this.

"Lighter, you mean." Janet had come in behind us.

"It's the same thing," Laurel said.

"Not always," Janet said. She walked out of the bathroom and, as she passed through the doorway, paused and flicked off the light. Girls squealed in the stalls.

Listen, I know what you're thinking, but the Buddha was never fat. He was first a handsome prince, and later an ascetic—well, you've heard the story. For six years, he lived on a single grain of rice a day. He gave up his fast only when he realized that if he didn't, he would die before reaching enlightenment. I'm saying he was pretty trim. That fat, laughing man whose belly you rub for good luck and whom Westerners call the Buddha is not the Buddha at all, but a Chinese folk deity whose name—Budai—means "Cloth Sack." Some traditions do identify Budai as an incarnation of Maitreya, the Buddha of the future, who will only appear on earth when the dharma has been utterly forgotten, but I don't know about that. It has always seemed to me that Budai is only Maitreya in the sense that any of us might be.

As the days passed, I began to dream about food. I found that I missed the sensation of eating even more than I missed the taste or nourishment. The fact that we had to fill our plates to fool the staffers didn't help: we stared at our rolls and pads of butter and slices of quiche, and then slowly transferred them into our napkins, and our napkins into the trash. In the mornings, Laurel would bring over a bowl of sugar cubes and we would dip them into our tea, watching the smooth white squares soak up the liquid, become warm and delicate. We sucked the tea from the cubes; they dissolved in our mouths. We didn't tell Serena. It was cheating, yes, but it was only cheating a little. I still felt light. I still felt empty. Fasting was like living in a series of tiny victories, with the feeling of building toward something—every meal we missed was like a coin saved, a moral claim on the future. Our fortune would buy us nothing but lightness.

Luke missed three more days of rota. I pocketed three more notes. When I finally showed up to find him on the bench, waiting for me, my heart flounced maniacally. Yes, flounced: *flounced* is a perfect word for itself—extravagant, absurd, a little embarrassing, like feeling. While we're on the topic: *thronged, fluttered, quivered*. Being hungry made it infinitely worse. I tried to make it stop as I approached. I was lighter now, I reminded myself. I was closer. I wasn't here for Luke. I was here for levitation.

"I want you to forgive me," he said by way of greeting. He pulled up his knees and hugged them with his arms. It was such a childish posture, like a little boy fitting himself into an even littler hiding space.

"You kissed me," I said. Oh, but how could I believe in anything but this? It was right in front of me, and I could touch it.

"I am trying to be tender," he said. "I am trying to be open to everything I can, to let myself be utterly raw, bare-hearted. My teacher says this is the way to true fearlessness. But I shouldn't have let things go so far. Even though we both know it was *you* who kissed *me*." He smiled and took my hand and held my fingers almost to his mouth. I imagined them inside of it, all five in a fist. "So, Buddha Hands. Forgive me?"

"Maybe I will," I said. "If you help us." For once, I remembered where my loyalties lay.

He let my hand drop, the brute. "Listen," he said. "I know levitation pays the bills around here. The Levitation Center, right? That's what the tourists call it. Dominique encourages it. But levitation is a trap. It's what we call relative siddhi, as opposed to absolute siddhi. It's only a side effect, a marker on the path to liberation."

"That doesn't mean it's bad," I said.

"It's not bad," he said. "It just doesn't mean what you think it does."

It was then that Serena appeared yet again, this time wearing a bright red dress. I saw that she had let Laurel do her makeup. Her eyebrows were dark, her eyes lined. She looked as though she were wearing a mask of her own face. The ends of her hair, usually lank and long, were curled, as if curious. How much had she heard? How had she known he would be there today? But she smiled at me.

"Stay back from the fence," Luke said.

She took a step forward. "I've missed you," she said.

"I'm serious," he said. "Don't come any closer."

Serena laughed. She blew a kiss at Luke and rested both her hands on the fence, but then immediately shrieked and pulled them back into her chest. The sharp electric snap made the whole fence shudder.

"I told you," Luke said. He was smiling, and I thought of a boy I'd known, one of the neighborhood scrum, who in the height of one dissolute summer caught a fat, lazy bumblebee and tied her to a string. He patrolled the sidewalks, whistling and swinging the bee in circles around his head. You could hear a faint buzzing when he came close, the complaint of hot air forced through those cellophane wings. You could hear the girls screaming as he lassoed them with his bee-tipped lariat, layering one small torture on another. When no one was around, he let the bee walk dizzily over his knee, and told her jokes, and petted her fur with a finger. He didn't untie her until she had been dead for days.

I shook away the memory. Serena was no tethered insect, no screaming girl. If anything, she was the boy. Wasn't she? I waited to see what she would do, how she would turn it back on him, but she just stood there for a moment more, her hands over her heart, before collecting herself, throwing back her shoulders, and marching away.

"Why did you do that?" I said. But this repudiation of

Serena had, I admit, thrilled me. I thought he might take me in his arms now, as though we were forbidden lovers left alone for the first time. (Now, of course, I see it for the goad it was, the invitation: *Try harder, little girl.*)

"Electric fences don't work unless they're electric," he said. He did not move any closer to me.

That night, obsessed as I still was with my image in the mirror, I barged into the bathroom when Jamie was hurriedly changing in there. It was late, and I suppose she'd felt safe enough to es- chew the extra safety of the stall. As it was, I walked in and she quickly pulled down her shirt, but not so quickly that I didn't get a glimpse of a series of regular, raised bubblegum slices, all perfectly parallel, all the same length, stacked in a column to the left of her belly button.

"Please don't say anything," she said. I found that in fact I couldn't. I turned around, my own stomach forgotten, and left her there.

10

At the moment of the truly unbearable, I once heard someone say, you can't help but change form. In the old stories, there are two kinds of transformation: punishments and escapes. The brutal King Lycaon, who was turned into a wolf (hence: lycanthrope, if you're keeping score) after serving his own son to Zeus at a feast; Actaeon the peeper, whom Artemis reshaped into a stag, bending his knees backward so his own hounds would rend him limb from limb; Medusa, who was once so beautiful, as the story goes, that Poseidon could do naught but rape her—which he did in Athena's temple, after which slight the goddess punished the victim with an ugliness so profound that all who looked upon her turned to stone. (This ancient allegory holds.) On the other hand: the virginal Daphne, whom I think I've mentioned before, became a tree to escape her suitor; the virginal Pleiades were shaken out into stars to escape theirs; poor Io, "the horned virgin," whom Zeus turned into a cow so his wife wouldn't catch them out. (As if Hera, by then, really thought him above bestiality—she knew who she'd married.) You see there's a pattern here: virgins transforming at the moment they would have been deflowered, or else, if they're unlucky, at the moment just after. Is *this* the moment of the truly unbearable? Or is the threat of transformation merely another way to contain us, to keep our legs swaddled closed with fear?

In fact, there's a third kind of transformation: one that seeks to change not only you but everything. A final, desperate effort to get that deepest desire. The Little Mermaid, Sandra Dee, William the Bloody. All of these threw themselves out for the love of another. For Sandy, it was just a makeover, but the Little Mermaid walked on broken glass to be loved, and ended in dissolution, sea foam smashed against the rocks. (She could have saved herself, if only she had been willing to cut out her foul prince's heart. But alas.)

After my father moved out, my mother waited. To me it seemed that she had almost no reaction to the end of her marriage. She was friendly with the movers who came to take away his things in a small number of boxes. She tipped them well. I remember she was on the phone more often than usual. Sometimes she played records. Sometimes the house was silent, which was the only fact in all of this that made me think she had been hurt at all.

Two months later, she threw a party. An enormous one, bigger by far than her old Saturday night gatherings. From the stairs, I watched each guest step carefully into the house, not quite sure what awaited them—a tearful wronged woman? A sinner licking her wounds? I suppose they were curious. In any event, they came. She greeted each one warmly, loudly, with a joke, and the fear melted off them—I could almost see it, pooling at the threshold—and they slapped her on the back, and kissed her on the cheek, and told me how grown-up and beautiful I was, the filthy liars, and drank and danced and stayed out in the backyard past four.

One of them had a guitar. He asked me questions about my classes, about what I liked to do on the weekends, about whether I had a boyfriend, and why didn't I, because clearly, I was a catch. A catch! I offered to bring him a beer, and he told me I was the best, truly the best, and after I brought it to him, he let me sit beside him while he played and played. He was young, a law student. My mother didn't seem to notice him, or me, until she told me to go to bed. In fairness, I was barely thirteen. When I left, the guitar player squeezed my hand, and his calluses made me blush. I was wrong, before. Luke wasn't the first man to touch my hands. At least there's that.

Yes, I remember his calluses, and the fat, underwater sound of his guitar, and also the fat, underwater sound of his breathing, later that night, as my ear was pressed against my mother's bedroom door.

In the morning, she was sitting by herself at the kitchen table. The guitar player was gone. She looked like an elegant statue that had been forgotten on the beach for many winters, warped by wind and sand, leaving only the vague shape of itself behind.

"Is that why Dad left?" I asked.

"Is what why?"

"I heard you last night," I said. "With someone." *With him*, I could not bring myself to say. (Of course, I can't even remember his name now.) She got up and poured herself more coffee, added cream, and leaned against the sink.

"I have never been unfaithful to your father," my mother said. She drummed her nails against the counter once, and then took her coffee upstairs, to drink in bed. I didn't realize until much later that she hadn't exactly answered my question.

She didn't get out of bed for three days.

When she finally emerged from her room, she had changed. She was diminished no longer—in fact, the combination of the party and the days in bed seemed to have made her even taller, if such a thing were possible. She no longer looked as though it was possible for her to cry. She no longer looked as though it was possible for her to be hurt, or to be sad, or to be silent. She marched out of her room and went straight to the garage.

In the days and weeks and months that followed, she became utterly obsessed with the Fatties. She had always worked on them in her spare time, but now she spent hours with them, hidden away, the radio she kept in the garage turned to full blast. She would come home from the advertising firm, where she did nothing, she once said, but staple things together, tear things apart, and change the size of words, and then go straight to the Fatties without even entering the house. She stopped making dinner; I lived on pasta and toast. I think she stopped eating, but even this did not diminish her. She would get up early in the morning to be with the Fatties before work, and she would stay with them long into the night, even as the air became edged with cold. The Fatties doubled in number and then grew into a horde, crowding the garage. When I looked inside, I saw heavy clay body parts on every surface, a fat face at every window. Eventually, the finished Fatties began to spill out into our backyard, first congregating around the garage doors and then spreading out over the grass, a Middle American Medusa's garden. Even then she couldn't stop. She kept building. She kept smoothing back the clay skin, forming the clay hands to fit her own, looking deeply into the hollow, carved eyes.

What was she looking for? What form would satisfy her? Or was it just that she was trying to fill the space my father had left with creature after creature who might finally accept her love?

• • •

Maybe the latter, because the only hours she spent away from
the Fatties were spent with men. I almost never saw them, the
men who stopped in the kitchen for a drink before following
her upstairs, the men who dropped her off in the middle of the
night, the men who called, or who didn't call. All different
men, all with the same face.

I was paranoid about them. I thought they stole things, small
things we'd never notice, or maybe left things: wadded-up bits
of newspaper in the drawers, business cards in the books, belly
lint under the rug. Sometimes I would search the house after
one of them had gone, turn over all the pillows, peek into the
cabinets. I never found anything amiss, but even still, I couldn't
shake the feeling that something had changed.

If it had just been the men, that would have been all right. I
could have learned to live with the tiny inaccuracies. If it had
just been the men and also the Fatties, that would have been all
right too. But if my mother had been hibernating somewhere
inside of herself for those two months, for those three days—
well, then she'd woken up angry.

Here: her hair was everywhere. She squatted in the living room
and thrust an imaginary knife up between her frogged legs.
"You're doing this," she said, thrusting. "This this this." Thrusting, thrusting, stabbing herself to death from below, both hands
clutched around the phantom blade. I can't remember now what
I had done or said to inspire this; I know it had involved a boy.
Maybe one of the men who all looked the same, but maybe not.
"This is you," she said, thrusting. Her wrists and ankles were
coated with clay. She pointed to a chair with her invisible knife
and told me to sit. And I said no, I wouldn't, because I was afraid

that if I sat, she would hit me. "I won't hit you," she said, softening her voice. "I promise." And so I sat.

Then she hit me in the face, so hard the room went dark.

"See?" she said. "You see what happens?"

I know others have had it worse. I know it's a little thing, finally, to be hit in the face by your mother. She didn't beat me, not really. Not in any of the ways I know children can be beaten. She didn't starve me. She didn't pimp me out to her friends and creditors. But I was indignant, like all lucky girls. Not long afterward, she dug her fingernails into my arm so hard it bled, and I stood in the stairwell and screamed until one of the neighbors called the cops. It was the middle of the afternoon, a Saturday. When the two uniformed men rang the doorbell, I was elated. I ran to explain, to show off the slim lunar wounds on my arm. My mother, exasperated, her robe opening, followed me to the door.

"If I'd talked back to my mother, I would have gotten the belt," one of them said.

"My father used to hit me across the face with his shoe," said the other.

"Don't be a brat," said the first.

"Your mother's a delight," said the second.

I gaped at them, my arm still lifted in evidence. My mother shut the door. I was alone with her again.

Anyway, this is not a sob story. These are only the facts. After my father left, my mother began to hit me, and after a while, my pleas to live with him first ignored and then impossible, I did something so that she wouldn't hit me anymore.

• • •

"Sometimes," Serena said once, her toes digging into the warm grass, "I think just rage would be enough."

We kept meeting at the rock palm. We drank our nettle tea. We focused on our empty stomachs. We fainted dead away. Serena did not want to talk about what had happened with the fence. It didn't matter. During that time, I felt that the space between lifting our bodies and not lifting them was so infinitesimally small, a sliver really, one that could be transcended at any moment. It was the same feeling you might get when faced with a deeply desired object that is only barely out of reach. Pony backpack, etc. The difference between having and not-having is so thin you imagine you'll break through it at any moment, like a film of soap. If I can stretch this far, why not stretch a little farther?

One night, Serena stood at the edge of the rock palm, looking out into the darkness. Daring herself, I thought. She got close, closer than I had ever been, shuffling her sandals against the rock. She lifted one leg, and then another, shifting her weight experimentally.

"Careful," said Laurel.

"Maybe I'll float," said Serena. She spread her arms. She was facing away from us, and her voice sounded much farther away than her body.

"Maybe you'll fall," said Janet. She stood and went over to the edge to retrieve Serena, but when she reached her side, it was as though she had stepped into a sphere of hypnotic influence. Her shoulders dropped. She pressed her hip against Serena's. They stared out into the darkness together, their arms entwined. I felt the urge to join them, and I must have moved to do so, because Laurel grabbed my wrist. Her eyes were wide. She'd been drinking again. I could smell it on her. I could always smell it on her, now. I thought I should say something, but

I didn't know what to say. I stayed where I was, and eventually both Serena and Janet returned to us.

"We're close," Serena said. "We're so close."

Much later, I would think about this moment, and whether I should have known to take it for the sign it was, whether I should have read the portent in their toes edging toward the ledge, in the panicked look on Laurel's face, in the unforgiving black of rock and air. But how can you blame me? Back then, I feared nothing. I didn't even believe it was possible for girls like us to die, cliff's edge or no. Death was for goldfish and grandmothers, disappearance was for fathers and fortunes. Girls like us would only go on forever.

The first time we all bled together, we pretended we were wolves. It was the hottest part of the summer; the midpoint was past. We were restless, reckless. Our bellies were already sore, but this was a new soreness, and a new lightness, too. We ached—wombs, hearts, backs, thighs, bitten fingernails, our bodies unsolvable proofs wanting impossible things—and so we spent one night on the rock palm not trying to levitate at all, but lying on our backs, hands on our empty stomachs, howling at the moon. We'd heard the wolves singing on the mountain all summer, their voices far-off and hollow, like men lost at sea. So we sang too, to show the wolf-men that all hope was not lost: we could be a port, a sleeve, a mirror. What could our bodies do? They could do anything. We felt only moments away from truly sprouting claws and fur, our fangs growing to enormous proportions. What big eyes you have, etc. Why not? We were above the things that other girls did for fun. Did they even have fun, or plans, or teeth like ours?

At the end of that night, Serena presented us all with thin glass vials, the kind that might have come with a kiddie chemistry set. The most powerful kind of magic, she told us, was blood magic. The most powerful kind of blood was menstrual blood.

"Well, sure," Janet said, but she examined her vial with interest.

"Collect some of your own," Serena instructed us. "Keep it somewhere safe."

"Are we goths now," Laurel said, but she took her vial too.

The moon was impossibly bright that night. It looked enormous, closer to the earth than I had ever seen it, and for the first time in my life I had the impression of it as a real celestial body, a curved gargantuan rock shackled to us by an invisible tether.

Serena did not look at the moon. She was inspecting her own legs, drawing her hem up and down like a curtain. "Apparently I'm not being alluring enough," she said. If she'd been another girl, I would have expected a whine, an edge of self-pity. But Serena sounded almost clinical, as if noting which element in a complex recipe or mathematical equation had gone wrong. My stomach turned with guilt, and also a deep pleasure.

"You are," Laurel said. "You're being so alluring that he doesn't trust himself. That's why he turned on the fence."

Janet lay on her back, folding her arms into a pillow.

"Besides," Laurel went on. "You witnessed his most profound spiritual moment. Men are deeply affected by that kind of thing."

"Don't be disgusting," Janet said, without raising her head. "She was eleven." In her black clothes, so close to the ground, she was nearly invisible.

"I'm not the one who's being disgusting in this scenario," Laurel said. "And that's not what I *meant*."

"What do you think, Olivia?" Serena asked. "Has he said anything?"

I swallowed. *Eye. Leaf. Fireplace.* I shook my head. "Something is definitely holding him back," I said.

Serena reached into the pocket of her dress and pulled out her own vial. I could see that it was already half full of a dark red liquid. "I know," she said.

She had a new plan, she explained. One that would finally make Luke tell her everything. We would sneak some of her blood into Luke's food. Laurel worked in the kitchen; I worked in the garden. It shouldn't be too difficult. If Luke had redoubled his defenses, she said, we had to respond in kind.

Even I had heard of this old magic: if a man eats your blood, he's yours. If he's yours, why wouldn't he tell you all his secrets, teach you to fly? If he's yours, why would he ever even look at another girl, no matter how close to him she stood?

"This seems a little extreme," I said.

"Not to mention unsanitary," said Janet.

"It's unnecessary," said Laurel. "He's already in love with you. You just have to take the next step."

Serena stroked Laurel's head fondly. "This is the next step," she said. Then she tucked the vial into my bra. She took both of my hands and kissed my cheek, hard. "I know I can count on you," she said.

As I walked back to the dormitory, the vial rubbed and squeaked against my breast. Now I wonder: Had she heard me after all, there in the garden? Or did she simply guess that I dreamed about Luke every night? Did she realize that as hard as I tried to scrub myself of desire, to realize the truth of emptiness, to gear my body and mind toward levitation, I still wanted him, as badly as I had ever wanted anything? If she did, her response was brilliant and cruel: to make him love her with magic and therefore unimpeachably, and even worse, to make me cast the spell.

• • •

Or maybe it was nothing like that. Maybe she was only trying and trying and trying to put off the moment when she'd have to do something real. When she'd have to give something up.

The next day, Harriet and Nisha cornered me outside, in the dregs of lunch. Harriet had an enormous red spot on her chin. "What happened to your face?" I asked.

She pressed two fingers to the angry mark. "I was drinking tea while walking," she said. "Nisha always says I should watch where I'm going."

"It's the kind of thing that could only happen to Harriet," Nisha said fondly, petting her friend on the head.

"Sorry," I said. "It looks like it hurts."

"Not the point," Harriet said. "Listen, we're worried about you."

"We don't want you to come to any harm," Nisha said. Her voice was absent its usual pillowed quality.

"That's sweet," I said. "I like you guys too."

"I hear you leave with them at night," Harriet said. *Sometimes*, I thought bitterly, but I smiled at her. "Where do you go?" she said. I kept smiling, and Harriet scowled. "Serena's a liar, you know," she said. "She's always been a liar."

"What do you mean?" I said.

"She manipulates people. She uses people. She pretends to be your friend and then she isn't."

"Oh," I said. I suddenly felt immense pity for her. Was Harriet one of the girls they hadn't kept? I remembered the Kyūdō range, the way Harriet had looked at Laurel.

"She has a history," Harriet said. "I'm just saying, you're new."

"Is it really Serena you have a problem with?" I said. "Or is it someone else?" Harriet's face closed. She narrowed her eyes at me.

"It doesn't matter," Nisha said, moving slightly in front of her friend. "They're all the same. But you're not really one of them, are you?"

At that, I turned on my heel and walked swiftly away. Jealous! Unkept! Burned by tea! Wrong about Serena! And wrong about me. So, so wrong.

Funny how *come to harm* can mean itself and also its own exact opposite. I've been harmed. I've come to harm you.

Speaking of harm: for a while after my father disappeared, I burned photos of him in the bathtub, watching the edges of his face curl and scroll, leaving a black stain on the porcelain that afterward I'd sit on, imagining that his destruction could power me like a battery. I didn't tell my mother. I didn't want to encourage her. She was so angry already. Later, I was sorry not to have those pictures, but isn't that always the way?

But of course my mother wasn't always angry, even after her transformation. That's just a story I tell. I remember one afternoon when she burst into the house from the garage. "Let's go on a walk," she said.

I pulled away from her. The night before, she had held me up by my hair, yelled into my face. "I'm eating," I said.

She reached out and took the sandwich from my hand, ate half of it herself in two bites, then handed it back to me. "Hurry up," she said.

"God," I said. But it was funny, and I softened toward her and slipped on my coat. It was early spring by then, March or April, wet snow in the seams of the sidewalks.

We walked through the neighborhood, looking into people's windows.

"I used to do this all the time when I was your age," she said.

"Spy on people?"

"Imagine what my life might be like if I were someone else. Look in there," she said, grabbing my arm and pointing into the picture window of a white Craftsman. "Boring home, boring soul. Never trust anyone with cottage furniture. Or a sitting room."

My mother had strong but mutable opinions about furniture. At least once a week, I would come home from school to find a completely different house than the one I'd left. Chairs, artwork, rugs would appear and disappear, or emerge in a different room, in a different form, painted or dyed or cut into new shapes. My mother liked to buy things, especially things we didn't need, especially when there was no money for it. Her own mother had never wasted a cent in America, had kept cans of Sprite in the cabinet long after their expiration dates, so when you opened them, she told me once, they had nothing but stale, flat water inside, all the sugar and flavor sunk to the bottom, but that was no excuse; if you opened it, you drank it—and so my mother bought things.

"What would you do if you lived there?" she said.

"I don't know," I said. "The same things I do now, probably."

"I'd tear down that wall," she said, moving closer. We were already on their lawn, and the frosted grass complained beneath our boots. "Get an oak dining table. They have nice moldings but terrible taste. Their house could be beautiful, if only they knew it was ugly."

"Mom," I hissed. I imagined cops, dogs. The neighbors already hated her. Loud parties, irresponsible lawn management, a shy shadow of an accent, and worst of all, a husband no one had seen for months, maybe longer, and well, you know what that says about a woman.

"Oh, come on," she said. "I want to imagine myself in there."

"Why?" I said. "You don't even like the house." She was stand-ing right in front of the window now—she could have pressed her nose against it—while I waited, shivering, a few yards back, looking over my shoulder. I imagined her hair growing enor-mous and sentient, breaking in through the windows and invad-ing every part of this ugly house, filling all the rooms like thick black water before spreading, searching, stuffing itself into every house in the neighborhood, smothering all the occupants and pushing their desiccated bodies out onto their lawns. I imagined my mother's calm face in the middle of the black mass, her sigh of relief as she filled up every space around her, as she reached farther, farther, farther.

She stepped away from the window. "It's only a game," she said. "My mother used to play it with me. We would walk around our neighborhood together, and dream about the lives we might have someday. Every house was my dollhouse. I never had a real one, like you did. I never had a single doll, and you always scream when I try to braid your hair."

I pointed to a green Victorian at the end of the block.

"Oh," she said. "You're my daughter after all."

Yes, sometimes she was like this: conspiratorial, kind, desirous of my love. Other times, she would storm into my room, push me, slap me, grab an arm in her hot fist, curse me, throw me to the floor. But after a while, I began to be able to predict her moods. They seemed to have something to do with the men who continued to come in and out of our house at night, with the parties she threw nearly every week, with the Fatties, who kept appearing, each one bigger, meaner, and closer to the house than the last. (Poor old Beth was looking slim and benign now. My mother had achieved grand new heights of grotesquerie.) I found I could map her anger, skirt to the edges when necessary. I could often escape this way. Yes, even like this, even though she had become this monstrous, unbridled version of herself, I could plot her. She made sense to me. I was her daughter, after all. That's why I had to leave.

When Tenzin finally made the meal we'd been waiting for—her "famous" vegetarian chili—I followed Laurel to the kitchen at the beginning of rota. I waited in the doorway as she ducked in to get a bowl, but just as she was handing it over, Tenzin noticed us. "Laurel," she said. "What are you doing?" She was standing before a sideboard covered with tiny green pots, mixing spices to see which combinations she liked best, and in which proportions.

I stepped forward. "I was wondering," I said, "if I could bring Luke a bowl of chili."

"Ha!" she shouted. "Does someone have a little crush on Luke?"

"No!" I looked around. The other girls who had their rota in the kitchen were not even pretending not to listen. Svetlana's look of outrage was somewhat mediated by the enormous rubber gloves she had on. "I do rota in the garden, and I know he missed his lunch today," I said. This was actually true, or at least it had a good chance of being true. Luke often missed lunch, preferring to meditate inside at the hottest parts of the day. We had missed lunch too, of course, preferring to starve ourselves, but Tenzin didn't know that.

"All the little girls love Luke," Tenzin said. She dipped her finger in one of the bowls, dabbed it into another, and then put it in her mouth.

"I'm just trying to practice, you know, loving-kindness," I said. This was a phrase Shastri Dominique had been saying a lot lately in our meditation sessions.

Tenzin snorted. "Well, good for you." She turned to let a few of her sous-chefs bustle past, and I was hit sideways with the scent of rosemary. "I don't know what you're up to," she said, "but I didn't see Luke at lunch, so you're in luck. Bring him a bowl. But don't make me regret it, or this one will be scrubbing my ovens for the rest of the summer." Laurel filled a glass bowl with chili, fitted a plastic lid on top, and handed it over, her face carefully blank. I left without waiting for any more discussion.

When I was out of sight of the main building, I stopped and sat down behind a tree. I put the bowl between my legs and opened the vial above it. The blood was thick; I had to tap the sides to get it out. Even then, the glass was still red by the end. I thought about using my finger to scrape with—the vial was wide enough that I might have gotten it to fit—but instead I screwed the cap back on and kept the dregs for myself. Just in case.

The blood sat, viscous and dark, on top of the chili. I waited for it to sink in, but it wouldn't, and I hadn't remembered to bring a spoon, so I stirred with the first two fingers on my right hand. I winced when I plunged them in; the chili was still hot. I had to knead a little bit to integrate the blood. When I pulled out my fingers, they were stained pink. I thought of Jamie, whose right index finger was always burned to a raw-looking red from nail to joint. But that was another thing entirely. That was the opposite of what I was trying to do now.

I looked down at the chili, suddenly hungrier than I had ever been. So what if I had already mixed it with Serena's blood? No one would see. And in fact—

No. I slammed the lid back on.

Luke was cleaning his tools when I arrived. He looked up. "I wondered if you were coming," he said.

I held up the bowl. "Tenzin wanted you to have this," I said.

"Ah, a lovely woman." He wiped his hands and took the bowl from me.

"I forgot a spoon," I said, hiding my hand behind my back. But he only winked and retrieved one from the shed. Then he sat down on the bench, bowl cradled in his lap. He stirred, but didn't take a bite. I couldn't take my eyes off the chili. I thought of Serena's blood cooking in the hot mess, steaming up into Luke's eyes.

"I'm worried about you," he said.

"It's a really good batch today," I said, pointing at the bowl.

"All right," he said. "I get it."

Then he began to eat.

He ate quickly, greedily. When the spoon hit glass, he licked the bowl. I could see his wet, pink, sea-creaturey tongue flattening itself again and again against the clear bottom, lapping up the stray bits of Serena. Lap lap lap lap lap lap.

I wondered if he would change immediately, if it would be something I could see. Would he sprout wings, or take off his clothes, or grow enormous or small, or declare his love for Serena, or become Serena, or turn the color of the hibiscus flower, which is also the color of blood?

"Thank you for this," he said. "You're too good to me." I felt the silver string again, pulling at me. I was overheating. There were no clouds in the sky. It was unbearable. I would fit into his lap so easily. I didn't move. He was full of Serena's blood. What would happen if I kissed him now?

I stepped forward, and he smiled. I came closer, and he reached a hand toward me. I moved slightly to the side, plucked the bowl from his lap, and turned away from him. "I'll go return this," I said, and then I walked out of the garden without saying anything else, and whatever Luke felt about that, I couldn't say, because I didn't look back to see his face.

How can I explain? I felt charged with power, run through with it, my bones turned to hot iron. I had forced something upon the world. I had changed something. Yes, I had fed Serena's blood to Luke, but it was more than that. I had wanted something, with my whole body, and then I had refused it. *Snap the flower arrows of desire and then, unseen, escape the king of death.* The king of death had nothing on me. I was not a peach!

I walked back to the dormitory, the bowl under my arm. The heat was suffocating that day, but inside it was cool and empty, everyone else still at rota. I lay on my bed. I held the bowl over my face. I could still smell the chili, and maybe even the blood, a faint metallic brightness. I moved the bowl to the pillow beside my head. I turned onto my stomach and let the bowl kiss my forehead. I reached down and pressed my hand between my legs, and felt an electric current run through my body, all my muscles turning toward that spot. I could see it so clearly: the shape their bodies would make together, now or soon, skin on skin, their long hair mixing. Serena had said she wouldn't really do anything, that it was all a trick, but what if she did? I would, if I were her. I would let him touch me. I would let him lift me into the air. I could see how her chin might fit into his neck, how his rough fingers might encircle her corded wrists. The muscles of his arms, her smooth shoulder, the slope of her small breast. Exposed, exposed, everything shown and touched and used, and I made it happen. I pressed harder. I thought of him, but I also thought of her. Right at the end, I thought of myself, leaving him there on the bench, wanting more of me. Yes, yes, I thought, yes: this feeling would build, and then I would rise.

11

The last time I saw my father, he took me to the movies. It was the thing we did together most often after he and my mother separated: sitting in silence in the dark. I'm not complaining. I wish we had done it more. I've forgotten what we saw that day, though I remember not liking it very much. I remember not buying into the tragedy, whatever it was meant to be.

On the way back, I began talking about nothing, complaining: there'd been a small slight at school, a fight with my mother. "Can't I live with you?" I asked him for the thousandth time.

"Your mother wouldn't like that," he said.

"I want to be a Buddhist," I said.

"I'm going to tell you a story," he said.

The story goes like this: there was once a young monk who traveled from monastery to monastery, hoping for enlightenment. Geshé Tenpa, a great old teacher, met him and said, "It is nice to tour holy places, but it is much better to practice the sublime Dharma."

The young monk took the master's words to heart, and began to study the sutras night and day, putting their teachings into action whenever he could. One day Geshé Tenpa came upon him as he was bent over a page, and said, "It is worthwhile to study scriptures and accomplish virtuous acts, but far better to practice the noble Dharma."

So the monk began to focus all of his attention on meditation. He meditated day in and day out. Inevitably, soon Geshé Tenpa found him, sitting on a cushion, concentrating with all his might. "Meditation is good," the old teacher said, "but genuine Dharma practice would be even better."

The monk, as you might imagine, was very confused. He had tried everything. "Sir!" he cried. "I wish above all else to practice the Dharma. What should I do?"

"Simply give up all clinging to this life," Geshé Tenpa told him, before continuing on his way.

I made sure to hide the bowl under my bed before everyone else filtered in from rota. It was too hot to go outside for free hours that day. Even sunbathing would have been too laborious in heat like that. I lay on top of the sheets in my bunk with my face in my book: *The Life of Saint Teresa of Ávila*, her autobiography. It was an old, attractive hardcover with green edges that I'd borrowed from Serena a few nights before. I'd pulled it from her shelf on a whim, for something to do with my hands, but Serena nodded gravely when she saw what I'd chosen. "She knew everything," she said.

When Laurel disappeared to take a shower, I climbed up on Janet's bunk. She had taught me to play gin rummy in addition to poker. She usually won, of course, but I didn't mind. Not least because when she didn't win, we'd have to play three more times, until she was satisfied that her loss had been a fluke. After what Laurel had said about her father, her brothers, I had tried to lose a couple of times on purpose, but Janet could always tell what I was doing. She would refuse to play until I was willing to do my best.

"Cards?" I said now.

She pulled out the deck. It was decorated with vintage photos of boxers: Floyd Mayweather Jr. was the king of spades, Muhammad Ali the ace of diamonds. Laila Ali, the only woman in the deck, was assigned the lowly two of clubs. Sometimes Janet would take the cards out to the lawn and turn them over, one by one, using the value to dictate how many push-ups she'd do before she rested for a few seconds. Kings were high at twelve, she said, but she always did thirteen for Laila. She could get through the whole deck that way.

"How did it go?" she asked.

I looked around as she dealt. Two bed-tops away, Nisha was trying valiantly to plait Harriet's messy hair. I thought they kept sneaking glances at us, but I wasn't sure.

"He ate it," I whispered.

Janet grimaced. "Draw or pass?"

"Do you think it'll work?" I asked.

She tapped the cards.

"Pass," I said.

Somewhere in the beds below, Margaret and Evie were exchanging dirty pick-up lines. If your left leg is Christmas and your right leg is New Year's, can I visit between the holidays? Are you a hard worker? Because I've got an opening you can fill. Have you ever kissed a rabbit between the ears? Would you like to? Would you like to? Would you like to?

"It doesn't matter," Janet said. "Serena is used to getting what she wants. If this doesn't work, I'm sure she'll find another way."

The bitterness in her voice surprised me. "Everyone wants what they want," I said.

"Some more than others," Janet said.

On the other side of the room, I could see Paola and Jamie sitting close together on Paola's low bunk. Paola had her fingers threaded through Jamie's fragile toes. Samantha was staring at them, her face drawn. I had no idea what was going on between them. They slept so close to me and still I hadn't noticed whatever saga of love or friendship or betrayal was playing out between their beds. It struck me how isolated I was, even in this mass of girls, how my loneliness hadn't decreased so much as widened its scope ever so slightly.

"I thought you wanted this too," I said.

"I do," Janet said. "It's just—look, I sacrifice a lot to come here. My aunt pays for it, but I lose all the wages that I could have made over the summer. It's a lot of money for me. And Laurel waits all year to come. She doesn't really have anyone at home, you know."

"Come on," I said. "I've seen the pictures. She's got a million friends."

"Most of those pictures are at least two years old," she said. "All those kids she goes to school with—they're not really her friends. Not anymore. She made a mistake, a couple years ago. They don't say anything outright, because her father's important, and their mothers make sure they don't burn bridges. But they all hate her, and she knows it. I don't know how she can sleep like that, with all their faces around. Or why she wants to."

"What kind of mistake?" I said.

"Exactly the kind you'd think."

I laid down my cards.

"What I'm saying is that if the Center burned to the ground, Laurel would be devastated. I would be, too. But Serena doesn't need this place. She doesn't even like it here. I don't blame her. She's done a lot for me. But we could get in actual trouble for this. If he gets sick. Or, I don't know. And who knows what's next? I'm just saying, don't ever think she's actually thinking of anyone other than herself. Not Luke, that's for certain. Not you. Not even me. She's playing her own game, and nobody but her even knows what it is."

I had the distinct feeling that Luke getting sick wasn't really what Janet was worried about. "She cares about us," I said carefully. "And why wouldn't she like it here? She's like the queen of this place."

"True," Janet said. "But don't forget that it also killed her mother."

Then Evie jumped up onto her bed, ignoring us but too hard, and we played in silence until Laurel came out of the bathroom and made us touch her newly shaved legs, which were so smooth, she said, look how smooth everywhere, so smooth, she said, they could burn you.

When I approached the garden the day after Luke ate the chili, Serena was already there. She was inside the fence this time, sitting on the bench next to him. She looked particularly lovely, I thought. She wore no makeup, and her dress was almost sheer. How I wished I could look like her, in those or any clothes. I felt a pulse between my legs at the idea.

"The Buddha said to work on your own salvation with diligence," she was saying. She placed her hand on Luke's bare knee.

"Yes, well, the diligence is the hard part," he said. He didn't move her hand. Instead, he reached out and touched her cheek. Despite everything, my first thought was triumphant. It had worked.

I stepped on a stick and they both looked up.

"Perfect timing," Serena said. I came through the gate and stood in front of them. I felt awkward, like a dingy chaperone, looming over two pretty young dancers. *Leave room for Jesus!* "I've remembered something," she said, turning her attention back to Luke. "I know exactly what you need to teach us."

"What's that?" Luke said.

"*Tummo.* That's what my mother was studying, right?"

Luke grimaced. "She really shouldn't have told you about that."

"It took me a while to remember. And then I wasn't sure, because I can't find it in any books. I've been looking."

"It is written in a few obscure places," he said. "But it's a sacred, secret practice. It's not for beginners."

"I am not a beginner," Serena said.

Luke began to laugh, but stopped at the look on her face. "It doesn't matter," he said. "The tummo teaching is self-secret. You can't learn it from a book. You need a guide, and even then, the practice will only make itself available to you once you're ready."

"*You* can guide us," Serena said. She moved her hand slightly higher on his thigh.

He looked down at it. "I'm not really qualified," he said. "I've received the transmission, but that doesn't mean I can pass it along."

Serena leaned over and kissed Luke on the cheek. "You'll teach us," she said. Luke said nothing, only smiled at her with half his mouth, and Serena kissed him again, almost climbing into his lap this time. Luke slipped an arm around her waist. I examined the rosebushes. I am, actually, interested in roses. I don't understand why they are held in such high regard. They are beautiful, yes, but like the rest of us, they all hide something ugly at the center.

After a few moments, Serena extricated herself and left, opening the door delicately, as though she feared that even the wooden handle might shock her fragile skin. Of course she cared about us. Look what she was doing. She didn't even want him, and look.

"You girls are relentless," he said once she had gone.

"Yes," I said.

Luke dropped his head into his hands. "I do want her to have what she wants. Whatever that is."

I kept my body completely still. "She wants you to have what you want, too."

"I don't want it to be a transaction," he said.

"She's in love with you," I said. "She's just pretending she isn't." It was a lie, and I thought he knew it, but as the words came out, I wondered if there was any possibility that they were true.

He looked up at me. "Can I tell you a secret?" he said. He didn't wait for me to respond. "I still believe in fate. Not like karma. Like destiny. I know I'm not supposed to. It's not a Buddhist concept. But I think the universe has plans for me. I think I'm going to do something big."

"So are we," I said.

Here's what I have learned. In 2002, Harvard researchers found that Himalayan monks practicing tummo, also known as inner fire, had the ability to raise their body temperatures as much as seventeen degrees at will. For a sacred, secret practice, they weren't particularly precious about it: sometimes, in their spare time, the monks would dip blankets in ice water, drape them over their bodies, and hold contests to see who could dry them the fastest. (Monks, I've noticed, love this kind of thing. The closer you are to enlightenment, it seems, the more easily amused.) Tummo is thought to not only allow meditators control over their bodies' metabolic processes and hormones, but also to enhance their strength, sexuality, and creativity. And yes, their ability to levitate—but not only that. Serena's mother had been right all along. "Inner fire is the real chocolate!!" wrote Lama Zopa Rinpoche. "It is the direct path to enlightenment that you have heard about. It is the secret key that opens you to *all* realizations." However, it is widely agreed that tummo should not be taught to beginners. The techniques are simple enough to understand, but it is dangerous to attempt without training and competent supervision. Of course, there are always those who ignore such warnings, and forge ahead without bread crumbs or ropes or guides. But there are tolls, you know, on the roads that go off the edges of the map. Here be monsters, etc.

The next day, I found myself sitting on the lawn alone after breakfast, though close enough to Harriet and Nisha that I could hear them talking about which tattoo Harriet should get next, and where—a white lotus on her rib cage, a dinosaur on her wrist, a bear, an eye, a ball of twine, her shoulder, her ankle, the smooth place behind her ear. I was only half listening to them. I could see Janet out at the edge of the white sand driveway, about as far away as you could get from the main building while remaining in sight. She hadn't been at breakfast. She had her hand on one of the boulders, and she looked, with her purple hair and black clothes, like an alien astronaut who had landed on an unknown planet. Alien Janet: blinking impassively at an unfamiliar world, observing its dress codes and government structures and waste protocols, making dry comments under her breath. This was essentially how she behaved anyway, I realized. She kicked at the sand and a little cloud bloomed at her toe. I felt very fond of her in that moment. I didn't understand why she would say that Serena didn't care about us. Serena cared, she did, and especially about Janet. I was overwhelmed by the urge to tell her this, except I knew I would ruin the scene by entering it, so I stayed where I was.

Who am I kidding? I have never in my life come across a beautiful image without deciding to force myself into it. I can't help it—show me a pretty patch of daisies and I'll immediately sit down in its center, so all the stems break beneath me, so all the petals smear and fold, but at least for that moment I am part of it. Just look at what happened that summer. Look at me now. I stood up and crossed the driveway.

"What're you doing?" I asked as I approached. She looked much paler than usual. She was pressing two fingers absently to the side of her neck, right below her birthmark. Standing in the expanse of white sand, it seemed as though the sun were coming from every direction at once.

"Taking in the sights," she said.

The sights: the golden seal on the main building; Harriet and Nisha still sitting together on their favorite rock; the mountain pitching upward, almost over our heads; a small clutch of girls practicing their Mudra Space Awareness on the grass. But these were as usual.

"I'm fine," Janet said. She let her hand drop away from her neck, took a step toward me, and then stopped, inhaling sharply. She pressed her fingers back into her neck, hard. She walked away from me, and then back, and then away. "I'm probably not dying, right?" she said.

I didn't know whether to laugh. "Probably not," I said. "Why would you be dying?"

"People die all the time."

"Old people. People in cars."

She stopped pacing. "You know what's really fucking terrifying about this place?"

I could think of a number of things.

"If someone had a heart attack here, they'd almost definitely die. Even if, somewhere else, they might have been saved. Rushed to the hospital. If it happened here, they wouldn't make it. We're too far away."

"I don't think you're having a heart attack," I said.

"When I was little, my dad took me to the top of the Statue of Liberty," Janet said. "Into her crown. I couldn't believe how different the city looked from there. They even used to let people into her torch. But there was an attack, once."

"What attack?" I said.

"Olivia," she said. "I don't think you understand what's going on here."

I felt a cold prickle in my throat. Her pressed fingers seemed to be growing white around the edges. I heard someone shout my name. It was Laurel, striding toward us, her eyes hidden by a pair of enormous pink sunglasses.

"Leave her alone," Laurel said. She marched up to us and pressed her fingers to the other side of Janet's neck. Janet pushed her face into Laurel's hand, and Laurel stroked her cheek with her thumb. "It's normal, darling," she said. "Strong."

"Okay."

"Say it," Laurel commanded.

"I don't need to say it."

"I swear to fucking God, Janet."

"This has happened before, and I was fine then, and I'm fine now," Janet said.

"Good. Let's walk," Laurel said. She put her arm around Janet and steered her back toward the main building. I followed behind them uselessly for a while and then stopped. They didn't notice. They kept on walking. I stood on the lawn, where I had started, and watched Jamie step carefully through the small forest of girls, weaving around their bodies. She looked more substantial than she ever had before, her skin sun-kissed, unbroken. When she was finished, they all smiled and hugged one another.

They fit together, Janet and Laurel. Not only physically, although that too—Janet slipping neatly under Laurel's arm. I hadn't understood it at first. They were so different; they made no sense together. But Laurel already knew what was happening to Janet. She didn't have to ask. She already knew what to do, what to say. They were a pair. I was extra. I could have come here or not come here, and they would have been the same. Complete. I realized this with a sort of dull ache; after all, I'd always known it. I was necessary to no one. Look: not even my parents needed me.

Later, Janet would apologize and tell me she'd been having a panic attack. She'd been getting them for a couple of years, she said, and when she did, she had to walk, sometimes for hours, it didn't matter where. Nothing else helped, except sometimes remembering that it wasn't the first time. I wanted to tell her then about the naming, the counting, and the way it kept me from falling apart at night, though I knew instinctually that her problem was not understanding her body too little, but rather the opposite.

"Is that where you are," I asked instead, "when you go off on your own?"

She nodded.

It finally made sense: all her disappearances, her refusal to explain. Or almost. "What about Laurel?" I asked. "Does she go with you?"

She looked at her hands. "No," she said.

I didn't ask her, then or ever, exactly what it was I didn't understand. Of course, in the end, I didn't have to ask. I found out soon enough.

When I got back to the dormitory, I found a note on my pillow:

Dearest O,
   Come tonight, please. Let L & J sleep, we won't need them.

Instead of her name, she'd scribbled at the bottom: *Where there is a sign, there is deception.*

Finally, it was my turn to sneak out alone, to leave the other two, if they were awake that night, to wonder where I was going, and why they weren't going along. I waited until the room was silent. I showed Magda my tongue. I shut the dormitory door. I kept my eyes on the trees as I climbed to Serena's tent. I was used to the forest at night by now, but not alone, not like this. I had the sensation of walking on a tongue, spongy beneath my feet. I had the sensation of magic. Could a certain patch of ground turn you from girl to bird? Could one misstep take you sideways, to an identical mountain in an identical world? You would never know, if it did.

But no. I'd walked this path many times, and I knew where it led.

Halfway up the mountain, I came across Ava, who had nestled herself between two bushes about a foot from the path. I would never have spotted her if I hadn't heard her yowl. When I held up my lamp, I saw that she was curled around three tiny kittens, each one sucking busily at its own personal teat; she looked smug, smugger than I would have thought possible with only one eye. I knelt, and the kittens all turned to look at me too. One of them had two perfectly enormous blue button eyes, and I gasped involuntarily (*destroy destroy destroy*). His brother, though, had only one—his right eye was crusted over and red. But the worst was the third kitten, who looked blind, both eyes raw and ruined. He looked as though he had no eyes at all, only little pink blisters, ready to burst. I recoiled. The three kittens struck me even then as symbolic. (But who—? And who—?) I had always assumed that Ava had lost her eye in some violent way—cat, mountain, hawk, hunter—but now it seemed that it was a sickness, a genetic flaw that had half blinded her, and this seemed worse somehow. I reached out to pet the two-eyed kitten. I couldn't force myself to touch the disfigured ones. Beauty moves us, after all. This we know. But ugliness moves us too.

Serena unzipped her tent as I approached, letting the flaps fall open. Inside, a carton of cigarettes leaned against the tent wall. A box of chocolates lay open on the ottoman, its little paper doilies strewn around like wandering ghosts. She had kicked all of her luxurious blankets and pillows and sheepskins onto the floor. She had her shoes on.

"What's going on?" I said.

"Once there was a man who wanted to fly around the world," she said. "But over Tibet, his plane lost power, and the man jumped out into the air. As he fell, he begged for help from his god, but none came. Then he looked down and remembered that Tibet was a Buddhist country, and so he began to pray to the Lord Buddha to save him. After a few moments, an enormous hand materialized and caught him, in midair." Serena held out her hand, palm cupped, and clicked her tongue. *Oh, thank God*, said the man. And then—" Slowly, she tipped her hand, letting the ungrateful man fall to his death.

"Serves him right," I said.

"Yes," she said. She lit a cigarette, but for once she didn't offer me one. Her eyes seemed to be all corners. "I want to try tummo tonight."

"Just us?" I asked. Something was interfering with my ability to feel excited about this—the story of the falling man, maybe, or the expression on her face, like barely bottled contempt.

"Janet's a spoilsport these days," she said. "Laurel's becoming a liability. She thinks I can't see what she's doing, but I can. God knows where she's getting it all. You've noticed."

I nodded.

"Besides, I don't think either of them really believes in any of this. Not the way you have to, to make it work. But *you* believe, don't you?"

I didn't say anything.

"Come on," she said. "You're my only goddamn hope."

Luke was waiting for us at the rock palm, as I suppose I should have known he would be. He was sitting cross-legged on the ground, his hands on his knees, his back straight, eyes resting on the rock in front of him. He was clean again, which made me shiver. Next to godliness.

"Hello, girls," said Luke. Serena sat beside him. Luke leaned over to whisper something in her ear. Serena tapped his knee with a finger and then looked up at me. Something had obviously changed between them, and not only because of the blood.

"I thought tummo was secret," I said. "I thought you didn't know how to teach it."

"What can I say?" Luke said. "You girls are very persuasive."

Serena gestured to the ground, and I sat, obedient to the last. First, we meditated. Luke led us through the bird visualization yet again. Serena led us through the Feeling. Finally, after an indeterminable period of time, we began.

"You begin by visualizing yourself as empty, completely hollow, a balloon," Luke said. "Outside you're glowing, but inside is nothing. You are a balloon with a shimmering face."

I closed my eyes and tried to imagine myself hollow. At first, I could only picture myself filled with blackness. Black sand, heavy and glittering. But after a while, I thought I could scrape it away, replace the scrim of colored-in, covered-up organs with real nothingness, negative space. I imagined air inside, pushing against the skin of my stomach, and then the opposite of air, pulling.

When Luke spoke again, I nearly jumped. "Now visualize a channel," he said. "The channel begins between your legs and goes up through the top of your skull. Take all of the energy from your body and make it into a ball of heat. The ball of heat will start at the bottom, at your sacrum, but then you can move it up, toward your crown, where there's a *hum*. Don't let it out."

I pictured a small white-hot ball with a little red tail, like a comet. I let it rest in the bowl of my pelvis. I thought I could hear the noise it made, a hot whir like a gas stove. I held it down between my legs until I couldn't hold it there any longer, because I didn't know what would happen if I did, and then I let it go, and it jumped up into the channel I had made, which was blue, and filled it with red light. The light climbed up through my body. I wanted it to go slowly, but it wanted to go fast, and I could barely control it.

"Breathe deeply into the space four inches below your navel, and focus on the ball of heat, let it rise, and then let it fall. Hold the heat in your mind and the breath in your body."

I had to keep the ball from escaping through my mouth by gritting my teeth. Rebuffed, it found its way into my head, and for a moment I thought my skull would explode. Then I remembered what I was meant to do next, and I started pushing it down, back toward my pubic bone, which seemed cold, and so far away, as though my body stretched forever between the two.

"Don't let it out," Luke said again, or maybe it was only an echo.

My eyes were closed, and I could see the ball of light, but I also thought I could see Luke, who had begun to speak in a language I didn't know, or in a language I knew but couldn't understand. I opened my eyes slightly and saw only darkness. It wasn't frightening; it was inviting, a bedroom darkness. I closed them again and the world looked the same. Open, closed. If we're inventing our reality, why not do it in the dark? The light inside of me was blocking out everything else; the pressure was building, blinding.

"Okay," I heard him say at last. "Let it go, and exhale through every pore in your body."

And so I let the light escape through my skin, and as I did, I felt an immense release, and as I did, I felt myself lift off the ground.

Saint Teresa: "It comes, in general, as a shock, quick and sharp, before you can collect your thoughts, or help yourself in any way, and you see and feel it as a cloud, or a strong eagle rising upward, and carrying you away on its wings. I repeat it: you feel and see yourself carried away, you know not whither. For though we feel how delicious it is, yet the weakness of our nature makes us afraid at first, and we require a much more resolute and courageous spirit than in the previous states, in order to risk everything."

My eyes flew open, expecting mountaintops, clouds, continents. But I saw only trees, barely blacker than the night they cut into, and I saw that I was seated securely among them, a root or rock digging into my right thigh. Again? Still? I crawled toward Serena, who was sprawled out on her back, her hips raised, moving her head slowly back and forth in the dirt.

"You see," she said. "You see, you see, you see."

I suppose it was only at this point, so late in the summer, that I truly began to believe. I should remember this: no matter what else, no matter the end we were speeding toward by then, no matter her real motives, her master plan—she did give me what I came for. Later, when Luke had gone, I lay stiff and flat beside her on her narrow mattress, barely wide enough for two bodies, if they don't move, if their breaths are shallow. I heard somewhere that if you lie next to someone for long enough, your hearts begin to beat in unison. I wonder if the weaker heart slows to mirror the stronger, or if the stronger softens for the weaker, or if both drift slowly together, toward a new rhythm neither has felt before. Sometime in the middle of the night, I woke. I thought I'd heard a sound, seen a shadow. But then it was gone, or it had never been there, and soon I was dragged swiftly back down, down, down into the deep sleep of a girl whose heart at last has a twin.

12

This is how my parents met: my father was standing on a table, a smear of blood across his cheek. My mother told me this story. He used to throw parties in his apartment, parties like the ones she threw, like the ones he used to come outside for, instead of turning the pages. Only his parties were even wilder, went even later. He was enormous when they met, she told me once, fully bursting at the seams. Yes, physically too, but that wasn't what she'd meant. He'd just been hit with something, the first time she saw him, and his face was bleeding, and apparently you should have seen the other guy. He'd hopped down to greet her, the new girl, the friend of so-and-so, and she had kissed his cheek, her lips coming away bloody, and then he'd wanted more, so he'd buried his hands in her hair and kissed those bloody lips, and that had been that had been that. Plath herself would have wept.

"But that was before," she said.

"So he's better now," I said.

"Your father didn't become a Buddhist until after we were married," she said. "If I had known what was going to happen, you probably wouldn't even be here." I stood to leave then, because I always hated to hear her talk this way about him, and she knew it. "I'm glad you are, though," she said as I walked away. I didn't say anything. I went up the stairs and shut my bedroom door.

My father never told me any stories about my mother. The only thing he ever said about her wasn't even true, as it turned out. "Being married to your mother," he said, "has been the greatest test of my spiritual practice. That's why I can never leave her."

Think of it as a system of vectors: my father and mother were connected. My father and me. My mother and me. But there was no triangle; somehow that shape never made sense for us. Instead, the two of them were like tectonic plates, drifting slowly away from each other. I didn't try to choose a side until I was almost completely lost between them. I think I did get lost. I think when I finally jumped it was already too late, and there was nowhere to jump to, or from.

I know I should say that everything changed when my parents separated. That's the narrative to which I should cleave. But it didn't feel like that to me. My father had a new house, that was all, a bigger shrine room. It was my mother with whom I spent the most time, both before and after. Art projects and music, that's what I remember, my mother dancing in her bare feet until my father came home. After the separation, the only difference was that I went to him.

Serena was right, you know, about desire. Now that I've seen this story to its mortal end, I know she was right. We were all

sick with want that summer, stupid with it. I wanted Luke. I
wanted Serena. I wanted my father. I wanted belief. I wanted
transcendence. It's not as though I was unusual. In fact, I was
trite. But now, I think this is what disturbs me most about religious seekers, as a group—they want so badly, so obviously. They
want enlightenment, they want release, they want connection.
They are like baby birds, their mouths and necks stretched to
impossible sizes, their eyes enormous in their soft skulls, watery
and blue with desire. They're waiting and waiting and waiting
for a strange foreign man in authentic robes to come and pour a
bucket of pure light marked Real Religion down their cold crying throats. It's gross, in the end, to want something so badly.
And look, after all, where all that wanting gets you.

Now I prefer not to want. It is much more dignified. I guess I
turned out to be a Buddhist after all.

But maybe not quite, because these days, waiting in bars after
a dull day of work to meet other unhappy strangers, or in my
cold, empty apartment, reading desperate novels in the bathtub, it's the act of desire and not its object that most effectively
seduces me. It's not strong shoulders or soft lips or kindness, or
whatever it is women supposedly want in men, when they do,
but simply being desired. What I'm saying is, I would get wet for
a slab of granite if I was convinced it wanted me badly enough.
Lithophilia, etc. This doesn't change any of my above feelings
re: want. It only makes me say, what a fucking masochist.

Serena and I began meeting Luke every few nights for tummo.
Each time I let the ball of light go, I felt closer to flight, but each
time I opened my eyes, I found myself still on the ground. Luke

talked more about himself at the rock palm than I had ever been able to coerce him to do in the garden—another of Serena's small sorceries. He told us about his own dharma teacher, a woman who had changed everything for him. He told us, finally, about his sister, Eleanor. He described the color of her hair, and the way she had died, in an accident that he might have prevented, only he was out drinking, only he couldn't be reached. She was supposed to be with him, but he left her at home. He thought she could take care of herself, but it turned out that she could not. She thought he could do no wrong, but it turned out that he could. He played the guitar at her funeral, a pretty song, his favorite, theirs—*I'm in love with the world through the eyes of a girl*— but the rest of his family only narrowed their eyes and waited for him to stop. "I don't blame them," he said. "But I don't blame myself either."

I was confident that the tummo would work eventually. It *was* working. During yoga, I closed my eyes and imagined the comet, the channel, and found that I could raise my legs into the air with no assistance. This, on its own, was a miracle. Shastri Dominique clapped and cooed. Even Janet was impressed. And when the four of us met to faint and fall and give ourselves the Feeling, to play our lightness games, I felt we were all getting closer, lighter, smaller, that the tummo had spread to them too, somehow. Janet's jaw set, her muscles straining. Laurel's fingertips moving through the air. Serena was wrong. They believed. They wanted this, each in her own way, each desperately. They both wanted more power for themselves, more control of the imperfect lives they lived outside of this. Who wouldn't? But as far as I knew, they still had no idea about the tummo, a fact that made me want to touch their hair and cheeks whenever we were together, and also made me want to slap them and laugh at the mark I had made.

One night we climbed into a tree, all four of us, and lay

with our spines pressed to its thick branches, our limbs dangling, heads spinning from the nettle tea and the whiskey Serena had let us drink and the number of times we'd fainted and awoken, fainted and awoken, the world becoming more hypothetical every time we looked at it.

"Admit it, Janet," Laurel said. "You feel it now. You *feel* it."

"I feel it," Janet said. Her voice was softer than I had ever heard it. I could see her arms swimming. "Something is happening."

"We're close," I said. The branch seemed to disappear beneath me. I could feel myself rising, or maybe the ground was falling. "We're so close."

"We are what we think," Janet said.

"We are everything," Laurel said.

"Form is emptiness," I said. "Emptiness is form."

But Serena was getting impatient.

"I've been thinking about Empress Consort Wu Zetian," she said when we'd climbed down.

"'Consort' being the nice word for 'whore'?" Janet said. She leaned against the tree, as if loath to leave it entirely. Laurel dropped her head onto her shoulder.

"She was the only woman who ever ruled China completely on her own," Serena said. "She *was* a whore, I suppose, but that only makes it better."

"Well, everyone loves a good whore," said Laurel, without humor. Janet squeezed her knee.

Empress Consort Wu Zetian, Serena explained, was the favored concubine of the seventh-century Chinese emperor Taizong, and when he died, she married his son, and when the son had a massive stroke, she took control of China. She is said to be one of the most beautiful women who has ever lived.

"She had an affair with a monk," she said. "He betrayed his god for her."

"The best god is the one between a girl's legs," Laurel said. She reached into her pocket and slipped her button into her mouth: pop.

"The only true religion," Serena said.

"People must be praying wrong," Janet said.

"She also installed secret mailboxes in government buildings so people could more easily inform on her enemies," Serena said. "When she found out that three of her grandchildren had been talking shit about her, she forced them all to commit suicide."

"That's not really suicide, then, is it?" Janet said. She was sitting up straight now, the dreaminess of the tree forgotten.

"One does what one must," Serena said imperiously. "Her specialty was this thing she called the human pig. She did it to one of her rivals. A traitor."

"Don't tell us," said Laurel.

"She cut out her tongue and poked out her eyes and cut off her arms and legs and then kept her alive, fed her slop, and left her to roll around in her own shit," said Serena.

"Pigs have legs, last I checked," Janet said.

"The point is," Serena said, propping herself up on one elbow, "I'm tired of waiting." Laurel put her button behind her lips again. Serena reached over and snatched it away: pop. "And I'm tired of this," she said. "It makes you look ridiculous."

I looked at Laurel, waiting for outrage, but she was examining her own knees. "I never said it didn't," she said.

"What is happening right now?" Janet said.

"Nothing," Serena said. "*Nothing* is happening. Nothing at all." She stood, walked to the edge, and threw Laurel's button over. "Nothing," she said again. She looked out into the air for a long time. When she finally backed away, she didn't return to the blanket. Instead, she walked past us and into the woods without a word. I had the feeling of being shipwrecked.

"It's not nothing," I said, but they didn't seem to hear me.

"You're not being careful," Laurel said. "You're antagonizing her." She was looking into the woods, as if waiting for something.

"I'm not asking you to do anything," Janet said. "You know what I think."

"Careful about what?" I said.

But they both looked at me in surprise, as if they had forgotten I was there.

The next day, during our free hours, I came into the dormitory to find Laurel rooting through my things. My bed was a mess; the clothes in my cubby were all over the floor.

"What are you doing?" I said.

"You have no sexy clothes, did you know that?" Her eyes were glassy, unfocused. "You dress like my aunt Pearl."

"Serena said we're not supposed to drink unless it's for a reason," I said primly.

"Who said anyone's drinking?" she said.

"What happened with you and Harriet last summer?" I said, to hurt her.

She set down the pair of jeans she was holding. "Oh, please. What did she say?"

I raised my eyebrows, a bluff. She seemed to sway a little on the spot.

"It wasn't going to work," she said.

I still said nothing and Laurel looked down at her hands. "She didn't fit in. Not everyone liked her."

"Janet liked her," I said, and then as if summoned, Janet appeared at Laurel's side.

"Come on," she said, tugging at the t-shirt in Laurel's hand. "There's no point in this. What are you even doing?" She looked apologetic but did not offer to help me pick up my things. Laurel pointed at me and narrowed her eyes, but she let Janet tug her through the door.

It was only when I started to replace my clothes, folding jeans and rolling shirts, that I noticed Nisha sitting on a bed in the corner, watching me and eating something out of a jar. MAMA'S FIRE TIBETAN HOT SAUCE. I wrinkled my nose.

"Transcendence, right," she said, and put another spoonful in her mouth.

By then, we hadn't eaten real food in weeks, only sugar and nettles. When we walked back up to the rock palm the following night, I thought I could see spots in the dark, green and watery blobs with empty centers, and then the spots clarified into faces, leering out from the woods with swollen tongues. I tried to keep my head down, but that made me dizzy, and so I put my hands around my waist again to comfort myself. Was this what all beautiful girls saw when they looked out into the night?

"Tonight," Serena said, once we had settled around her on the blanket, "is the night." She kept flexing her fingers, pulling her hands into fists and then loosening them again. She passed around a bottle of whiskey. "I finally figured it out," she said as we drank. She looked at each of us, one by one, meeting our eyes, taking her time. "I mean I really did it," she said. "I levitated."

Laurel sucked in her breath. Janet only raised her eyebrows.

"How?" I asked.

"It was an accident," she said. "I was on the ledge, alone, and the ground was wet, and I slipped and fell. I thought I was going to die. But then I just—stopped. Floated." Her voice sounded sweet again.

"What did it feel like?" Laurel whispered.

"Like there was a hook inside me, right here." Serena held her palm against Laurel's solar plexus, the same place we pressed to make each other faint. "I felt it lift."

Janet frowned.

"I think you can only really levitate when you *need* to,"

Serena said. "And then only if you've practiced. Everything we've been doing, the fasting, the fainting, the Feeling, everything *else*—" She cut her eyes toward me for the briefest moment. "That's why I could do it. Otherwise I would have fallen." She was twisting a lock of hair around and around one finger; when she'd pinned her hand to her scalp, she let it unravel and started again.

"What about when you saw Luke?" Janet said. "When you were a kid? He wasn't in danger, was he?"

"I don't know," she said. "Maybe he was. Maybe there's more than one way. But it doesn't matter. We're doing it. Together this time." She stood and walked slowly toward the eastern edge of the rock palm. We followed, a little behind her. It made me dizzy to stand there, even a few yards back. Across the empty drop, the branches of the weeping willow–girl were still. The darkness below us felt like a vacuum, deleted space, although I knew it was not, that it was full of air. It must have been eighty feet of air at least. The rock close to the edge looked flat and soft, like mica. I imagined walking up to it and peeling back a layer with my fingernails and hurling it into the void. But of course it was not me but Serena who stepped up onto the lip.

"What now?" Laurel said. She was leaning on Janet's shoulder.

"Now we step off," Serena said. She looked unstable, listing slightly to one side. For the first time, there was something uneasy about her. Now I wonder how many of her own rules she had broken.

"It's a long way down," Janet said.

"Exactly," Serena said.

"What if it doesn't work?" I said.

"Then we'll die," Janet said.

"Luke only thinks he's the most powerful person here," Serena said, almost to herself. She raised her arms above her head. "He thinks he's the chosen one, that he can do anything he wants. But he's wrong. *We* are the ones. And this is going to transform us," she said. "This is going to turn us into beautiful, wrathful, whole new creatures."

Nobody moved. She lowered her arms.

"Laurel," she said, her voice soft now. "After this, you won't have to let anyone touch you. Unless you want it. Imagine what they'll say. Or don't, because you won't have to listen." Serena reached out her hand. "Come on, dearest," she said. "Don't you know I love you?"

Laurel only hesitated for a moment before she took Serena's hand and stepped forward to join her on the rock lip. I could see her trembling from where I stood.

"Janet," Serena said. "You need this too."

"Do I?" Janet said. She sounded like she really wanted to know.

"I know you didn't break your arm falling off a bicycle. Since when have you ever fallen off a bicycle? Please. You're strong, but they're men now."

I looked at Janet, but she was staring straight ahead.

"Consider the possibilities," Serena said.

Janet didn't move.

"Janet," Laurel said. "I need you to come." And it was only for this, for Laurel, that Janet finally stepped forward. Laurel reached for her and held her tightly to her side.

Then Serena turned and looked at me. "What about you?" she said. She was relaxed now. She already knew she had won. "Your dear old daddy will be so proud."

Thrall is an almost perfect word. Old Norse for "slave." Shades of Dracula, and that persistent, tiresome Anglo-Saxon bleat about evil and sex being inextricable. In thrall. The word is like the sound a sudden change makes, or like a spell resolving. Say it out loud and listen: *thrall*. That guttural glissando. Like all real magic words, it's a little hard to get out. Mechanically,

I mean. The tongue, asked to roll two ways at once, revolts. Don't worry; she gets there in the end.

What I mean to say is: no one ever tells you how good it feels.

What I mean to say is: I stepped toward the edge.

"Imagine yourself standing on a ledge above a canyon," Serena recited. "Imagine yourself stepping off. You don't fall, you hang there. The earth's energy holds you up. Imagine yourself as a feather, floating upward. Imagine yourself as a bird, hollow-boned and small. Imagine the distance between yourself and the ground growing, growing, growing." Serena reached out her hand, and I took it, slotting in beside her, my toes toward the edge. I couldn't see the bottom.

Her hand was cold and dry in mine. The wind had begun to blow. It was unusual for summer, wind like that. I thought of the sand twister from the first day, and wondered if it was spinning now in the empty driveway. If a twister spins on a mountain, and no one is there to see it, etc. A few strands of Serena's hair flew into my face. She began to lead us through the tummo visualization we'd been doing with Luke. If they were surprised by this, Janet and Laurel did not react. They both had their eyes closed. I tried to conjure the ball of light whirling in my pelvis, but the wind distracted me. Serena distracted me. She was more like herself than I was like anybody. She could lead three girls up a mountain and make them fly. I knew then that if I stepped off this cliff, at this moment, my body would become perfect and holy at last. All my charmed particles would light up and rise.

"We are what we think," Serena said. "Are we ready?" She seemed to be faceless, there on the ledge, her features darkened by the shadow of the drop.

"Yes," I said quietly. This is what it meant, belief. I saw Laurel nod. We were four figureheads on the prow of a ship, all holding hands, all facing outward, our chests raised, our hair whipping and writhing in the freakish wind.

Unbidden, I saw an image of our bodies smashed down at the bottom of the crevasse, limbs all mixed together, reddening the sharp rocks. I shuddered. I wondered vaguely if the wind was a warning, if the mountain was trying to stop us the only way it knew how.

"Don't look down," Serena said, reading my mind again.

Om tare tuttare ture soha, I thought, but it brought me no release from the fear that had begun to clutch at my throat.

"What if," Laurel started, but Serena only pulled her closer.

"Death comes without warning," Serena said. "This body will be a corpse." She spat into the abyss. "But not today." She laughed. "We didn't need Luke after all."

Om tare tuttare ture soha. Om tare tuttare ture soha. Om tare tuttare ture soha.

I couldn't get the image of our broken bodies out of my head. I thought of my father, who had said something so similar once, before wrapping me in his arms. Death comes without warning. But this isn't what he had meant. *Om tare tuttare ture soha.* Where was Tara, to pull me back from the edge? To save me from fear of fear? Still trapped in the wall in my mother's house, I realized with a jolt. I'd forgotten about her after all.

"On the count of three," Serena said. "One. Two."

Serena paused, and I felt in that brief moment that Tara had come despite my negligence—my fear was gone. I was ready to jump. I might have even done it. But our imminent deaths were interrupted by a loud crack that echoed across the valley. Even in the dark, I knew it was the willow, its gnarled trunk forced prostrate, bending to the wind past the point its body would allow, forced over the edge, falling to the cold rocks below, as Harriet had predicted it would.

Something else had broken too. Janet scrambled backward, away from us, onto the grass. "This is ridiculous," she said, but the look on her face was one of longing, as if someone she loved had just left her forever.

"It's only the wind," Serena said. "You can't be afraid, Janet. Not you."

Janet ignored her. "Laurel," she said. "Do you want to die right now?"

Laurel kept looking out into the air. She seemed like she didn't quite know the answer to that question.

"I'm surprised at you, Janet," Serena said, pulling Laurel closer, rethreading her fingers through mine.

At some point in her story, every true heroine realizes that she is fundamentally unlike other people. She may be the chosen one (*we're going to choose ourselves*) or have trained for many years, or be merely damaged, or merely strange. She may have had an accident involving radioactive material or nuclear waste. She may have natural abilities. She may be molded by circumstance. But I have had to realize that no matter how much I desire to be different, I am not. That I am, finally, just like everyone else. I cannot be the heroine, even of my own story. (Is that what this is?) I could tell you that it was me, and not Janet, who pulled away first. But it wasn't. I could tell you that I was still ready to leap, even then, to face the fall. But I wasn't. You know this. My body seeks safety every time. My body only follows.

I unclasped my hand from Serena's. If I never saw my father again, fine. I would live. I crawled backward and sat down heavily on the rock. "I don't need to levitate," I said. "I'm okay with the idea of not levitating." I felt completely sober.

"And here I thought you really believed," Serena said. I had been thinking the same thing, which is what hurt the most.

"Come on, Serena," Janet said. "This isn't you."

"Is it not?" Serena said, as if amused. She was still looking at me. "I know what you did, Olivia," she said. "Even after I told you what might happen."

Janet stiffened at my side. "What's she talking about?" she said.

"It was an accident," I said. How long had she known? Was that why she had brought us here, to the edge of the world? Was it me she wanted to throw off?

"He told me all about it, you know," Serena said. But she didn't look sad, saying this, or angry. She looked hungry. "He was trying to make me jealous. But it didn't work—at least, not the way he wanted." She smiled, her hair whipping out behind her.

No, it wasn't revenge. Now I think she just needed more, as she always did: more sensation, more power, more meaning. She wasn't satisfied with tummo. She wasn't satisfied with Luke. She was tired of waiting, of wanting, of opening her eyes and finding herself still on the ground. She had to change something, anything, even if the change was a violent one. Especially then. I'm not saying I don't understand.

"Come to us, Laurel," Janet called. "Come back."

"Okay, Laurel," Serena said. "You and me."

Laurel looked back at Janet, and then at me, and then at Serena.

"Wait," she said.

"Laurel," Serena said. "Don't you love me?"

"Yes," Laurel said. She had started to cry. "But let's go down. Please let's go down."

"No," Serena said. "We're going up." Then she grabbed Laurel by the shoulders and pushed her hard, out into the empty air. Laurel screamed, but at the last moment, Serena seized her by the back of her shirt. The wind caught in Serena's hair, and it streamed outward across the void, mixing with Laurel's.

Janet lunged, and I held on to her wrist.

"You know what worked, that first time we fainted?" Serena said, her voice cold. "Spilling a little blood." Laurel was crying, her tears dripping into the emptiness, her arms held tight to her body. Serena was holding on with one hand. I was shocked at her strength.

Then, all of a sudden, she laughed, and this time it sounded sweet, so sweet, bluebells and coffee cake. "Oh, you babies," she said. "I'm only kidding." She hauled Laurel back up onto solid ground, wrapped her arms around her and kissed her wet cheek, and then pushed her toward us. "You're all so gullible," Serena said, as Janet stroked Laurel's head. She looked right into my eyes. "Come on. I was never going to let you jump." I would think of the look on her face in this moment later, as the police scoured the Center grounds, looking for bodies: it was open, girlish. There was nothing to distrust here. There was nothing to question. She looked utterly, completely believable.

But for once in my life, I didn't believe her.

Because yes: beauty, in the end, it hurts us.

13

For the record, here are a few ways in which levitation can be reliably achieved:

There's the classic Asrah trick, in which the magician drapes a sheet over a prone assistant, whom he then appears to levitate and, after a moment, instantly disappear. This relies on a precise plastic mold of the assistant, which is snuck under the sheet, then raised up by wires, while the real girl disappears through a trap door. Trap doors, which may seem like the opposite of levitation, are often essential to its practice.

On the other hand, the Balducci method is essentially advanced tiptoeing.

David Copperfield, I'm sorry to tell you—for all his grand old speeches about the age-old human desire for flight—is also invariably raised up by wires, though they are very sophisticated, as wires go.

There's always mirrors, smoke.

Yves Klein's *Leap into the Void* is a beautiful hoax, an early example of photo-manipulation. But despite the lie, Klein's heart was in the right place: in the air above Fontenay-aux-Roses. "We shall thus become aerial men," he wrote before his jump. "We shall know the forces that pull us upwards to the heavens, to space, to what is both nowhere and everywhere. The terrestrial force of attraction thus mastered, we shall literally escape into a complete physical and spiritual freedom!"

The image in question is now stored at the Metropolitan Museum of Art, labeled as an "artistic action," as if one could keep an action in a drawer. Obviously not: at least one artist tried to copy Klein's feat by throwing himself casually out a second-floor window, expecting to fly. In some accounts, he breaks a leg. In others, he escapes unharmed.

Scientific attempts have been rather more convincing. An artist in Barcelona recently developed a system that uses electromagnetic feedback and coupled resonant wireless power transfer to suspend a lit bulb between two blocks. The bulb will last for years, he says, floating there, and use half the energy of a regular incandescent fixture.

There are ways to do it with magnets. That much should be obvious to anyone. Magnetic quantum forces are currently being researched for use in nanomachines, which could, sometime soon, have tiny levitating parts whirring along within them.

My next-door neighbors have a trampoline, and their children spend hours on it, bouncing and bouncing, never satisfied. They too want to renounce the earth. They too feel the edges of something when they're at the apex of a bounce, something that, if they could only get a little higher, a little longer, they know would change them.

Look, any Buddhist would be quick to tell you: levitation isn't the point. But it fascinates.

After that night on the ledge, Serena removed herself from our lives. She stopped coming to meet us. We stopped going to her tent. Whole days went by without her. But just when I'd start to think that she'd evaporated entirely, she would appear in the shrine room for a moment or an afternoon. When she did, she did not try to speak to us. She meditated with intent. She nodded to Dominique, who blinked back. She looked far away, too tangled up in her own thoughts to even notice we were there.

This was worse, of course, than her not being there at all.

It's hard to explain exactly how my feelings about her had shifted. If violence is primarily authoritarian, violence deferred should be a triumph for the intended victim. Why then did I feel so disappointed? I can liken it only to the moment when, during a climactic scene in a film you're watching in the theater—perhaps it's a horror, perhaps a romance—you notice, for an instant, the texture of the screen itself. The result is a kind of dissociation, stemming from the realization that the drama in which you've been so invested is merely a projection of light onto a flat, imperfect canvas. Which, of course, you knew all along. You understand what movies are. You're not an idiot. But thereafter you can't focus on the shimmering images because you keep returning to the worn spot in the center of your vision, the unseemly sight of that old gray screen, stripped of all its charming artifice.

Well, I wanted to go back to the shimmering world. For once, I had no interest in the man behind the curtain.

Another kind of levitation: in Nepal, a little girl is chosen when she's three years old, and recognized by some as the Kumari, the embodiment of Durga, goddess of destruction and blood sacrifice. They say that she is a god, and also that she is a girl. They say she can see into the past and future. They say that if the Kumari smiles at you, it's an invitation to heaven, and that you will die within the day. The Kumari has her every wish attended to. Her feet must not touch the ground, so she's carried everywhere, covered in jewels and the finest fabrics. She is held in the air and worshipped.

But when the Kumari reaches puberty, she becomes mortal again. The Nepalese believe that the energy of the goddess goes out with the girl's first blood. So they put her down—but by then, her legs are unsteady. She has no social skills to speak of. She may not know her family. She's mortal, but worse than mortal. She is an infant alien jammed into the newly bleeding body of a twelve-year-old girl.

There are other legends about the Kumari: that if you try to deflower one, even years after her descent into the mortal realm, snakes will slither from between her legs and eat your penis whole. The legend goes that because of this legend, no man who knows a Kumari's past will have her, and many must turn to prostitution to survive. But in all truth, there are some ex-goddesses

who live quite normal lives. One of them opened a bank. A bank!
I find this comforting.

Without Serena as our center of gravity, my connection to Janet and
Laurel began to fray. Laurel gave me up without a second glance;
she forgot me so thoroughly she didn't even think to avoid me. I
remember her bumping into me once in the dining hall, jabbing
her tray into my side. She was carrying a bowl of strawberries and
two mugs of tea. Janet was waiting for her. "Oh," she said, her face
blank, her eyes wide and watery. "Sorry." The smell of alcohol was
overpowering, and when I looked into her mug, she pulled it away.

    Janet was different, but Janet, really, was Laurel's. I knew that.
Though the two of them seemed uneasy together too. Their
bickering had turned sullen. Their silences had legs, fingernails.

I began to hang around Harriet and Nisha, trying to catch up
on their inside jokes, to remind them that they'd once been my
friends, or almost. They mostly ignored me too. Girls who try to
elevate themselves and fail are never much loved by those they
crash-land among. With no reason not to, I began attending every
activity again, and I could see that these weeks at the Center had
been good for most of the other girls: they seemed relaxed, happy.
All that mindfulness therapy, contemplative art, meditation—the
girls who had really transformed were the girls who hadn't tried
to force it.

    I started eating again. Oatmeal and blueberries, kale and
black beans. I felt heavier than I ever had in my life.

There was no more tummo practice. No more nights attempt-
ing levitation. There was no more Serena coming by the garden
unannounced, or at least not when I was there to see it. There

was only me, moving dirt around, grinding my molars into paste, saying nothing, my hairline burning as I pruned. There was only Luke, asking concerned questions, but letting more and more time pass between them.

I blamed him, of course. If he had simply done what Serena had asked, had bent to her desire like the rest of us, none of this would be happening. Instead, we would be together on the rock palm, holding hands, all four of us with our feet in the air. All five of us, maybe.

"Isn't there anything else you can do?" I asked him once. All I wanted was to go back, to repair whatever ineffable structure had been broken. "Some other teaching? Couldn't you at least show us, so we can see?"

"Trust me, I'd love to," he said. "She's driving me crazy." So she was still seeing him, at least. She was still trying, without me.

"Then do it," I said.

"I would," he said. "At this point, I would give her anything she wanted." He shuddered a little—at what? This admission? His own desire? "But like most people," he said, "I have no earthly idea how to levitate."

"Come on," I said. "She saw you do it."

"I've heard that story," he said. "I wish it were true."

It took me a few seconds to understand what he was saying. Did that mean Serena had imagined it? Had she misremembered—or had she been lying all along? "What about tummo?" I asked at last.

"Tummo is real," he said. "I've just never taken it all the way. I haven't been doing this all that long, you know. I'm just some guy." He put his hands in his pockets, and smiled, as if he didn't quite believe what he was saying. I didn't contradict him. I didn't ask him why he didn't tell us the truth from the beginning. I didn't need to. I knew what Serena was offering.

• • •

When I left the garden, I walked down to the koi pond, thinking I might sit for a while, or kneel and let the jeweled fish suck on my fingers. I needed to think. But when I approached, I found that Janet was already there, stretched out on the muddy bank amid the nettles. I noticed, seeing her from that angle, that her roots were growing in, that signature purple finally admitting to being not of her, not entirely, not originally. The effect was of someone wearing an inexpertly attached wig, the glue peeling and stretching. She was showing her seams. She was not yet, but almost, exposed. Despite the fact that she too had been eating again, she seemed even further diminished, as if boiled down to her essential parts, all marrow.

She didn't notice me, and as I watched, she pushed herself forward and began to drink from the pond. She slapped the water into her face, letting it splatter her skinny chest. When she dunked her head in, the purple spreading out, I quietly turned and left her there.

Later, I woke in the middle of the night, needing to pee, and went into the bathroom to find Laurel in the tub. I said her name. She didn't move. I came to the edge, and tried to stop myself from looking down at her; in the stillness the water was perfectly clear. She ignored me. I put a hand in the water to disturb it, a way of touching her without touching her, and found that it was cold.

"Laurel," I said again.

"What?" she said at last, her voice drawn up into its haughtiest register, the one she'd used with me the very first time we'd met. It made me sad to hear it, nostalgic even.

"The water's cold," I said.

"Oh," she said. She looked down. She began, silently, to cry.

I knelt by the tub. But she wouldn't answer me, wouldn't explain, wouldn't get out of the cold bath. Finally, I said I was going to wake up Janet.

"No," she said. "Leave Janet out of it." Then she stood in the bathtub, bare and tall and towering over me, swaying only slightly. She was covered with goose bumps, like a pointillist's Venus. I wanted to hold her, wrap her in a towel, warm her by the fire, even though there was no fire, even though it was a hot night like all the others, and we didn't have that kind of love. But she stepped around me and disappeared naked into the dormitory. I still had to pee, and once that had been accomplished, I came back to find that her bed was empty.

I slid my body between her sheets. Her pillow smelled like the plasticky jasmine of her shampoo. Her sheets were silky and cool. I kicked my legs back and forth to feel the smoothness against my skin. I turned my face down into the pillow, but something didn't feel right. There was no thrill, no promise of closeness here. I didn't know what I was doing. I crept back to my own stale bed.

Ritual cleansings are common in both Eastern and Western religions. Ablutions are often required before worship, as though our gods cannot be trusted to see us as we are, as though the soap we scrub into our outsides might filter down to clean our filthy souls, or at least shine them up a little. Baptism, mikvah, misogi, punyahavachanam, ghusl, an evening in the sweat lodge. Cleanliness/godliness. But it seems to me that the closer we get to our natural states—the muddier we get, the more savage, the more covered with semen and silt and scratches—the closer we are to whatever elemental force created us. It does not seem likely that the gods are civilized, that they take their tea with one blue pinkie finger held aloft. It does not seem likely that they were looking down at Laurel, kindly or at all, no matter how she splashed and shivered in that cold dead tub.

14

I found out the way anyone finds out anything: I had a dream about Rasputin. He sat at a high table and fed the four of us crumbs and crusts from his plate as we fought and scrambled beneath him. When the crumbs and crusts were gone, we sucked meat juice from the dirty fingers he dangled down to us. Rasputin's thumb was in my mouth when Serena began climbing, digging her toes into his heavy robes for balance. Up, up, up she went, and soon I heard Rasputin scream, and then I heard the screaming muffle and stop, and I knew she was crawling into his mouth, that she was going to force her body into his head, fill it up until it exploded. I could hear the kicking of his legs, the desperate scratching of his hands against the table. He clutched at my hair, my breasts, my neck, trying to gain some purchase, but I was smooth, too smooth, a peach after all. I could hear the squeaking of his skull, the sound of the plates coming apart at the seams, and I knew it was coming, it was almost there, she had done it, she was doing it now.

I woke up. I pulled myself out of bed and went into the bathroom to wash the dream off my face. When I came back, my eyes adjusted to the darkness, I could see that neither Laurel nor Janet were in their beds. I tried to go back to sleep, but the dream was sticking in the back of my throat. Rasputin's face had been familiar. His hands had been rough. I could still feel where his calluses had burned the inside of my cheek, where his fingertips had grazed my clavicle.

It occurred to me for the first time that it was possible our little group hadn't so much fractured as I had simply been excised from it. That my rotten apocalypse was only their pulled tooth. Their relative estrangements could be fictions, meant to fool me, to keep me from following them. I knew Laurel was a good actress, more than capable of deception. I didn't think Janet would lie to me. But I didn't think a lot of things. If the two of them were meeting Serena as usual, if they were all doing tummo right now, I would never know.

But I also knew something about Luke now, something they didn't. Looking at my wet reflection, I was overcome by an urge to see him. I didn't see any reason why I shouldn't, middle of the night or not, go down to talk to him, just talk, or maybe kiss him again, the fraud. It was late, but I was sure he would be awake. Back then I figured grown men were always awake. I still basically figure that. Certain kinds of men, at least.

Sure enough, when I approached Luke's cabin, the lights were on. His leather sandals were outside on the mat; I could see the smooth black imprints of his feet in their soles.

Instead of knocking, I walked around to the side of the house and put my face to the window. I wanted to see what he did when he was alone.

But he was not alone. In fact, I couldn't see him at all. In the slice of light between the two inexpertly pulled drapes, I could see only Serena, lying face down on Luke's bed. The skin of her bare back was clear, the rest of her hidden by blanket. She was still, as if dead. I shifted a little to see more. And then I could see more: I could see that her hair looked strange, and maybe it was the light, but no—the hair tucked against the pillow wasn't black at all, or long, but a smear of dark, earthy purple. Those shoulders, hard and strong, like a boy's.

Somewhere to my left, I heard Luke wrench the front door open, heard him ask a question into the night air. I froze, but after a few seconds of silence he retreated, leaving a thin scent of lavender behind. My face was still at the window when he entered the room, leaned over, and kissed her on the head. It wasn't actually until this movement, which was so tender—the way his lips descended into her hair, the way her hand curled around his leg in response to his touch—that I really understood what I was seeing.

But I was to understand it better, because then he slid under the blanket and put his arms around her, and they began to move. She sat up, straddling him, and he tried to sit up too, and she pushed him down again. It was some time after this, his arms wrapped around her small body, her chin on his shoulder, that, for the first time, for the only time, I saw her smile. I won't say she looked beautiful, because she didn't, and aside from the blush of youth, wasn't. But she looked happy. She looked perfect. It was her smile that made me unstick my fingers from the windowsill and slink back to the dormitory. It was a long time before I heard her climb up into her top bunk and push her face into her pillow.

In the morning, I ate my cereal between Harriet and Nisha, but I didn't hear anything they said. I was looking over at Laurel, whose makeup was not quite hiding the dark circles under her eyes. Where had she been, if Janet had been with Luke? Where was she ever? Twice, her spoon clattered against her bowl. I was about to approach her, to touch her arm, even struggle through some kind of argument if it would keep her from being alone, when Janet finally appeared, her hair wet. I thought her usual scowl seemed hung inexpertly in place, like a surgical mask about to slip from an ear. More likely the face was the same, and I was seeing it differently now. To be honest, I had never even considered Janet as a sexual creature. Not like Laurel, not like Serena, not even like me. Not for a moment. Can I be blamed? She rolled her eyes at every allusion. She wasn't interested in tanning her stomach, or the tops of her small breasts. She had no stories. She had no questions. It seemed she had no desires. But all that meant nothing. All that meant was that she didn't need to talk about sex with us, she didn't need to make jokes, to assert herself in that way. She knew she had something we didn't.

We had Kyūdō again that day, and I watched Janet carefully, taking in her strong arms and the concentration on her face. She looked the same as ever: as calm and hard as a machine. I was lying before, you know. She was beautiful, in her own way. We all were. I couldn't see it then. I was too cocooned in my own relative judgments, too disappointed at my own dull bone structure, too enamored of long limb and bouncy hair and cookie-cutter exactitude, but now I see us clearly: we were young, smooth, clean. Or at least younger and smoother and cleaner than we are now. Those of us who are left, I mean. Janet hit the target again and again, her shots increasing in power as the lesson wore on, while I fumbled, still, with the steps, and Laurel gave up and sat down in the grass. She hadn't even put on her glove.

"Sarah's going to yell," I said.

She looked at me like I was a tree that had opened its mouth to speak. Maybe I was.

"It doesn't matter," she said.

And it didn't. Sarah didn't even reprimand her. She must have been tired, that far into the summer. Like all of us, she must have been so tired.

I skipped my rota that afternoon. The reasons for this should be obvious to anyone.

That night, both Janet and Laurel fell asleep immediately, or at least turned their faces into their pillows and stayed that way. I rolled onto my back. I could feel every square inch of fabric that was touching my body; I thought I could feel every fiber. I wished for sleep. I wished even for Rasputin.

I'd have this feeling many more times in my life, but this was the first: I was overcome by the certainty that choosing any path would by necessity eliminate the others—eliminate them as choices, yes, but also somehow obliterate them, erase them from the world. I pictured the different paths dissolving as if in acid. I pictured them burning. I felt that any choice I made now would be a destructive act. As essential as Hamlet's query, if not ultimately the same: to tell or not to tell?

Eventually, without ever actually making the decision to do so, I sat up and pulled on my shoes. Laurel was whimpering in her sleep (what a word, *whimpering*: the cutest, saddest little word, except it's not little, it's long and thin, like a dachshund being tortured) and I hesitated over her. I had to stop myself from smoothing back her hair. I took her flashlight and crept toward the front door.

As I walked, I told myself that I still hadn't made any decisions, that every step I took forward wasn't a betrayal of Janet, wasn't one of those choices that bombs out the rest of the world, but was only a step forward, an innocent step on an innocent path in the dead of night. I was going to see my friend, my best friend, yes, still, no matter what she had done or not done. Why shouldn't I?

The smile may be overrated as a device, overused. I have overused it in this accounting, no doubt. In Russia, they don't trust people who smile too much. In America, it's obligatory to smile at strangers, lest you be perceived as mean-spirited or, worse, unhappy. Showing one's teeth—well, Janet was right, it's a strange gesture, one that shouldn't mean friendship. But Janet's smile— that was not overused. That meant something. Didn't it?

On the other hand, I was angry. And yes, I was jealous. I can admit this to you now, today, a day when I have touched no one, and can't imagine when I will again. If no one had Luke, I could live without him. I could sacrifice him for the chance at transcendence. If Serena used him, flirted her way into levitation lessons, or did more, fine. Fine. She didn't love him, didn't even want him, so it didn't count. He was a means to an end. But what did Janet think she was doing?

Serena had the real power among us. I had always known this. Now I wanted her to use it. Hadn't we learned that she would? Hadn't we learned that she would lead us all over the edge at the least provocation, with a smile on her face?

Did I want that for Janet?

Oh yes, I wanted it.

Perhaps you will blame me, by the end. It's all right if you do.

• • •

Here, this will help: almost a year after my father left, my mother called me into her bedroom. She was yelling. I can't tell you now what it was I had done; it hardly matters. She was yelling, and she was trying on clothes in front of her enormous walk-in closet. She was always doing two things at once, my mother. This closet was a space that held immense interest for me, and not only because I was forbidden to enter it. There were so many different colors, so many textures inside. My mother had silks and brocades, leather and velvet and nylon and lace and suede and satin and other things I touched and touched but have never identified. Because of course, yes, despite being forbidden, I had been inside, and had buried my face in all of her coats, raked my fingers through all her sleeves. I had even, while she was out, tried things on in her giant mirror, but of course nothing looked right. Everything of hers was too long, too tall, too small in the waist for me. Although there was one dress—black silk, with a low front—that, when I pulled it on and stood the right way, made me feel beautiful, or if not exactly beautiful, then at least worthy of being looked at.

Anyway, I can't remember why she was trying on clothes. There was a party that night, maybe, though not at our house. It was a Friday, I'm sure. That I remember, because of what happened next.

What happened next: she raised her arm, a blue satin–covered arm, to strike me. Just one of a thousand times that she did. She raised her arm to strike me and I had this sudden thought, a new thought: I am bigger than she is. Not taller, no, but wider, and certainly heavier. Maybe stronger. I had this thought and then she struck, and I caught her arm in my hands. I caught her arm in my hands, and then I pushed, hard, and she fell backward into her closet with a thump and a crack that might have been her head against the dresser, and a gasp that might have been her response to the pain. She fell backward into her closet, and I shut the door. I did this without thinking:

I shut the door, slammed it, and then I turned the key. It was an old-fashioned closet door, with an iron key that was always in the lock and never used. My mother found it charming. I didn't know if the key worked, but I turned it anyway, and pulled it out of the lock, and then I stepped back, clutching the thing to my chest as if she could somehow suck it out of my hands and back through the door.

"Olivia," my mother said. "Let me out." I heard her scrabbling, trying to open the door. But it would not open. There was no handle on that side.

"No," I said.

"You're going to have to let me out eventually," she said. "Better do it now."

"You brought this on yourself," I said.

"I hurt my head," my mother said. Her voice sounded far away.

I told you, already, what happens when I am given any amount of power. I turned on my heel and walked out of the room.

It is possible that I should not be forgiven for this.

In the kitchen, thrilled and raving, I looked for the matches. They weren't in their usual place. I began opening drawers at random, picking up knives and cheese graters and dish towels and putting them down again. I looked in the cupboards, under the sink. I looked in the freezer, where things are found in films.

Finally, I saw the battered matchbox, sitting next to the telephone. (What had my mother been doing? Talking to creditors, lighting them up one by one?) I stood in the middle of the kitchen, opened the box, and lit a match. I was for a moment transfixed by the fire, the way it ate the stem so purposefully, and as a reward I let it burn me a little. Then I shook the match and dropped it onto the tiles. I lit another. This one gave a little flare of green. I could hold it to anything—the roll of paper

towels, the hanging apron, the curtains—and it would be over.
I would walk out the door. She would not hit me again.

I cannot be the only woman who fantasizes, sometimes, about
spinning the wheel, driving her car off a cliff. It seems impossible to do, and therefore I long to do it. If only to make a hole
in the preordained. If only to do something other than follow
along, bumper to bumper, a dutiful mirror, for once in my life.
If only to destroy something, even if it is myself.

I say this, but I can't even take a leap into the goddamn ocean.

I imagined what it would be like, to stand across the street and
watch my house burn down. The house where my parents had
fought. The house where my mother had hit me in the face with
all her strength. The house with the empty room in the attic.
The house with the empty hole in the wall. The house where
my father had read to me, book after book, as I curled against
his warm shoulder. The house my father had decided to leave. I
imagined the whole thing burning at once, as even and bright
as a match head. I imagined the fireman approaching me, asking
if there was anyone inside.

"Yes," I would say, closing my eyes as the heat came off
the house in waves. "Upstairs, on the left." I wouldn't give him
the key, but it wouldn't matter, he'd have an ax. I wouldn't
be the one to kill her, not me. If it happened it would be the blaze
(an accident), the inexperience of the fireman (budget cuts), the
slow traffic between the new fire station and the old house on
fire (can't be helped). If it happened, it wouldn't be because of
me, the bereaved, the new orphan standing on the curb, shiny
and sore as a burn. But it wouldn't happen anyway. They would
save her. Probably, I mean.

I blew out the match and dropped it to the floor. I put the matchbox back into the drawer where it belonged. I reasoned with myself that if my father came home, which he could still do, at any time, despite everything, I didn't want him to return to a hole in the ground. I didn't want him to be angry with me.

Before you ask: I don't know if I could have done it. I do know that I wanted to punish her. I wanted her to know what it was like to have something she loved taken away. (As if she didn't know—but I wasn't thinking about that, not then. You can't expect so much from me.)

I went out to the garage. Inside, the Fatties were waiting. I had the distinct sense that they were judging me—not for lighting the match, but for letting it burn out and take nothing with it. They leered at me. They whispered among themselves. Their clay eyes were rimmed with pity. Furious, I began to destroy them. All of my mother's work. Some were hard and dry, and I beat at them with my mother's sledgehammer. Many were still soft, and I twisted their limbs, massaged their shoulders onto the floor in clumps. I smashed and tore and clawed and cut until I was standing in a room full of clay mounds and dust with a group of rebar skeletons, some of them knocked prone, but most still standing, bare and scraping as winter trees. The Fatties had thin dead women inside of them the whole time. Well, it figured.

I spared Beth. I am sentimental in that way.

In the morning, my arms were sore and I was ashamed. I went downstairs and made coffee, the way my mother and I liked it, much too strong for my father. I cleaned up a little, picked the spent matches from the floor and sent them down the garbage disposal. But when I finally approached the closet door, key in hand, I couldn't hear her inside.

"Mom?" I tried. Nothing. I turned the key and opened the door. The closet was clean and organized. Nothing was on the floor. My mother's shoes were in their boxes. The overhead bulb burned. I couldn't see her. I felt a stab of panic. Had she been transported or simply transformed? Had she deserved punishment or escape?

"Hello?" I said.

And there she was, coming from behind the coats, as though being birthed whole and enormous from folds of wool and fur.

"What have you done?" she asked, stepping out into the light. She had changed her clothes, but her face was drawn and tired. I was sure she already knew. She could sense that the Fatties had been murdered. Now I realize that, like the fire, their destruction was something she might have done herself. That's how she knew I had done it.

I said nothing.

"Why do you want to hurt me?" she said.

I thought, *How can I possibly hurt you when you have all the power?*

She ran her hands through her hair and winced. "I may have a concussion," she said.

As she pushed past me, I thought: *She would have done it right; she would have lit the draperies.* As her favorite author once wrote: *Harm is the norm. Doom should not jam.*

Two weeks later, I packed a bag and left. I signed up for the program at the Center online, with the copy of her credit card she'd given me for emergencies. I bought a plane ticket with it too. I used it to pay the cabdriver. She said nothing. She said nothing at all to me for two weeks, and then I was gone. You see I had to go. You see I had to find him. It wasn't her fault; it was mine.

• • •

Love can't be owed, you know, no matter the chain of reincarnations. Not to a parent. Not to a child, even. People are wrong about that.

"What are you doing here?" Serena said. She was slightly blurred from sleep. I said nothing, suddenly unsure of myself. Standing in the kitchen, holding the match. I wasn't used to seeing her look so flammable.

"Come in, I guess," she said. I followed her into her tent, and she curled up on her bed, tucking her feet underneath a blanket for warmth. Half-asleep, with no chance to plan or organize, she was briefly identifiable as that sad girl whose mother was dead, who slept in a milk barrel. She didn't look capable of hurting anyone that night, only of being hurt, of being left. It made me want to leave, seeing her that way. No: it made me want to caress and destroy her at once, like that pretty fish, like my own mother.

"I have to tell you something," I said.

15

It may not shock you to learn that in the years between that summer and this one, I've come to be suspicious of American practitioners of Eastern philosophies. There's something so rapacious about them: all those blond ladies sitting on cushions in their work slacks, the round-faced, dirty-haired college sophomores with their elastic mala bead bracelets—or else with spectacles and sweaters, high-chair philosophers spouting the Glass family values—the sweaty middle-aged men with framed pictures of their dead cats in their pockets, looking for Inner Peace. All that performative kindness. All that practiced calm. I'm sounding like my mother, I know. I know, I know, I know. But I don't mean that there are no American practitioners who are truly engaged in the concepts. There are. Of course there are. I only mean that I've seen a pattern. Upper-middle-class white people, looking for meaning. Looking to hook themselves to someone else's old magic. (*fig.1:* the booming yoga pant industry. *fig. 2:* the glut of mindfulness apps.) Even Buddhism's emergence in this country, primarily via the Beats, leaves something to be desired. Sure, Ginsberg was on the level, despite being probably a pedophile, and Snyder was a true believer—that beautiful man, still in the woods somewhere, because sometimes the good do grow old—but Kerouac, most famous of them all (typing), was a terrible Buddhist. He couldn't even sit for meditation because he had knee problems, and on his deathbed, scared as hell of hell, he renounced his heretic Eastern practice and converted back to Catholicism. Like, as Serena put it once, a fucking punk.

I sat with Janet and Laurel the next morning at breakfast. Laurel ignored me, but Janet began telling us how Sarah had asked her to come back to the Center as part of a Kyūdō exhibition that winter, how she was trying to figure out a way to scrape the money together, how she was the only one to be asked. I couldn't bring myself to respond. I swirled my spoon around and around in my oatmeal. "What's the matter?" Janet asked me. *What's the matter, what's the matter with you?*

What's the matter? we ask. *Nothing*, we answer. It's a strange question, forward or backward. What's the matter? Nothing is the matter. No thing is matter. There is no matter here. Only emptiness.

matter (n.) from the Latin *mater* "origin, source, mother," or possibly from the same root as the Latin *domus*, "house"; see also: no one ever leaves the house where they were born. See also: my mother believed in nothing.

That afternoon, I went to the garden. Luke was watering the plants, his shirt tied around his head. He had his back to me, and with his head covered like that, he could have been almost anyone. Anyone with blue cloth hair, any kind of magical cartoon space prince.

But then he turned, his face snapping into place. "There she is," he said. He untied the shirt from his head and dropped it over his body. The patchy sweat marks made it look like it was patterned with large flowers.

I came around to the door and he went back to his work. He was putting in three plants with wide, oval leaves. I stood behind him.

"What is the traditional view of sex?" I asked.

He didn't look up, or miss a beat. "How traditional are we talking?" he said.

"The traditional Buddhist view."

He thrust his spade into the ground and sat back on his heels. "It depends on how you look at it," he said. "The earliest texts are not very permissive, I'm afraid. A number of the more explicit ones were written by monks, and you know what they're like. Shantideva is *very* crotchety on the subject. The body is a bag of filth, and all that. Serena loves him." Finally, he turned and squinted up at me. "On the other hand—do you know the Tibetan concept of Yab-Yum? You've seen the copulating iconography, I expect. Those are meant to represent the divine union of feminine and masculine, of wisdom and skillful means, and to offer a path toward transcending our sense of duality."

"Okay," I said.

He laughed and stood, brushing the dirt off his knees. "I think the answer to your actual question is this: Western Buddhists are fairly open when it comes to carnality. The teacher who was most influential in bringing Buddhism to the West was—well, he enjoyed sex, let's put it that way."

"What about you?" I asked.

"I enjoy sex too," he said lightly. "Most people do. The body is not something to be afraid of. It's only a tool." He reached out and rested his hand lightly on top of my head.

"I saw you and Janet together," I said.

He pulled his hand away, as if burned. "Ah," he said.

"And I will tell," I said, though I had already told the only person I had any intention of telling. "I'll tell Shastri Dominique. I'll tell the police. You'll be locked up. It's disgusting."

"Is it?" he asked quietly.

"Yes," I said.

He tilted his head. "Why?"

I had a thousand answers for this and no answers at all.

"You were supposed to be good," I said instead. I sat down on the far end of the bench.

"I don't suppose you want to hear how *good* is an illusory construct, empty of actual meaning," he said. "Though maybe you should. I could bring you some literature." I almost laughed, thinking of my father holding out the book. But then Luke stood and came to sit beside me, so close I could feel the hard electricity between our hips, our shoulders.

"Besides," he said. "I *am* good. You know I'm good, don't you?" He moved the hair off my face, and then reached down to pull it away from my neck too, grazing my skin with his fingertips. "I didn't mean for it to happen," he said, softening his tone. "But there's something about her. She's so tough, it really breaks your heart."

"What about Serena?" I said.

"Serena and I have known each other for a long time," he said.

"Since she was a little girl," I said.

"Serena was never a little girl," he said.

"Yes, she was."

He bit his lip, exquisite. "None of the girls I've met here are exactly normal," he said. "It's a special place."

"Do you love her?" I asked. I couldn't move. I wished he would either kiss me or burst into flames.

"Look," he said. "You're a virgin, aren't you?"

"No," I said.

"I know you are," Luke said. He pulled on my earlobe and then traced his fingers down until he was pointing at my heart. "So you can't understand, not really. You want, but the want is undefined. It doesn't know itself."

"What's going to happen?" I said.

"Death comes without warning," Luke said. "This body will be a corpse." He nestled his large hand between my legs and pressed, hard, and I was shot through, and I'm ashamed to tell you that after everything, this, *this* was the closest I would ever in my life come to flight.

When my mother wanted to hurt my father, she'd bring up the sins of his teachers: the alcoholism, the drug use, the manipulation, the sleeping with students. The Buddhist leader who knew for years he was HIV-positive but continued to have unsafe sex with his students, men and women both, including at least one straight man who resisted his advances but was overcome, held down; including at least one who later died from AIDS. The Buddhist leader who trapped women at parties, forced himself into their mouths, who told them this was the only way toward the illumination they sought, who reminded them of the vow they'd taken, to believe in the absolute purity of the teacher, no matter what. Because yes, even in Buddhism, there has been scandal. There has been abuse. That old slog: men with power. Every community has some bad apples, my mother said, but these are the men who are leading by example. How can the reins not rot in their hands? How can you still follow them?

"You don't know what you're talking about," my father would say.

"Is what I'm saying not true?" my mother would say.

"You don't understand it," my father would say.

And this, this, the way he held the line no matter what— this is what disturbs me most now. I suppose it's possible he was right, that my mother really didn't understand, that there was some absolving circumstance that my father knew but couldn't discuss, something that changed his perception of the truth, or even changed the truth itself. That old-world mysticism runs deep, even in contemporary Buddhist traditions. The tantras and sutras are complex and contradictory, and of course there are advanced teachings, secrets that students are strictly forbidden to share with anyone, especially their angry wives.

"It's complicated," my father would say. "I can't explain."

"Alcoholism is alcoholism," my mother would say. "Rape is rape. Bullshit is bullshit."

In these moments I always felt the desire to protect him. My mother had always been a bully. She didn't understand when to let things go. She didn't understand that my father was inherently good and therefore deserved the benefit of the doubt. She didn't realize the alternatives. But she did, of course. I see now that she realized everything. She was only demanding that he look at the facts, that he account for himself, and face his own ego, his own belief, without self-deception. (A Buddhist goal indeed.) When she spoke, everything my father loved seemed to be made of glass. I didn't want it to break in his hands. But then, if it was so breakable to begin with, maybe it should have.

Here is what I have come to believe: in the end, religion has done more harm than good. For one thing, there's war, ethnic cleansing, genital mutilation, abused altar boys, the systematic oppression of women—the foundational text of Christianity locates women as the source of all evil, do not forget this when interacting with the faithful—as well as anyone who doesn't fit into its narrow moral straitjacket. Hierarchy breeds corruption. Patriarchy cultivates debasement. Believing in something—anything—so blindly is corrosive. You follow a recipe instead of inventing your own world. There are certain corners you can't see into. My mother used to say that raising your son or daughter to believe in God is child abuse. I have repeated this often, to shocked looks, even from my secular friends. I'm sorry: I believe it. Religious belief may be a pleasant distortion, a comfort, for a while, but too much, unexamined, for too long and it eats away at your body, turns you stupid, kills you. Serena was right: the effect is not dissimilar to alcohol.

Is that what happened to my father, in the end? Was he simply obliterated by all his believing? I think it is what happened to me.

The last time I saw my father, he kissed the palm of his own hand and held it up to me. I didn't know what to do. Was I meant to mirror the gesture? Kiss his hand? High-five him? Press his hand to my face? It didn't matter. There was no time. He was already in the car.

If even now, after so many pages, you have no mental image of him, no solid grasp of his personality or his form, I will say this: exactly. There is no tree; there is no forest. My mother knew: there's a hole in the bottom. How can you binge on emptiness?

You may be asking: why have you been working so hard—all these weeks, all these years, all these pages—to sew yourself to a stranger?

I have no good answer for you.

• • •

That night, I heard Laurel's breaths become deep and regular. I heard Harriet toss and toss and eventually start to snore. Then I heard Janet get up. She climbed quietly down the little ladder, but she didn't immediately sneak out into the night. Instead she knelt by Laurel's bed and kissed her on the forehead. Laurel moved a little, and Janet straightened. She seemed to waver for a moment before she turned and crept through the door of the dormitory.

I knew where she was going. I should have closed my eyes and nestled under the covers to furiously masturbate or cry or sleep, whichever came to me first. But instead, I threw off the blanket. The feeling I'd gotten from seeing them together had already started to dissipate. I could barely remember what her breasts had looked like, or where he had laid his hands. The bruise had already begun to heal. I wanted to press down, to repurple it. I wanted to see more.

Outside, I almost tripped over Ava. There was only one kitten with her. It looked up at me, the moonlight turning its two blue eyes to mirrors. I wondered, briefly, if the others had been drowned. Wasn't that what you did with eyeless kittens? Or maybe they'd simply wandered off when their mother wasn't looking, and fallen down one of the mountain's cracks. Maybe they'd been snatched up by a hawk; maybe they'd flown for a moment before the end.

I leaned down to stroke the final kitten. *(But who—? And who—?)* Before I could touch him, he swiped, scratched me. *Beauty, it hurts us.* I swore, stood. I put my finger in my mouth and started across the grounds.

My very earliest conception of sex was this: my mother systematically placing my father inside her body, one bit at a time. First his hand, then elbow, then shoulder. Inserting each part evenly,

carefully, and holding it there—*there* being an undefined opening in the stomach region—for a moment before removing it
and inserting the next piece.

I could still feel Luke's hand between my legs, hot and enormous. I had wanted to let him leave it there. I had wanted him
to press harder. I had let him grin at me, knowing I had lost.

But then he had moved, just a little, a stroke, that thumb,
and I thought of Serena, of Janet. I had pushed him away, both
of my hands on his. Not because I felt guilty. Not because I was
loyal. Because I wasn't the only one, and I hated myself and
him for this. He had shrugged and gone back to his work. I had
run from the garden. He had stood and laughed at me, at my
ineffectual fleeing form. For some, the only thing more alluring
than sex is self-righteousness.

When I arrived at his cabin, it was dark. I hurried forward to
press my face into the window, but his bed was empty. No
Luke. No Janet. I took a step back, confused. A wolf howled
somewhere on the mountain. My long-lost sailor.

Then I heard something moving, much closer, from the trail
behind me. Janet—had she been detained? Was Luke inside
after all, waiting for her in the dark? There was nowhere for me
to hide now. But it was Laurel who stepped out of the woods.
She looked at the empty cabin, and then at me.

"Did you tell her?" she said.

"Are you following me?" I said.

"Did you tell Serena about Janet and Luke?" she said, enun-
ciating as if to a child.

"You knew?"

"You don't think I know when people are fucking?" She
laughed bitterly. "It's been going on for weeks. I tried to make
her stop, trust me, but she's goddamn stubborn."

I lost my breath for a moment. "She lied to me," I said at last.

"So what?" Laurel said. "Everyone lies to everyone."

I couldn't explain my reasoning to her. I dropped my arms helplessly to my sides.

"Did you know," Laurel said slowly, "that Serena has somehow gotten rid of every woman Luke's ever been with? From the time she was eleven years old, I'm saying. He used to be with Dominique, did you know that? They were going to get married. And Serena ended it. No, let's be precise: Serena made *Dominique* end it. Janet knows all this, of course. But she's as much of an idiot as you, apparently."

"I hope she does end it," I said. "I think that would be best for everyone."

But then I had a vision of Serena straddling Janet, her knees bruising into the rock, her fingers around her neck. Serena, who knew everything. Serena, who didn't love us. There was only one other place they could be. I pushed past Laurel and started toward the rock palm.

"I talked to him too," Laurel said, following me. "I tried to tell him. Maybe she saw me, and that's why—" I heard her inhale. That night on the ledge still scared her. "But he's so caught up in himself, in his own holy fucking ego trip, that he didn't even think it was wrong."

I said nothing. We kept walking.

"How did you even know?" she asked. "I can't imagine he told you, despite your hot little make-out session."

"I saw them," I said.

"And you ran right off and told Serena? What made you think you should do that? Don't you realize what she's capable of?"

"Yes," I said, and we were silent for a while.

It was late. Those small hours, between three and five: the hour of the wolf. As the legends and Ingmar Bergman would have it, it is in this liminal time, this uneasy transition between dark and dawn, that most people die, and that most babies are born, and that the demons have their best access to your heart. (It's not true, you know: most people die at 11 a.m. Eleven! It surprises me that such a sweet hour can claim so many. Babies actually tend to arrive between 8 a.m. and 9 a.m., at least in America. The demon thing, though, could well be true.)

We arrived once again, for what would be the last time, at the rock palm, and they were there, all three of them; it was as though they had been waiting for us. I remember even then having the impression of theater. Serena and Luke were in a spot of moon-light, center stage. Janet stood separate, holding a lantern that gave her a ghostly affect, her hair glowing at the edges. Even their clothes, the same clothes they had worn all summer, seemed like costuming now: one girl in long white, one in cropped black. I can't remember what Luke was wearing. Gray, maybe. Gray would be appropriate here. They stopped talking as we approached.

"I thought you might find us," Serena said. "You two can never get enough." She reminded me of Puck at the end of the play. *If we shadows have offended, think but this and all is mended—*

"What's going on?" I said.

"Serena said she wanted to show me something," said Janet. "But now I don't think that's true." I was surprised at the tenor of her voice. She sounded angry, defiant. I had been expecting something else: shame, maybe. She had been caught, after all. She had been confronted. She had broken the rules. But she was standing straight as a pike, downstage, her hands on her hips.

"I don't understand," Serena said, turning back to Janet. "We had a plan."

"I'm sorry," Janet said. "It wasn't about you. Shocking as that may seem."

"We are what we think," Serena said, almost to herself.

"Serena," Luke said. He took a step toward her, looking

menacing or amorous, who's to say, either one, both. "It's not what you're imagining. You know how I feel about you."

Next to me, Laurel covered her eyes, and I thought of my father, who always covered his eyes at the disturbing parts of the movies we saw together, only to peek through his fingers. He did the same thing when my mother and I would argue: he covered his face, he peeked. I think he peeked less at the real world, though. He could keep his fingers safely closed there. There was nothing to miss; he'd seen it all before.

Serena ignored him, spoke only to Janet. "I thought you understood what we were trying to do. I thought you wanted the same thing we did." Her tone was cool, controlled, but her hands were in fists at her sides.

"Levitation isn't real," Janet said. "Or if it is, it doesn't matter. I don't know why I let you convince me it did."

"This wasn't how it was supposed to be," Serena said.

"This is how it is," Janet said.

"Don't you see who he is?" Serena said. She sounded almost sad. "Don't you understand? He's a bad person, Janet. He doesn't deserve you. He doesn't deserve anything good."

"Hang on," Luke said.

"Everyone has desire," Janet said. "You're the only one who thinks it's wrong. We would all just be enjoying our lives if you weren't here."

"Oh, would you?" Serena snapped. "Is that what you've been doing with Luke, enjoying your life? Or were you measuring yourself by what some man wants, like you always do? Or were you trying to win at everything, no matter the cost, like you always do?"

"At least I'm not delusional," Janet said.

"Just admit that you're jealous, Serena," Luke said.

There was a beat of silence. Someone in the audience coughed.

"Jesus Christ," Serena said.

"Then why do you knock on my door?" Luke said. He looked like a stranger to me now, harder, older. "Why do you beg me to come to your tent? To touch you?" I admit to being shocked by this. But of course, I knew nothing about any of them.

"You know why," she said quietly.

"You're a tease," Luke said. "That's the truth. You offer and offer and take your goddamn clothes off and twirl, but you never go through with it. You can see how a guy would get tired."

"They used to hold official ostracisms in ancient Greece," Serena said evenly. "Every year, the assembly voted on whether or not they needed one. If things were going badly, or if the crops were dying, or if someone was causing trouble, people would vote yes. Then they'd hold a meeting in the Agora. Every citizen would carve a name into a rock or a piece of pottery, and put it in a pile, and whoever got the most votes was exiled for ten years. Sometimes people need a scapegoat. One person to get sacrificed for the good of the group." Her face was blank, as if she were reporting a list of figures. "If we did it now," she said, "I wonder who would win?"

She moved toward the edge of the rock palm. There was a small boulder there. She climbed up on it and lifted a foot, like a dancer.

"Nothing has changed," Luke said, his eyes on her raised foot. "I still want to help you. I'll tell you whatever you want to know."

"See, Serena," Janet said. "Your plan worked after all. What do you care what I do in my spare time?"

Then I couldn't help myself. "He can't do it," I said, from the back. "He never could. He told me he doesn't know how." I didn't know whether Serena already knew this or not. I still don't know. She might have invented the memory of Luke's levitation to manipulate us. Or she might have wanted it so badly, imagined it so much, that slowly, slowly, over the motherless years, she began to believe it was true.

"I want you to know that I hate you," Serena said. I assumed she was talking to Luke, but it was hard to tell. "Everything I may have said or done to the contrary was a lie. But it doesn't matter. I don't need you anymore." She looked over the edge. She spread her arms wide. She turned her back to us. The threat was obvious.

Luke caught my eye. The question on his face was plain: *Will she do it?*

Would she?

I would personally never kill myself, she had said, weeks ago. *I'm telling you that now.* Even then, she had known it would come to this. The grand finale. Smoke, mirrors. Coupled resonant wireless power transfer. *I was never going to let you jump.* The boy, the bee. Had this been her plan all along? She had wanted us to be here for this. She had known I would follow Janet; she had known Laurel would follow me. She had set this up, clever girl. But I didn't understand my role. She had forgotten to feed me my lines.

I should have shaken my head, or smiled. I should have given Luke some indication that she wouldn't jump, not her. *Else the Puck a liar call.* But I gave him no sign. He looked at me, and I looked back. He didn't deserve my help. He didn't deserve to know anything. The wolves were howling again, somewhere on the mountain, like hungry ghosts. I wondered if they had been howling this whole time.

"What do you think, Olivia?" Serena said.

I raised my head to look straight into Luke's eyes, hating him and her and all of us, and whatever was in my face made him run toward her, even before I opened my mouth. I wanted to end this. I wanted to end everything. Car, cliff.

"Do it," I said.

After that, it was too fast. I couldn't see. He rushed toward her and grabbed her and his own momentum threw them both out over the edge. He rushed toward her and pushed her with two hands and then couldn't help but follow. He rushed toward her but didn't make it, and she jumped, and so he jumped after her. He rushed toward her, and she jumped, and she grabbed him by the throat and pulled him down with her.

What I did see: Serena's body twisting away from Luke's. What I did see: the smile on her face as she fell.

Then they were gone.

Curtain.

But no, because we were still there. In life, scenes don't end, they only bleed and bleed. Laurel and I were still standing dumbly at the center of the rock palm. Janet was still lit by the lantern. We were all staring, now, at nothing. Dead air.

"We have to go," Laurel said. "We have to go right now."

"No," I said.

"Do you want to explain this to Dominique? To the police?"

"No," I said again. My brain wasn't working. I was looking at Janet. Her face was so pale her birthmark seemed to glow. She was still staring off the edge of the cliff, into the abyss.

"Look," she said, her voice clear.

Laurel took a step toward her. "It's okay," she said. "It's not your fault."

"Look," she said again.

So we looked. And this is what we saw: Serena standing above us, in a space between the branches, where a moment before there had been only sky. The darkness around her was latticed with oak leaves. She was standing in the air, in that white dress, her hands stretched out beside her, her toes pointed downward. One rope of black hair cut across her body like a sash, letting in the night. Her eyes were closed, her face as flat and remote as the moon, a closed system that needed nothing, that could expose itself to you completely, without tremor, because you'd never get close to reaching it. *Levitation is good for the soul*, she had told me once. She drifted a little higher. I watched her, sure that if I blinked, she'd disappear, reveal herself as a dream, an illusion, a fata morgana. But her dress was flapping in the breeze, a soft slap slap slap against her legs. Was she dizzy, up there, higher than any of us had ever gone? Was her stomach churning? Did the altitude make a difference when you were no longer tethered to the earth?

"Serena," I whispered, and she looked down at me, though she couldn't have heard me. She tipped slightly in the air, and held up a small white hand, a miraculous hand, like a bird. Her wrists shone bare, almost blue. Her protection cords were gone. When had she cut them? She looked so quiet there in the sky, not angry or hurt or sad at all.

This is the thing. This is the thing I need to see, to understand. This is the crux of it all; I should not look away. And yet I want to tell you that the fata morgana is a complex superior mirage that occurs when light passes through a series of slices of air of different temperatures. Different temperatures mean different densities, and so an atmospheric duct is created, and so as the light comes through, it bends: refraction. The mirage appears when our eye-brain sees the kinked light and assumes it's coming on a straight path. In a fata morgana, the light reflecting from a distant object bends downward, but your eye doesn't know that, and so your brain raises the object in question into the air. It happens most often over water—sailors have seen floating cities, upside-down ghost ships (the *Flying Dutchman* is a famous fata morgana), mountain ranges, spaceships—but it can appear anywhere.

I also need to tell you that the phenomenon is named after the Arthurian sorceress and shapeshifter Morgan le Fay, the deathless nymph, who is capable of flight, who has something of the siren in her, who is said by some to live in a levitating castle above Mount Etna, from whence she beckons travelers. Morgan, who sought Lancelot's bed even as she sought his undoing, who was both healer and destroyer.

Except look, look at her bare feet, and the way they point, as if she's standing on tiptoe on an invisible platform far above mine, which used to be ours. Look at the moonlight hit them. Those feet: I am close enough that I can see the bones and tendons suspended, straining. Now I want to tell you how my father always told me that a girl's happiness was directly proportional to the amount of sunlight that hit the back of her knees, and how it was only at this moment, as I was writing it down, that I thought about it enough to realize that it wasn't, couldn't be, true.

I was watching her hair, the tips floating upward, as though she were suspended in water, when I heard her laugh. I laughed too, because I could never keep myself from laughing when she laughed. And when she threw back her head, I threw back mine, thinking about how wrong I'd been. She'd been telling the truth about levitation all along. Look, look: she had done it, and just at the moment she had needed to. Maybe we all should have jumped when we had the chance. Maybe the ending would be different if we had. But when I lifted my head to tell her, to apologize, to pledge myself to her forever, to follow her off the edge at last, she was gone. I closed my eyes and saw only the echo of her existence, shine-seared into the backs of my eyelids.

16

I don't remember how we got back to the dormitory. I don't remember the climb down the mountain, or taking off my clothes, or getting into bed. But I must have, because when I woke, I was curled around my pillow, and it was bright. Everyone else was gone.

I had no idea what time it was. The grounds were silent. I walked to the empty garden and sat on the bench. My fingers felt cold, despite the sun. Exhaustion, perhaps. It was August. I stretched them, pulled them to pop the knuckles, the way Luke had once done. Maybe he would come. I would wait for him to come. The sun would warm me, bring back the feeling. The Feeling. I may have fallen asleep. But if I did, my dreams were the same texture as the world: I was lying on the bench in the garden, face turned to the infinite sky, dreaming about lying on the bench in the garden, face turned to the infinite sky. They say we're constantly dreaming, not only during sleep. It's only that during the day our conscious minds overrule our dream minds, so sure are they of the rightness of their reality.

What had Serena said, holding Laurel over the abyss? *You know what worked, that first time we fainted? Spilling a little blood.* Luke did not come.

It wasn't until the next morning that we were called into the shrine room. The space was heavy with people: all the girls were there, plus every staffer I recognized, and a few severe-looking adults I didn't, who I think now must have been board members or similar. Sarah kept fiddling, twitching, squeezing her left thumb with her right fist as if it were a lever. Magda whispered incessantly to Colin. Harriet kept her back to us; Nisha couldn't help but stare. Only Shastri Dominique looked calm, easy, her face empty, her hands gathered loosely in her lap.

We were told that Serena was missing. To the best knowledge of the Center, she hadn't been seen for two days. She hadn't taken a cab, she hadn't appeared anywhere in town, or used a credit card, or made a call. We were asked to come forward with any information we might have. We were asked to think about the last time we'd seen her, what she had said, what she was wearing, or carrying. Her father was on a Greek island for the summer and couldn't be reached.

About Luke they said nothing. At the time I thought this was a good sign. Now I suppose they just didn't want to build a bridge between them.

But, wait: "Her father?" I whispered to Laurel. *Gone*, she'd said. Had I assumed? "What does she mean?" We hadn't spoken much since that night; we had kept our distance, like thieves. There was too much to say. We couldn't say anything.

Laurel laughed. It came out thin and shrill, and smelling

like gin. People looked at us. "Did she tell you the story about the creamery?" she said. "Or the one about the houseboat?" She didn't wait for me to answer. "The truth is that her father is alive and well and remarried to a nice wealthy woman named Karen, and they live in Los Angeles in a huge mansion, and they give the Center millions so Serena can keep coming no matter what she does, and so she can have the run of the place," Laurel said. "How do you think she gets everything she wants? Why do you think she never gets in trouble? Why do you think they leave us alone? It's because her dear old daddy basically owns it all. This whole program, Special Teen Retreat? It's all for her. Her daddy bought it. He *invented* it."

It was the banality of this explanation that hurt me the most.

"Poor Olivia," Laurel said. "What will you do with your little comb now?"

My stomach twisted. She must have come across it that night she'd drunkenly gone through all my clothes. "I was just borrowing it," I said.

"I knew it," Laurel said, walking away from me. "From the beginning. I knew you were going to ruin everything."

The atmosphere at the Center changed after that. How can I put this? It seemed that the grounds themselves had tensed, that the Center, which I had grown to love so much, had been peeled away in the night and replaced with another version of itself, almost the same, and nothing like it at all. I was sure that even a stranger would have been able to tell something was off just by setting foot onto our chalky driveway. It was that charged, that basic. When the staffers counted us at the start of an activity, they made sure to touch us, each one, on the head or the arm. When they had us all together in one room, at meals or during group meditation, they paired off among themselves, heads together. When they gave us directions, their voices were near-screams.

What was known, now, about Serena: that she was lost in the woods. That she was dead in the woods. That she was pregnant, and Luke was the father, and that they'd run off to be together—that old slog. That Luke had married her. That Luke had killed her. That she had killed Luke. It didn't have to be Luke, though. Anyone could murder us up here, anyone. That she was caught in a bear trap, caught in a web, caught in a crevasse. That she had hitched to the nearest town, only to get drunk and murdered and chopped up and hidden in some townie's walls. That she'd been walking down the road, on her way to freedom, and a car had hit her, and kept going, and her body had rolled off into a ditch. *What would you do?* we asked one another, and ourselves. *What would you do if you were the driver, and the girl was clearly dead, and no one was around to see? Turn yourself in, ruin your own life, or?* That she was hanging by the neck out in the woods somewhere, in a noose of her own invention, her toes brushing grass—that long-desired levitation, in that long-imagined stance. That she was just playing with us, and would appear in the next day, in the next hour, in the next five minutes, blinking, smirking, asking *what.*

What was known about Luke: still nothing, officially, but we all had our suspicions. Men and girls only disappear on the same night for one reason, we all knew, no matter what Shastri Dominique said or did not say.

It could have been a bird I saw, a white bird, a cloud, a scrap of something floating in the wind. A dream, an illusion, a fata morgana. It could have been the moon itself, barely camouflaged by clouds, so that it took on the shape of a girl. The moon can easily take on the shape of a girl, given the right circumstances. Or could it have been the ghost of that girl abandoned on this mountain so many years ago, making her sweet sorrow known once again? If I were that girl, I wouldn't be content with letting my tears speak for me, even if they spoke by splitting the earth. I'd come back again and again, to enact my revenge on lovers who weren't the lovers they should have been.

In Marc Chagall's *The Birthday*, Chagall is the floating man, lifted by his love for the wide-eyed woman, a doll-like depiction of his first wife, Bella Rosenfeld. She is running toward the open window, her face white, her expression unreadable. She still touches the ground as he contorts to kiss her. She has flowers in her hands. Her dress is black. Is she about to take flight as well? Why is she running? Is it a game? Will she escape? Will she survive?

Serena said you couldn't levitate unless you had to. She was full of fictions in the end, but I don't think this was one of them. Our bodies can issue imperatives. Anyone with a body knows this. There are stories of mothers performing superhuman feats, raising cars to save their children. There are stories of mysterious misfires, instant deaths. The human body is only a parcel of particles assembled in an uneasy alliance, hanging in tandem for a few years before they dissipate back into the universe. Their nature is to be separate. Chaos rules. We hold ourselves together by force, natural or otherwise. But all forces are inconstant. There's no reason why any set of particles might not decide: rise.

This is how I've tried to straighten it in my mind, you see, to square a thing that cannot be squared, to put the round peg in, to reify the emptiness. I have piles and piles of pages on my desk: lists of rumors, eyewitness reports, science projects, photos, fairy tales. Things are falling apart. Things are bleeding together. On my desk and in my mind. The stitches I make don't always hold, or they dissolve. The stitches I make spell out messages. If I were to tell you I made it all up, you would be forced to believe me.

Was it a final display of rage, of sorrow, the force that lifted her up at last? The sublime ecstasy of pain? Did she finally find that feeling of control, her eyes closed, *as one ground to pieces*, only to lose it, because *yes, beauty, it hurts us*, lose her grip, *like Niobe, all tears*, and fall to her death?

That's how it is, she'd said. The heaviness, the black sand. Did she slip free from all that weight, all that want, for a moment and rise, and did it rush back into her organs and bring her down like a thrown stone?

Was it belief that raised her, finally? Is there any way it might have been enlightenment, real and actual?

Or did she just jump?

Because of what I told her?

17

Here's a version: Serena was nothing but a snake oil salesman, a cheap magician, silk tie and spit-slicked eyebrows. It was all a trick, a series of mirrors, a set of false bottoms—even the end, her grand finale. The wonder show of the universe! Key-mouthed Houdini herself. The Great Serena. Watch her beat the Devil, one night only. She wasn't looking for enlightenment. She wasn't looking to avenge her mother's death. She believed in nothing. She was merely whiling away the hours, the days she was forced to spend at the Center, doing her best to keep herself entertained. Reading her books. Working out her old grudges. Pulling us like rabbits out of hats, coaxing us through hoops, starving us, dangling us in the air, on strings oh so cleverly hidden against the black backdrop, as we squealed and shit and dove desperately for her breast, and the audience clapped and clapped.

Here's a version: my father loved me. He just loved his religion more. And here's a version: he was right. He made the right choice.

• • •

Serena had said she would find out where my father had gone, whatever holy place had been next. Maybe she had forgotten. Maybe she had found out, and kept it from me. Maybe she had never intended to help me at all. Now it was too late. When I finally mentioned him to Janet, she furrowed her brow. "Why didn't you say?" she said. "This place keeps files, you know. Forwarding addresses. Credit card information. We've had the key to the office for years. How do you think Laurel knows everything about everyone?" The key to the office: where Harriet had worked all summer, if only I'd trusted her. If only I'd chosen her. I might have asked Janet to take me there, but we both knew it didn't matter anymore.

Buddhists do not believe in a soul, you know. Which is not to say that nothing remains—though nothing remains forever. Buddhists are comfortable with death. The Buddha taught Anatta, the doctrine of No-Soul, which identifies a cluster of forces within us—body, sensation, perception, mental formations, and consciousness—as that which makes us believe we have something unmoving and eternal at our cores. But we do not.

What, then, is reincarnated?

Nothing, my father told me once. Reincarnation is just one candle lighting another.

Taoists, on the other hand, believe that if you do all the right things, in the right order—well, you'll die, of course, but if you've been very good, you'll skip the afterlife and become immortal. Hindus have an eternal atman, similar to the Christian soul. A couple of Mormons came to my door recently, and I asked them about death. They said we'd definitely be corporeal in heaven (I would be included if I'd only read a certain book, give them my telephone number, maybe a donation), but they couldn't tell me how far up heaven would be, or how our body parts would get there from our graves, or whether we'd be healthy again, our bodies fixed and fused, or whether we'd also get space suits. *I think this is all there is*, I told them. *But it's all right. It's not so bad, the world.* Their faces fell. *This can't be all there is*, the paler one said. *If that's true, that's the most depressing thing I've ever heard.* They were so young; razor burn and starched collars.

When we saw the truck drive up, the men unloading equipment to dredge the pond, it was impossible to understand it as anything other than an admission: they were no longer looking for Serena, or for Luke. They were looking for their bodies. Even the peonies that had lined the paths so brightly at the beginning of the summer hung their heads, left petals in the dirt. It was just as well. They were spoiled now, overfat. They would die and be reborn.

Somewhere off to my right, Jamie was talking loudly to one of her friends. She laughed, clearly unmoved by the dredging, and I was surprised by the way her voice carried, her calm squared shoulders, the new solidity in her form. It suited her. She caught me looking and nodded once before turning away.

That was the day Dominique called me into her office alone. I had never seen her look so small. Even her magnificent breasts seemed deflated behind her desk.

"I'd like you to explain the nature of Luke and Serena's relationship," she said when I had closed the door. I sat down in the chair in front of her desk; it offered a weak plastic protest. *I am so heavy now*, I thought. I stretched out my legs and pulled them in again. "You were there every day, in the garden. Serena was your friend," she said. "They're both missing. Explain it to me."

"She is my friend," I said. "Currently."

"And what kind of a friend is she?"

I didn't answer. There was a large chip in the wood on the side of her desk. I squinted at it. I imagined putting my tongue there: the sharp ridged feeling, the danger of splinters.

"Were they sleeping together?" she asked.

"No." Janet had fooled everyone, even Dominique.

"Then what?"

The chair was growing more uncomfortable, as though the plastic itself were trying to punish me, to push me off. Did it matter what I told her now? "Serena wanted Luke to teach us to levitate," I said.

She remained impassive. "And did he?"

"No," I said. Whatever else, it wasn't Luke after all. I knew that much. Whatever else, she did it on her own.

"It's important that you tell me the truth," Dominique said. "You won't get in trouble. I know it isn't your fault."

"The truth about what?" I said.

She shifted slightly. "What were you doing in Luke's cabin that day?"

"What day," I said.

She picked up a pencil and pressed one soft finger pad against the lead. She sat back in her chair. "He has a history," she said at last. "You should know that. For a long time, I thought it was innocent, that he just liked the attention. It would be understandable." She gestured helplessly at the walls. "But it turned out to be more than that."

"You were going to marry him," I said.

"Ironically, he's much too young for me."

"Why didn't you do anything?" I said.

"It's complicated," she said.

I stood, because even at my tender age I knew that this answer was a bad one. She didn't protest. She thanked me and asked me to please shut the door—yes, all the way.

Well, she loved him, I expect. Can we blame her?
(Oh, yes.)

What else? I started dreaming the blackness. I won't tell you about that.

The police found Luke's body at the bottom of a gorge on a bright, dry afternoon, far away from the rock palm, a detail I couldn't understand then and still can't. A suicide, they said. Nothing to suggest otherwise. If not a suicide, perhaps an accident. The steep cliff, the shifting rocks. *When you see hoofprints in the forest*, the authorities said. *What would horses be doing in our forest*, we wanted to know. *Accidents happen all the time*, the authorities said. *We know you had nothing to do with this.*

They searched the area, of course. His was the only body there.

Even so, they weren't suspicious. *Girls almost never murder*, the authorities said. Psychologists, police officers, social workers, Freud. Everyone's parents. They're the wrong age, the wrong gender. Bullying is common. Bitchery. But premeditated brutality is usually the purview of boys.

No, girls are not supposed to kill. Maybe that's why when they do, they so often take their victims out into the woods, into the green world, where reality blurs, where they can unpeel from themselves. Where they cannot be found, because there is no them left to find.

What had Serena said, the first time we met? *There's nothing sad about destruction. Or oblivion.* In my secret heart, I think she had always meant for him to die in the end. But what about her?

• • •

At the news of Luke's death, the girls at the Center erupted in grief. They all lined up to tell one another about the times Luke had smiled at them, helped them, offered them flowers, brushed against them in one way or another. They all lined up to tell one another just how well they had known him. They all claimed injury, wore it proudly, with their hair down. Serena was not part of it. It was assumed now that she had simply run away at last, that it was unconnected to Luke's accident, a coincidence. Serena had never smiled at them, nor helped them, nor offered them anything except fuel for their ravenous searching tongues. Their tears were only for Luke.

After all, he was kind, our Luke. He was so kind. They were not wrong about that, the crying girls. But he also thought that he deserved whatever he wanted, just because he wanted it. He also thought he could do no wrong. And here he was, surrounded by adoring young things, *things* like the sister he had lost, the sister he had forgotten about, the sister who had died for his thoughtlessness, his irresponsibility. He'd left the burner on. Yes, anyone could make that mistake. Most people do not. She would have been the same age as we were, that summer. Yes, almost exactly. Serena never had to trick him into desiring her, you see. He wanted her from the beginning. He wanted all of us, any of us, but she was the best prize because she was the hardest to reach. The sacred is always obscure; the inverse is also true, in this case.

Of course we all have our weaknesses. We all have our burdens. A place like that would warp any young man's sense of self. This is not to say he should be forgiven.

When I finally asked Janet why she'd done it, how it had happened, she couldn't explain. She hadn't been lying about the panic attacks. They were the reason she was out of bed at night, at least at first. Like she said, walking was the only thing that helped. One night, she had walked until she found herself outside Luke's cabin. The next time, she'd found herself walking the same way.

"It just happened," she said, which is what they all say. It is a meaningless sentiment. That is why I believe it.

Here's a version: Serena was our savior all along. I had been right to worship her. She always knew who Luke was—her only mistake was believing that he had something she wanted. She may have been willing to sacrifice herself for levitation, but she had tried to protect the rest of us. She had even tried to protect Dominique. That's why she sought me out, the girl doing rota in the garden. It wasn't because I was like her. *We can smell our own.* It wasn't because she needed me, or any "inside man." It wasn't because she loved me. It was because she knew exactly what would happen to me if she didn't. And she was right. It almost happened to me anyway.

The Center sent us home a week early. There was no ceremony. The board sprang for the changed plane tickets. The staff hired vans to get rid of us quicker. The monks watched us go without a word. Coming down from the mountain in a clean white van full of crying teenage girls, I nearly choked on all the extra air rushing into my lungs. I knew I was supposed to feel stronger, more powerful with all that new, thick air inside of me. I knew I was supposed to feel as if I could run forever without stopping. But instead I felt weighed down, pinned to my seat, some old wound in the vinyl scratching at my thigh. Laurel was at the front of the van. Through the spaces in the rows, I could see her head against the window, smacking it hard with every bump. In the seat directly behind her, Harriet was making out extravagantly with a Tiger who I thought was called Penelope. Janet wasn't even in our van. She had gone on ahead. In the end we hadn't even said goodbye. We drove past an old church, moss and bricks. A flashing blue cross was stuffed into its crumbling roof, neon tubes bent into a symbol of salvation instead of EAT or OPEN or XXX. And why not? All are, finally, offering the same thing. There was a squadron of tall nuns circling in the courtyard, but when I looked again, their figures resolved into demure blue umbrellas, folded against the wind. The van swerved and squealed, but I felt nothing in my stomach. The summer had cured me of one affliction, at least.

Saint Teresa, on the moment after: "Here comes the pain of returning to this life; here it is the wings of the soul grew, to enable it to fly so high: the weak feathers are fallen off."

Poor Saint Teresa. On the day she died—young, only sixty-seven—the proximate cause likely being uterine cancer, she collapsed after communion and proceeded to hemorrhage from the vagina for fourteen hours. The gathered witnesses declared she died in ecstasy; her doctors interpreted her vaginal bleeding as evidence of the inevitable consummation of her long relationship with God. They were overjoyed, the lot of them, to see that God was taking her virginity at last: look at all this blood to prove it, the moment of the truly unbearable; put a veil on her, a new bride, her blush seeping away. This was everything she wanted, they told one another. Praise the Lord.

Later, when I was in college, a boy would go missing in the middle of winter. He'd be missing for months, while the search parties tracked parallel lines through flat sheets of virgin snow, while the campus erupted in histrionics, in candlelit vigils, in collections. Missing while his ashen parents moved across the country to our small college town with their other (their only) son, enrolled him in grade school, rented an apartment, posted flyers, waited and waited and waited and waited. Someone would find the boy in the spring, at the end of a long river, a long winter, long dead. He'd drunk too much, he'd wandered, he'd slipped. A freshman. How cold I must have seemed to the people I knew then. I did not engage in the vigils. I did not help in the search. I did not hold a candle. Why, when this boy's death could only be an echo?

But it wasn't the familiarity that chilled me, not really. It was my own relief. It was my own ecstatic, overwhelming relief that this time, at least, it had nothing to do with me.

Even later, my mother would ask me: can you imagine what it is like to have your husband renounce passion, aggression, and ig- norance? To renounce desire? "For a while, after he left, I tried to embody them all," she told me. "I let myself indulge in every base instinct. I only wanted to feel human again." We were sitting in a restaurant. I'd been drinking, she hadn't. "I'm sorry for hitting you so much," she said. "It was what I needed at the time."

You may think I only saw her jump—that I have stretched the moment in my memory, pulled out her trajectory like taffy, so that she seems to float, to wait for me to see her fully before she goes down. You may think that I made her catch my eye, wave goodbye, my own personal Berryman sailing down into the Mississippi River mud. You may, if you are a remarkably attentive reader, think about the height of that overhang, which I only mentioned once, and whether anyone could have distinguished it, in the darkness, from air. You may simply think the whole thing was a hallucination, or perhaps a dream. *Folie à trois*. Sometimes I would agree with you. But at night, when I close my eyes, I think she did it.

Now I keep a Post-it with the definition of levitation above my paper-strewn desk: stuck there indefinitely with glue, an uncertain magic (polyvinyl acetate emulsions or, barbarically, animal collagen) all of its own.

Levitation (n.) to rise by virtue of lightness, from the Latin *levitas* (lightness itself).

This definition, like the pressure cooker, dates back to the 1670s. It was only some two hundred years later that we began using the word to refer to the mystical ability of humans to lift themselves or one another off the ground. Now, levitation is practiced by charlatans with staffs on Prague street corners and young YouTube mountebanks and scientists with mice and magnets, and perhaps (perhaps, perhaps), also in some secret places by the genuine, by the truly light. No, you say, you're thinking. No. No. After everything, no. You're probably right.

Not so long ago, on a night when I was sure that no amount of bristling or therapy or little white pills would ever shake that summer from me, I tried to give myself the Feeling. I was in the back seat of a car—whose, I can't remember, but the leather seats were gray and tattered and I was alone. I pulled the seat belt toward my face and ran my fingernails along it: scritch scritch scritch. I felt nothing. Desperate, I made long scratches, then short, staccato ones, taps. I tensed my fingers, making the sound as small as possible. Then I felt it, what I hadn't felt in so long: that tingle walking its way up my spine. I focused both on it and away from it; the Feeling had always been something like a Magic Eye image, only legible in the middle distance. The tingling grew stronger as I scratched faster, but as soon as it hit the base of my skull, it exploded into blinding pain, as though something hot and pointed had been driven into that spot. I let go of the seat belt. It hit the car door with a cold thwack, and I curled into myself again.

Sometimes I think: *Well, at least he didn't get me.*
Sometimes I think: *In my heart of hearts, I wish he had.*
Sometimes I think: *He did, of course. Look around, girl.*

There is a map of the Center, creased and left over, pinned up next to the definition of levitation. I study it often, though it hasn't offered me anything new in years. I trace my finger from our dormitory to the garden, from Luke's cabin to Serena's tent, from the rock palm to the place where they found him, trying to square the paths, to find something new in the pattern. It looks like a tangram, only without the puzzle pieces. And there's no solving a puzzle without the pieces. It will only ever be empty, unfillable space.

Does this constant tracing and retracing make me less the witness, or more? I mean, I have to do something, even after all this time.

Alone at night, I slide my hand between my legs and think about the black sand. Even on those rare occasions when there's someone next to me, on top of me, inside of me, the black sand is what I want. To be pressed down, down, down, to where there is no light. To where I have no control, to where my limbs are pinned, to where I can be blamed for nothing. Serena's slow voice, her fingertips on my neck. I think about those too. I still keep her comb in my bedside drawer, though all remnants of her hair have long dissolved.

They never found Serena, or her body. The summer program at the Center was discontinued. What she told me about her father was a lie. But it was true in its own way. He might as well have been dead, *gone*, because he sent her to the place that had killed her mother every summer, paid to keep her quiet and contained, so he could be alone with his new wife, a wife who didn't like this sullen, beautiful daughter, no, not at all. That old slog, indeed. It was a punishment. In my darkest moments, I think it was also an invitation. Serena didn't want to be there at the Center, chasing her mother's ghost into the trees. She wanted to stay with her father. He didn't want to be bothered. She wanted to be loved, kept, important. He wanted to forget her, to live his new life, to pretend to be childless, careless, free.

Well, he will not forget her now.

As for her mother: I found out much later that she was desperately in love with that famous teacher, the one who swore levitation was possible for those who followed his instructions. I heard that she snuck into his tent every night until the end. He was old, yes, but holy, which changes things. She believed in something. It was an open secret; everyone at the Center knew. Then suddenly he was gone, and her husband despised her. I see how it could have happened. Serena was too young then; she couldn't be expected to understand. Would you blame her if she managed to confuse things?

Laurel told me that Janet moved out of her father's apartment. She left her brothers there. She showed a judge her medical records; she became officially emancipated. Harriet told me she'd heard that she ended up going to Yale, but no one knew for sure. It might have been the University of Chicago. This was back when Harriet and I emailed once in a while, before she died in a car accident. It was the other driver's fault, said Nisha, but I couldn't help thinking of the burn on Harriet's chin, the way she tumbled out of bed. I didn't go to the funeral. I heard she was cremated. I heard her mother flew across the country to scatter her ashes at the Center. I never realized how much Harriet loved it there.

The word *cremate* comes to us quite directly from the Latin *cremare*, "to burn," but I've always been a little swayed by the overlay of *cream* I hear in English. Cream-ated. A body creamed. A body reduced to that silky white-gray ash that slides sweetly between your fingers.

In recent years, companies have gotten fairly creative about cremation. Now, your survivors can shoot your ashes into space. They can make your ashes into jewelry. They can have your ashes pressed into a record, so anyone who spins you can hear—what? That's the question, always. What is left? And can we make it mean more if we arrange it this way, treat it in this fashion, bury it, burn it, embalm it, smear it across our faces, work it into our hair, ingest it bit by bit by bone-flecked bit?

Luke was cremated too, of course. I have no idea who scattered his ashes, or where.

• • •

I still hear from Laurel sometimes. It seems like she's doing better this year. She sent me a picture of her daughter. She's beautiful.

It's a miracle I didn't overdose, she wrote in her last message. I confess that at first, I didn't know what she meant. It took me some time to realize. But of course she had her own reasons for being out of bed at night, for being raccoon-eyed in the mornings. I learned the names just for her: oxy and Valium and E and fentanyl, which is a patch you can wear on your body, or the best lollipop you've ever had, developed for the battlefield and used on the front lines of our many wars, foreign and domestic.

My mother received a major grant and some degree of notoriety in the art world for her exhibition of the destroyed Fatties, each skeletal rebar sculpture presented in front of a blown-up photograph of the figure in its previous form. The Fatties, I realized only at the end, were perfect in every way. Beautiful, enormous women. I hadn't seen it before. The power in weight, in taking up space. Beth, the sole survivor, stood in the middle of the room in all her flabby glory. My mother invited me to the opening, and I went. It was nice. She complimented my dress. She squeezed my hand. She still filled the room, but then, there, she was meant to. She introduced me to everyone, and everyone told us how alike we looked. How lovely we were. How lucky.

The truth is, I always loved her the hardest. I just didn't know, for a long time, what love felt like. Children may worship the parent that isn't there, but they usually wind up loving the one that is. Love may be uglier than worship, but at least it has bones, fingernails, skin. At least it can reach back to touch you. At least it braids your hair, even if it tears at your scalp in the process. At least it can forgive you, no matter what you've done.

I didn't find my father for a long time. When I did, he was living with a woman named Clarissa in a one-bedroom apartment in Modesto, California. Yes, that old slog. The stucco exterior of the building had been painted a soft seafoam green, but inside all the hallways were pink as lungs. When he opened the door and saw me standing there, he put a hand over his mouth. The blueness above the hand was thin and faded. The hand was thin and faded too. Elsewhere, he'd grown slightly fat. He'd let his hair grow out, but it didn't look the way it had in the pictures from his youth. He was exactly the man I remembered. I wrapped my arms around him anyway, while he whispered something too quiet for me to hear, even with my head so close. I let Clarissa pour me a beer. She had light brown hair that was a little frizzy.

My father said: *It wasn't you I was trying to leave.*

My father said: *Didn't you get the letter I left you?*

My father said: *After a while it seemed too late.*

My father said: *Your hands are like the Buddha's.*

We sat. He didn't ask for my forgiveness. I didn't have the heart to bring up the Center. I knew by then that no amount of shared experience would allow me access to my father. No amount of listening, no amount of trying, no amount of Buddhism, Hinduism, Taoism, no amount of knowing. Facts do not work. Loving what someone else loves does not work. Closeness cannot be manufactured. It knits itself from unseen fibers, and we can crochet the ends with approximations of our favorite flowers, but we can't choose the color, or the kind of wool. It knits itself, or it doesn't. In the end, I didn't have to choose between my parents, because I couldn't have either of them, not really. I could only be this cobbled-together thing, this Garuda girl, this monster. I could only be my mother's daughter and my father's daughter both. I could let Serena levitate. I could let her jump. I could let her live.

I could let her die. It didn't matter what I chose. It wasn't that I
believed in everything, or that I believed in nothing. It was that
I had realized the limits. I think my father was a good person. I
think he was trying. I don't think it matters. When I left, I forgot
to give him my telephone number. He didn't ask for it, I mean. I
shook Clarissa's hand. She had long fingernails, but I don't mean
to imply she was trashy. I hugged my father a second time. He
kissed his hand. He held it out to me. It stayed there, hovering in
the air between us, its meaning still uncertain, as I climbed into
my car and drove away.

And maybe that would have been the end at last, but yesterday,
I saw Serena on the street. Though she was some distance away,
I knew her instantly. I recognized the way she turned her head
to look at things, the way the other pedestrians parted to let
her pass. She wore a long black dress. Her hair was tied up. I'd
never seen it that way before. It looked pretty on her. I crossed
the street. I quickened my pace. She stepped sideways to avoid a
small trash lake created by a dip in the concrete, the recent rain.
You can learn a lot by watching people when they think they
are alone, but in this city, everyone assumes a certain amount
of observance. She gave nothing away. I followed her for eleven
blocks, until she went into a small grocery and emerged with a
fresh clutch of cut flowers. I followed her for three more, until
she stopped to check her reflection in a large store window. She
grimaced into the glass, smoothed her dress down her thighs.
She was older, of course, like I am, but her face had lost none
of its coercive quality. I wondered who had died, and if she had
loved them.

"Excuse me," I said. I had looked for her, of course. In the
years following that summer, when everyone seemed to be
findable online, I looked for her. There was nothing, not even
a news story about the Center's summer program, or about her

disappearance, or about any of the schools and mental hospitals she'd supposedly attended or burned to the ground. I couldn't find her parents' names anywhere either. No address, no phone numbers. It was as though she had never existed.

She turned. "Yes?" she said. And was I, after all, sure that she had? I wasn't sure of much anymore. Janet and Laurel had seen what I had seen. There was a time we would have all sworn to it. There was a time we would have sworn to a lot of things. But now, so many years later, would it be the same? Does it even matter who saw what? Does it even matter what happened, and to whom?

"What are you doing here?" I said. It mattered, it mattered. I had dreamed about her for years. She looked the same now as she did in my dreams. Exactly like her old self; nothing like her.

Something passed over her face. "You must have me confused with someone else," she said. I saw that she was holding her purse tight against her body. The flower heads pointed at the pavement. Peonies.

"Those are lovely," I said.

She stared down at them as if she'd forgotten what they were. "They serve a purpose," she said. "There's a difference."

I took a step toward her. "Serena," I said.

"That's not my name," she said. She hid the flowers behind her back.

"I'm sorry," I said. "My mistake."

And so I let her go.

AUTHOR'S NOTE

I have quoted, referenced, and borrowed liberally in this novel. Many instances are indicated directly in the text; some few others I will mention here, and the rest will be left to the reader to notice, Google, or ignore.

The Tolstoy line referenced in passing is from "The Kreutzer Sonata," as translated by Louise and Aylmer Maude: "It is amazing how complete is the delusion that beauty is goodness."

The version of Giambattista Basile's "Sun, Moon, and Talia" from which I quote was translated by Richard F. Burton.

I first came across the story of Geshé Tenpa in Lama Surya Das's *The Snow Lion's Turquoise Mane: Wisdom Tales from Tibet.*

As for the quips about the parachute and the corpse, I've been hearing those my entire life; like so much else, I suspect they come to me thirdhand from Chögyam Trungpa Rinpoche.

It is Lama Thubten Zopa Rinpoche, writing in the introduction to *The Bliss of Inner Fire*, who describes tummo as "the real chocolate." (However, I should tell you that the instructions for tummo in this novel are somewhat inexact, and are unlikely get you anywhere, chocolate or nay.)

While writing this book, I consulted the Online Etymology

Dictionary, compiled by Douglas Harper, as well as Dzongsar Jamyang Khyentse Rinpoche's *What Makes You Not a Buddhist*, which is a book my father likes to hand out to young people.

It is, of course, the narrator of *Pnin* who prefers that doom not jam.

Finally, as far as I know, it was Sage Bierster who invented the term "pocketing." I hope she will not object to its usage here.

ACKNOWLEDGMENTS

There are so many people without whom this book would not exist. I want to thank firstly my agent, Claudia Ballard, who read an (embarrassingly) early draft and asked me—very politely—if I thought the novel was done, or if maybe I would be willing to work on it a little, and then proceeded to push me to write the much-improved version you have in your hands; and my brilliant editor, Jessica Williams, who understood me immediately, and who saw everything I could not, and who made this book shine. I am so grateful for the attention and effort and insight of these two astounding women.

My endless gratitude also goes to everyone at WME, William Morrow, the Borough Press, and HarperCollins, but especially Charlotte Cray, Julia Elliott, Carla Josephson, Eliza Rosenberry, and Molly Waxman. The same to Mary Karr, Téa Obreht, and Garth Greenwell, for their vital early kindness and support.

Thank you to my parents, Bob and Marisa, for a lifetime of love and care, for raising me in a house full of books, and most importantly—though some details were inevitably stolen, sorry, guys—for not being the parents in this book.

To everyone at the University of Virginia's MFA program, but especially Jane Alison, who "suggested" I write a novel for my thesis, and to all my many other teachers over the years, including Robert Cohen, whose Barthelme-heavy reading lists and early tolerance for my nonsense were invaluable.

To the very earliest readers of this novel, Jane (again), Chris Tilghman, Chloe Benjamin, and Bri Cavallaro, none of whom advised that I quit writing and go to law school, at least to my face.

To all of my friends for their endless love and patience, but especially to Maddie, Dan, and Bri (again) for being generous advisors and confidants during the whole terrifying process of writing and selling and publishing a book. Unfortunately for them it is unlikely that I will shut up, even now.

Finally, last but not least, and in fact most: to Raf, who has probably read ten versions of this book, bless him, and who made writing it possible in a hundred other ways, large and small. Lick, paw.

EMILY TEMPLE was born in Syracuse, New York. She earned a BA from Middlebury College and an MFA in fiction from the University of Virginia, where she was the recipient of a Henfield Prize. She now lives in Brooklyn, where she is a senior editor at Literary Hub. This is her first novel.